IS SHE
REALLY
GONE

ALSO BY A.M. STRONG AND SONYA SARGENT

THE PATTERSON BLAKE THRILLER SERIES

Sister Where Are You

Is She Really Gone

Coming Soon

All the Dead Girls

PATTERSON BLAKE PREQUEL

Don't Lie to Me

IS SHE REALLY GONE

A PATTERSON BLAKE THRILLER

A.M. STRONG
SONYA SARGENT

WEST STREET

West Street Publishing

Cover art and interior design by Bad Dog Media, LLC.

ISBN: 978-1-942207-25-2

For the doggies

PROLOGUE

IF MIRANDA OLSON had known that staying late at work meant she would be dead nine hours later, she might not have agreed to cover the afternoon shift when Stacy Capello called in sick. Miranda should have left the *Cherished Memories and Moments* gift shop at two in the afternoon, but instead, she was still there when the store closed at seven—a willing worker-bee grateful for the extra money her tired feet had earned.

At seven on the dot, and not a minute later, she locked the front doors against any last-minute looky-loos who might happen along and helped her boss cash out the register. Fifteen minutes later, she slipped on her coat and headed out into the dark and chilly January evening, blissfully unaware of the dominoes that were falling one by one to ensure that her life ended right on time. And all because Stacy Capello wanted a long weekend with her boyfriend at a romantic bed-and-breakfast and figured she was owed a sick day.

But Miranda was not aware of her coworker's deceit. All she knew was that Stacy's absence had put a few extra dollars in her paycheck, which meant she would be able to pay the electric bill on time for once.

Right now, though, she wanted to get out of the tan slacks and white shirt with the gift shop's logo embroidered on the left breast, slip on her jogging pants and the Nikes her parents had given her for Christmas, then hit the trail behind her apartment building for a couple of laps around the lake.

And that was precisely what she did, even though she knew it wasn't a good idea for an attractive young woman to be running alone on a secluded pathway after dark.

Miranda left her second-floor apartment, descended to ground level, and sprinted across the back parking lot. Her long brown hair was pulled tight into a ponytail at the back of her head. Her apartment key swung from her wrist on an expandable plastic coil—better than keeping it in her pocket. Despite the nippy air, she wore a tank top because she never got cold when running. Just the opposite. By the time she returned to the apartment after three laps of the mile-long trail, her clothes would be sticky with sweat.

That was a good thing. It meant she was working off calories. Slimming down. Only this morning, her fiancé had mentioned how much weight she'd gained, and he was right. She was lying in bed, willing herself to get up and pee, which meant leaving the bedroom and walking to the other side of the apartment, which was always too cold because she couldn't afford to turn the heat on. A journey made more daunting by the fact that she'd fallen asleep naked last night after they'd had sex. Something she rarely did because she was so self-conscious about her body. But no sooner had she pushed the covers back than he'd reached out toward her exposed belly and pinched the skin between thumb and forefinger, pulling it up into a fleshy tent.

"You're getting fat," he'd said, eyeing her nudity as if he were looking at the carcass of some dead and bloated creature that had washed up on a beach. "The wedding is in three months. You won't fit into your dress."

Every girl's worst nightmare.

The fitting had been in November, before the holidays. She was bound to have packed on a pound or two, which was why she was going to jog tonight, even if it meant doing so in the dark. And because it would please him, of course.

Right now, she needed to please him. Her fiancé had been in a bad temper when he left that morning despite the previous evening's frantic session between the sheets. His bad mood had started hours before they even fell into bed. He had dragged her to a bar across town where an up-and-coming band was playing—the Kings of Destruction. After a couple of years on the local circuit, they had scored a record deal and were about to start a country-wide tour opening for a much bigger group. They were, he assured her, going to be huge, which was why he wanted to get some signed merchandise now before they hit the big time. To this end, he had been pulling down posters advertising the gig for a week and took the opportunity of a break between sets to ask the band to autograph them for resale later. This was how he made his money. Hawking memorabilia.

And it was lucrative, especially since he wasn't opposed to creating his own if necessary. He could sign a mean Jimmy Buffett or Dave Matthews, mostly on old guitars or albums purchased from thrift stores and pawn shops. In this case, he had decided to go the regular route of getting the real thing. At least until he saw her talking to the band's drummer, who had bypassed her fiancé and gone to the bar for a drink. He got up in the guy's face and almost punched him before accusing her of flirting. He was still sniping on the way back to her apartment that night. When they made love—something she thought would calm him down—it was rough and quick, as if he were trying to reclaim her. Make Miranda his own again. But she forgave him as always, and now she would get back into his good books by making sure that wedding dress fit.

Miranda reached the gate that led from the apartment parking lot to the trail. Here she paused, eying the narrow path that weaved off into the darkness between the trees, praying for a fellow soul to appear and ease her misgivings.

But there was nobody.

The trail was empty.

And it felt darker than usual.

Trees pressed in on both sides, the space between them filled with impenetrable blackness that hid the lake she knew was there. She looked up at the light mounted on a pole that was supposed to illuminate the path, but it wasn't working.

Dammit. The bulb must have blown.

Further along the trail, she could see another pole casting a circular pool of light. But to reach it, she would have to run through the unlit gloom.

A twinge of apprehension wormed up Miranda's spine.

She looked back across the parking lot at the apartment complex. Maybe this wasn't such a good idea, after all. She could turn around, go back to her apartment, and pull the cork from that bottle of Shiraz sitting on her kitchen counter instead. But even as the idea formed in her head, she resisted, remembering the mortifying belly pinch that very morning.

No. She would push on.

Besides, it was probably safe enough. She would surely run into someone, even if it were only Mr. Blain, the older man who lived in 4C, giving his poodle a bathroom break.

Just one lap around the trail, she promised herself. Not the usual three. That would be enough to justify opening the wine.

Miranda sprinted forward, ignoring the growing sense of unease as the shadows wrapped around her like a shroud.

Ahead of her, the light pole stood like a beacon of safety. An oasis in a sea of black. Beyond it, there would be another pole, she knew, then another. And those would be lit. She hoped. And even if they weren't, she wasn't returning to the apartment and that bottle of wine until she'd achieved at least one complete circuit.

That was the deal she had made with herself.

Her footfalls sounded heavy on the gravel. Her breath came in short, sharp exhalations that fogged the icy air, which was doing its best to push below zero.

She reached the next light pole, and her unease lifted—just a little. There was a bench around the curve where she usually stopped to do squats and stretch her legs. Reach that, and she would be a quarter way around. The next waypoint would be a small public parking lot that sat on the other side of the lake. This part of the trail was better lit. There was also a jetty with a covered area at the end where folk could sit and look out over the water. After that, she would be on the homeward stretch, running back toward the apartment complex rather than away from it.

This thought gave her a lift, and she pushed her legs to work just a bit harder and get her home quicker.

She could see the bench now, coming up on the right. But she had no intention of pausing to stretch. Not this time. She blew past it and kept going.

From somewhere in the trees off to her left, she heard a lonesome cry—an owl hooting in the darkness. The melancholy sound did little to ease her frayed nerves.

Not long now, she told herself, and you'll be at the jetty, halfway around the loop. Just keep going. You can do it.

But despite the cajoling voice in her head, she was tempted to turn and retreat in the other direction. Why bother putting herself through this? Just get up an hour earlier in the morning and run when it was light out. Except she knew that wouldn't happen. Miranda was not a morning person. It was all she could do to drag her tired ass to the car and stop at Starbucks for a mocha latte on the way to work.

No. Best to just finish what she'd started.

Tomorrow was Saturday, the busiest day of the week at the store, but there would be extra help on hand because of it, so she wouldn't need to work two shifts. That meant getting home while it was still daylight. And if she didn't—if some inconsiderate person didn't show up for their shift and Miranda ended up stuck on another double—then she sure as hell wasn't jogging in the dark again.

Screw that.

Maybe she should just do as her fiancé wanted. Quit her job and move in with him right away, rather than after the wedding. He could support them both without her wage if they didn't have to maintain two separate residences. At thirty, he was seven years her senior. He was also a successful businessman. That was how he described himself to others— A businessman! Even though he just sold stuff online.

But she wasn't ready to move in with him yet. Miranda didn't want to lose her freedom. That would happen soon enough when they were married the following July. And besides, she still had four months left on her lease, which she would have to pay even if she did move in with him. He had brought the matter up again only this morning before he left her apartment, and she had said as much.

This only added to his sour mood.

Miranda hunkered down and kept going. The parking lot and the jetty were in view now. She could see the vague shape of the building that housed the public restrooms sitting at the edge of the asphalt. The parking lot was devoid of cars, as was the road beyond. She had the sudden feeling that she might be the only person left on earth, running through an empty landscape. She wished there were other joggers on the trail or teenagers hanging out drinking beer beyond prying eyes, as they sometimes did out by the jetty. Anyone to break the spell.

"Stop spooking yourself," she said aloud, mostly to hear the sound of her own voice. "Fifteen more minutes and that wine is yours."

That perked her up.

Wiping a bead of sweat from her forehead, she was tempted to stop at the jetty and catch her breath. But that would only delay the end of this torturous lap. Despite her aching legs, she resisted the urge to slow up as she approached the place where the slender wooden pier jutted out into the lake, indicated only by a break in the trees on her right.

She pulled her phone from her pants pocket—glanced at it to see how fast she'd made it to the halfway point. Twelve minutes. Not bad. She wondered if she could complete the other half in ten. That was unlikely. She never made the entire circuit in less than thirty. Miranda returned the phone to her pocket and glanced back up toward the trail.

Just in time to see a dark shape moving at the periphery of her vision, near the gaping hole in the trees that led to the jetty.

Her stomach clenched.

She wasn't alone on the trail, after all.

Someone was standing almost out of sight on the jetty. Pushed back into the bushes as if they were waiting for her.

Miranda dug her heels into the soft gravel underfoot, almost slipping as she tried to arrest her forward momentum. But not before she caught more movement out of the corner of her eye.

The dark shape moved from the trees and started toward her, a hoodie tight around his head, obscuring his face.

She opened her mouth to scream, but all that came out was a choked whimper as fear closed her throat.

Then the man moved toward her.

Miranda backed up, about to turn and flee back around the trail, when another shape, smaller than the first, came bounding out from the undergrowth.

A dog.

Now Miranda saw the leash in the man's hand.

Relief washed over her. This was no rapist waiting to attack. It was just a guy out walking his dog.

She almost laughed out loud and stepped aside to let him pass.

The man nodded a silent greeting as they crossed paths while his dog jumped at her, excited to meet another person.

Miranda patted the animal's head and continued on her way. Thirteen minutes later, she stepped off the trail and sprinted back across the parking lot and up the stairs to her apartment.

She pulled the key off her wrist and went to open the door. But it didn't turn. Surprised, she tried the handle. The door was already unlocked. She thought back, wondering if she had forgotten to lock it in her haste to go running. Or maybe her fiancé had come by. He had a key, after all. Except he was supposed to be in Tacoma trying to get memorabilia from some old rocker she hadn't heard of who was playing at Fawcett Hall. His friend worked backstage and had promised to get him in.

Miranda stepped inside and called out but received no answer. She glanced around, then decided that the apartment was empty. She must have just forgotten to lock up when she left, after all.

She closed the door, remembering to engage the deadbolt this time, then moved off into the bedroom, where she stripped off her sweaty clothes. She continued into the bathroom and turned the shower on.

While she waited for the water to heat up, she went to the kitchen and grabbed a bottle of water, drinking half of it before heading back toward the bathroom. On the way, she passed the full-length mirror in her bedroom.

She stopped and studied her naked body. She wasn't fat. A little soft, maybe, but probably not chubby enough to prevent her wedding dress fitting. Miranda turned sideways to view herself in profile. Still good. She rubbed a hand over her belly where her fiancé had pinched her. So long as she kept jogging each day, it would be fine.

Miranda stepped away from the mirror and was about to turn toward the bathroom when a sound caught her ear. It was nothing much—just a slight shuffle, like socked feet on a tile floor.

She paused, her eyes flickings back toward the mirror, and the room reflected in its glassy surface. Nothing was out of place. Even so, her gut tightened as she remembered the front door. Maybe she had locked it when she went jogging after all. Which meant . . .

Miranda took a step backward—was about to turn and run—when she caught a blur of movement in the mirror. A nightmare figure that reared up behind her with the face of a devil.

A hand slipped over her mouth.

The devil whispered in her ear. "You belong to me."

And then she saw the knife . . .

ONE

AT FOUR IN THE AFTERNOON, Patterson Blake stood under the portico of the FBI field office in Dallas, Texas. It was raining. A steady drizzle that had been falling ever since she arrived, painting the city a dreary shade of muted grey.

She was clad in the standard-issue agent attire. Plain black trousers and a white blouse under her unbuttoned navy-blue trench coat. Her blonde hair was tied back in a tight bun, yet strands kept escaping to blow in the breeze.

She had left Oklahoma City in her rearview mirror early that morning, saying a fond goodbye to Special Agent Mary Quinn, whom she had been staying with the past several days, and hit the highway in the borrowed Toyota Corolla that her boyfriend and line-boss, Assistant Special Agent in Charge of the New York office, Jonathon Grant, had arranged for her. After a long drive south, she reached Dallas in the early afternoon, later than planned, thanks to construction on Interstate 35. A frustrating five-hour slog that should have taken less than three.

Now she stood outside the FBI building feeling the chill of

unseasonably cold wind and rain as it wormed inside her trench coat and pierced the thin fabric of her blouse.

She took her cell phone out and called Grant to tell him she had arrived, as per his instructions the previous evening when they talked. Of course, he was in a meeting—no surprise there—but his secretary took a message and promised to relay it to him post-haste.

She hung up, tucked her phone away, and surveyed her new surroundings. The field office stood on Justice Way, a stone's throw from the interstate. Its dull five-story facade was an unremarkable grey, but for the white lettering that spelled out "FBI" above its main entrance. It was a large building by any standard, yet Patterson couldn't help but feel it was designed more to adequately house its occupants than to be even remotely aesthetically pleasing.

Three flags flapped near the entrance on poles. The Stars and Stripes, Texas State, and between them, a third depicting the FBI crest against a dark blue background. A similar trio flew outside her own field office, except a New York State flag occupying the rightmost position.

Turning her attention back to the matter at hand, she pulled the doors open and stepped inside. As she walked across the dark brown tiled lobby, her heels echoed, drawing the attention of a woman with straight red hair who sat behind a long reception desk.

"Hello there," the woman said at Patterson's approach, looking up with a fake smile. "Can I help you?"

Patterson nodded, flashing her badge and credentials. "I'm here to see Special Agent in Charge Harris."

"Do you have an appointment?"

"Yes. He knows I'm coming." Patterson took a moment to look around the lobby. It was pristine and sterile. The tile floor shone sharply in the fluorescent lights.

"May I take your name?"

"Pattersons Blake."

"Very good." The receptionist smiled and pointed to a row of plastic chairs to the right of the reception desk. "Take a seat over there. I'll let him know you've arrived."

"Thank you." Patterson stepped away from the desk and settled into one of the seats, which was as hard and uncomfortable as it looked.

A man wearing black trousers and a pressed white shirt passed by, carrying a thick file folder. He disappeared into an office without looking her way. Two more men stood near one of the glass windows to her right, talking in low tones. She could see the slight bulge of their guns in shoulder harnesses under their jackets and the badges clipped to their belts. They were field agents, of course, given where she was. And male, which was also unsurprising. Even in this day and age, most were.

One of the agents looked her way as if he could sense her wandering eyes upon him.

She dropped her gaze, took her cell phone back out, and checked her mail.

Five minutes later, while she was reading a message from Special Agent Quinn in Oklahoma City, an elevator door across the lobby slid open, and a slim, well-groomed man in his late thirties stepped out. His suit was dark. His tie and shoes perfectly matched. A pair of black-rimmed glasses framed his eyes. He strode towards Patterson and offered a hand as he reached her. "Special Agent Blake?"

"Yes, sir," she stood up, putting her phone away.

"I'm Walter Harris," he said, shaking her hand. "Please, follow me."

He led her back towards the elevator, and they stepped inside. He hit the button for the fourth floor, and they waited in silence as the elevator rose.

When they reached his office, SAC Harris held the door

open and allowed her to enter first, then followed behind. He settled into a leather chair on the far side of an imposing wooden desk.

Patterson took the chair in front of it.

Harris crossed his arms and steepled his fingers, letting them rest under his chin. His eyes drilled into her from behind his glasses.

"So, you're Marilyn Kahn's special project?" A faint smile touched his lips.

Patterson wasn't sure how to respond to that, so she settled for a simple nod.

Harris leaned forward in his chair and rested his elbows on the desk. "Fresh off catching a serial killer in Oklahoma City."

"I was a small part of a large investigation," Patterson said, suddenly feeling the need to defend herself even though she didn't know why. She wondered if Harris and Kahn knew each other, decided they probably did. The FBI was close-knit, at least on the SAC level, and they looked around the same age. Maybe they were even in the same class at Quantico. "It wasn't just me."

"Of course not." He picked up a manilla folder and browsed through it. "But you were the one who lured him out. A nice job, by all accounts."

Patterson nodded again, fidgeting in her seat. She had never really been comfortable accepting compliments, and she wasn't starting now.

Harris leaned back, dropping the folder onto his blotter. "And now, for better or worse, you're in our neck of the woods."

Patterson nodded a third time, suddenly aware of how much she was nodding. She made herself stop.

"And why is that?"

Patterson cleared her throat, tried to arrange her thoughts

into a coherent reply before she spoke. "I'm following the trail of my older sister, Julie. She went missing when I was a teenager. We never found her."

"And you think you can find her now, all this time later?"

"Maybe. I don't know."

"A case from over a decade ago with no new leads." Harris shook his head. "Colder than the Arctic in winter. Hell, there isn't even any real evidence of a crime."

"I disagree," Patterson said, not sure where the words came from. They just tumbled from her mouth. "I have leads. Julie sent postcards along her route. The last two—"

"Yes. I've read the file. I knew you were coming. Remember?" Harris gave her a long, hard stare before he spoke again. "What makes you think she was ever in Dallas? Seems like you'd be better off looking in Los Angeles. If at all . . ."

"Because of what I found in Oklahoma City," Patterson said, ignoring the slight dig insinuating that she was wasting her time. Instead, she proceeded to fill him in on all she had discovered, including the registration cards from the Welcome Inn.

Harris listened without interrupting, then he said, "All very interesting. And very circumstantial."

"Maybe. But I think there's something to it."

Harris shrugged. "Whatever. It's your time and Kahn's ass on the line. I've been asked to provide support, and I will."

"Thank you, sir," Patterson replied.

"Anything for an easy life. Right?"

Patterson resisted the urge to nod this time.

"I think that's about all for this meet and greet," Harris said. "You can go."

"Oh. All right." Patterson stood up, taken aback by the abrupt end to their meeting. She made her way to the door then stopped when Harris spoke again.

"A quick question."

"Yes," Patterson turned back toward him.

"Why is Marilyn Kahn so eager to open an investigation on this?" Harris observed her with keen intensity. "I understand the case is personal to you, but what skin does your SAC have in the game?"

Patterson opened her mouth, then realized she didn't know how to answer without telling him the truth that she had effectively gone rogue, and now her boss was using the case to further her own career prospects by piggybacking off Patterson's unexpected success in catching an unrelated serial killer.

In the end, Harris saved her the trouble. "Don't bother answering. I'm sure she has her reasons, all purely self-serving, I'll wager. And honestly, I don't care."

Patterson breathed a sigh of relief and went to leave, but Harris had one more thing to say.

"Be back here in the morning. Nine o'clock. If I must help you on this, then you can do me a solid, as the expression goes, in return."

"Sir?" Patterson was confused and more than a bit wary.

"Tomorrow, Special Agent Blake. Don't be late." Harris turned his attention back to the folder on his desk. "I assume you can find your own way out."

TWO

PATTERSON LEFT the FBI building behind and drove to the motel. It was a run-down joint on the edge of town, out near the highway, surrounded by nothing but poorly maintained roads and dilapidated warehouses.

She parked out front and entered the lobby, giving it a cursory glance as she stepped inside. Small, dirty, and worn down. It reeked of stale cigarettes and old coffee. An overweight middle-aged man with greasy black hair sat behind a dingy counter reading a dog-eared copy of Guns and Ammo. Patterson walked up and stood in front of him.

"Can I help you, honey?" he asked, without looking up.

"Checking in," Patterson said, almost turning around and leaving right then. Almost. But not quite. Because the motel was cheap, and the FBI per diem, which she could now claim thanks to Marilyn Kahn making her sister's investigation official, would barely even cover this room, let alone swankier digs downtown. She could have used her own money, but that pot was not limitless, and she might need the cash later.

"Do you have a reservation?" he asked, finally looking at her.

Patterson nodded. "Five nights. I might need more. I don't know yet."

He nodded. "License?"

Patterson reached toward her purse. Her coat opened, revealing the FBI shield on her belt as she did so.

"You're FBI?" he said, his tone changing immediately.

"Yes," she said, trying to shove the shield back while simultaneously digging for her wallet. She reached into her purse one-handed, then passed him her license.

"Patterson Blake." He said, glancing at the license.

"That's me."

"Odd name." He sniffed and wiped his nose with the back of his free hand.

"Yeah," said Patterson, unwilling to share the story behind her name with a stranger in a motel lobby.

"Still, guess it works the same as any other, huh?" He looked up at her, his expression unreadable. "You in town on personal business or for work?"

"A bit of both," she replied, sensing tension in the air, probably because of the shield on her belt. She wondered what the desk clerk did when he wasn't desk clerking. His wary attitude told her it might not be entirely legit.

The man handed the license back to her and pecked at his computer keyboard.

"Room twenty-three. Second floor," he said, handing Patterson a swipe card. "No breakfast, but there's a diner a block down the street. Open all night. Try the corned beef hash, but steer clear of the pot roast unless you want the trots."

"I'll keep that in mind," she replied.

"Check out is eleven on the dot. No later. If you want to extend your stay, just come on back here, and I'll get you all fixed up."

"Thanks." Patterson made for the door, sensing the clerk's eyes on her all the way out. She hurried along the breezeway and up a set of metal steps, then counted off the second-floor doors until she reached room twenty-three and let herself inside.

The room was dark, illuminated only by the glow from a streetlamp outside. It smelled musty, too, just like the lobby. But it was clean enough so long as you didn't think too hard about exactly what might have gone on in the room over the years.

She turned on the light and threw her travel bag down on a threadbare red and white patterned armchair, then tossed her purse onto the double bed closest to the window. Outside, all she saw were industrial buildings, and nearer to the motel, rows of small businesses. A shuttered convenience store with a rent sign hanging in the window. An auto repair shop. A laundromat. This last one Patterson would need soon enough even though Mary Quinn had let her use the washer before she departed. Then, somewhere further afield, beyond the window's viewing area, the diner recommended by the desk clerk.

Patterson filed it away for breakfast. She wasn't hungry right now, having stopped at a sub shop after leaving the FBI building. She purchased a turkey sandwich which she ate in a dining room with four tables that looked like it hadn't been decorated since Bush was president—the first one, not the second. The food wasn't much better than its surroundings. The bread was stale, the meat tasteless, and they forgot the mayo, which she had to go back to the counter and ask for. The pickle that came along with the sandwich was good, though, which was a bonus.

She walked back over to the bed, pulling her hairband free as she went, then undressed down to her undies and headed toward the bathroom to take a shower. But as she reached the door, Patterson caught sight of herself in the full-length mirror.

She looked like crap.

Her hair, usually blond and lustrous, looked flat and dull. Dark rings surrounded her eyes. She was still bruised, too, thanks to the abuse suffered at the hands of Scott and his crazy aunt back in Oklahoma City. But this paled in comparison to what the sicko had done to his months-long captive, Abigail. She would probably never be the same again. Even if she could put the physical trauma behind her, the mental anguish would last a lifetime.

Patterson pushed the depressing thought from her mind and pulled her gaze away from the mirror. She opened the door, then stepped into the bathroom. It was utilitarian and cramped. The kind of basic amenity that didn't care if its guests were male or female. She turned on the shower faucet, letting it heat up while she discarded her underwear, then pulled back the plastic curtain and climbed in.

Patterson didn't like motel showers, especially in cheap places like this. They always felt dirty, and she was never sure where to put her hands. She washed quickly and then stepped out, drying off with a scratchy towel barely big enough to count as anything but a hand cloth. Back in the bedroom, she pulled on a pair of sweatpants and an FBI Academy T-shirt.

After moving her travel bag from the chair to the bed, Patterson sat cross-legged, then rummaged around until she located the letter her sister had written to Stacy all those years ago. She read it several times, just as she had done every night since discovering it, even though she knew it would contain no previously missed information. It was enough just to hear Julie's voice, at least on paper. To touch the same item Julie had. It was like a bridge across the years. But the one thing it could not do was tell Patterson where her sister was or why she had disappeared.

Feeling defeated, Patterson slipped the sheet of paper back into its envelope and watched TV for the rest of the evening, before falling asleep a little after ten, still in her sweatpants.

THREE

AT NINE O'CLOCK THE following morning, Patterson returned to the FBI's Dallas field office. This time, there was no wait. No sooner had she entered the lobby and identified herself than an administrative assistant appeared and led her up to a small second-floor office that contained two desks, a couple of chairs, and not much more. There wasn't even a window because this office was buried deep in the middle of the building. Instead, the room was lit by stark white fluorescent light from a grill in the false ceiling. It looked more like a janitor's closet than a workspace to Patterson, and she wondered why she was there. She'd expected to be taken directly to the SAC's office, but Walter Harris was nowhere to be seen.

The administrative assistant—a lanyard around her neck containing an ID badge identified her as Vanessa Klein—must have read Patterson's mind. "Special Agent in Charge Harris thought you might need some office space. I know this room doesn't look like much, but it's all we had available at short notice."

"It's fine. I don't intend to be here much, anyway,"

Patterson replied. She was thinking about Walter Harris's words from their previous meeting. He had all but said he wanted a favor in return for helping Patterson but had not informed her what that favor would be. She had assumed all would be revealed this morning given his instructions for her to be back at the field office at nine, but so far, it had not. "I believe SAC Harris has an assignment in mind for me. He told me as much yesterday afternoon but didn't say what it was."

"Ah, yes. I was getting to that. *Assignment* might not be the best way to describe it . . ."

"I don't follow," Patterson replied, her curiosity piqued. "How would you describe it?"

"Well, it's more like—" before Vanessa could finish, there was a soft knock at the office door.

Patterson looked around to see a handsome man standing there dressed in a black suit. He appeared to be in his mid-thirties. He sported an angular jaw and a trim waist beneath a broad chest. His slate-gray eyes observed the pair for a moment before he spoke. "Sorry I'm late. What did I miss?"

"Nothing. I was just showing Special Agent Blake your new office." Vanessa stepped aside to let the newcomer into the room. "I guess I'll let you pick your own desks."

"Wait? What?" Patterson was taken aback, unsure what was going on. "I'm sharing an office?"

"Not sharing an office, Special Agent Blake." Vanessa shook her head. "This is your new partner."

"Hey. Name's Marcus. Marcus Bauer." The newcomer in the suit extended a hand.

She looked him over, then turned her attention back to Vanessa, ignoring the outstretched hand. "I appreciate the offer, but I don't want a partner."

"Not my call." Vanessa looked uncomfortable. "SAC Harris made the decision. The Dallas Field Office assigns a senior field agent to shadow all new arrivals during their first month. Special Agent Bauer is fresh out of the academy."

"Good for him. Find someone else to change his diapers."

Bauer looked taken aback. "I don't think you—"

Patterson cut him off. She glared at the harried administrative assistant. "This isn't what I agreed to."

"I get that. You've made it abundantly clear." Vanessa glanced toward the door, no doubt wishing she could escape through it. "But I don't give the orders around here. I just follow them. Right now, those orders are to deliver your new partner and get the two of you settled."

"I'm not so bad when you get to know me," Bauer said, leaning on the doorframe and watching the proceedings with an amused look on his face. "And for the record, I don't want a babysitter any more than you want to have me traipsing around behind you like a lost dog. I'm quite capable of performing my duties."

"I never said you weren't," Patterson replied.

"And just like Miss Vanessa here, I know how to follow orders," Bauer added, observing her with cool eyes as he spoke.

Patterson felt the accusation in his words. Everyone was following orders except her. She shook her head and turned back to Vanessa. "You need to make this go away. I don't have the time to break in a newbie. I have a cold case to investigate, and Special Agent Bauer will only slow me down." Her gaze shifted to the new agent. "No offense."

"None taken." Bauer shrugged.

"I don't know why you're still arguing with me, Special Agent Blake," Vanessa said in an even voice. "I'm just the messenger. If you've got a problem with having a partner, you need to take that up with the SAC."

"You know what, that's a good idea." Patterson started toward the door. She could feel the adrenaline pumping through her system. First, Marilyn Kahn hijacked her leave of absence and used Oklahoma City to further her own ambitions. And after putting her on administrative leave, no less. Now SAC Harris was using her as a stooge to free up his own agents. She didn't like being taken for granted and didn't have the patience to play nice. "I'll go see him right now and straighten this out."

"I wouldn't be so hasty if I were you." Vanessa tried to step between Patterson and the door.

"It's a good job you're not me, then." Patterson made a deft sideways move around the outmatched administrative assistant, pushed through the doorway past Bauer, and stomped off in the direction of the SAC's office.

FOUR

PATTERSON BURST into the SAC's office with all the fury of a human tornado, followed by the startled secretary who had failed to intercept her.

"I'm so sorry, she just blew right past me," the secretary said, frantic.

"That's okay, Jackie." Walter Harris waved her off. "Close the door on your way out."

The secretary retreated—no doubt relieved to escape the tense situation. Once they were alone, Harris fixed Patterson with a deadpan stare. "Please, sit down, Special Agent Blake."

"I'll stand."

"Suit yourself." Harris shrugged. "To what do I owe the pleasure of this unexpected visit?"

"That newbie you saddled me with. Find someone else to be his nursemaid. I don't need a partner." The rage in Patterson's voice, though controlled, was obvious.

"I'm sorry, Special Agent Blake. I wasn't aware of your sudden promotion." SAC Harris spoke in an even tone.

"What?" Patterson was caught off guard. "I don't understand."

"You just burst in on the highest-ranking official in this field office and started issuing demands. Either you need a lesson in the organizational hierarchy of the FBI, or the email confirming you as deputy director has not hit my desk yet."

Harris's words were as good as a glass of cold water thrown in Patterson's face. The anger subsided to be replaced by a sense that she had stepped over the line. Whether or not she liked it, Patterson needed Walter Harris on her side if she was to follow her sister's trail in Dallas. A gulf hung between them as the SAC waited to see what she would say next. When it became clear that his rebuke had stunned her into silence, he motioned toward a chair.

"Special Agent Blake, sit down. That's an order."

"Yes, sir," Patterson mumbled through gritted teeth. She parked herself opposite the SAC and waited for the tongue lashing she was sure would ensue.

Harris let another few moments tick by before he spoke again. "That's better. Now, please tell me, what's your objection to Special Agent Bauer? Is there something I should know?"

"No." Patterson shook her head. She fought to keep herself in check. "It's not about him."

"Then what is it about?"

"I'm here to investigate my sister's disappearance. I've already made progress in Oklahoma City, and I don't need a rookie agent who knows nothing about the case getting in my way."

"Please correct me if I'm wrong, but isn't your sister's disappearance an official Bureau investigation?"

It wasn't until Marilyn Kahn muscled in on it for credit, Patterson thought, but she didn't say that. Instead, she nodded. "Yes. It is."

"And as such, it falls under the supervision of the field office you are currently working out of. Is that not also correct?"

"Yes." Patterson was annoyed with herself for flying off the handle. She should have known better than to storm into the SAC's office like a crazy person. Her sister's case becoming an official investigation had its merits. For one, she was no longer locked out of the Bureau's resources. She could also flash her creds without risking a reprimand for improper use, or worse, losing her job. But she still didn't want a partner. "I can work faster on my own. That's all I meant."

"Maybe." Harris folded his arms. "But the FBI is not a lone gunman type of organization. We work as a team. Back each other up. A second set of eyes on this investigation will not be detrimental, at least during your time in Dallas. You might even find it useful."

"I don't have the qualifications to show a rookie the ropes," Patterson said, trying a new tack.

"Nice try, Special Agent Blake." Harris couldn't help a smile, although he quickly reined it in.

"But I'm not a senior agent."

"True, but you're also the only person I have available to do the job. Every other qualified agent is either tied up with a complex case or working on a joint task force. Like it or not, you're it."

Patterson said nothing. She could think of no other way to protest.

"Are we good here?"

"Yes." Patterson knew when she was beaten. Now she just wanted to escape the SAC's office with as much of her dignity left as possible. This had not been a good morning or a great start to her tenure in Dallas. She pushed the chair back and stood up. "May I be excused?"

"I didn't invite you up here in the first place. You took it upon yourself to make a house call. Please, take your drama somewhere else."

Patterson turned to leave.

"Special Agent Blake..." Harris waited until she was almost out the door.

Patterson stopped and looked back over her shoulder. "Yes?"

"For the record, you might not be a senior agent, but despite your modesty, the events in Oklahoma City prove you to be a talented one. You are an asset to the FBI and could go a long way if only you could learn to focus your enthusiasm in the right direction."

"Thank you." The unexpected compliment surprised Patterson.

"I wasn't trying to place obstacles in your path when I assigned Special Agent Bauer to your charge. I didn't have to provide you with a junior agent. After all, if you defy the odds and crack this case, it could help Marilyn Kahn in her quest for higher office, and then she wouldn't just be your boss, she would be mine, too. And between you and me, I don't find that thought very appealing."

Patterson smiled despite herself. "I understand."

"I thought you would," Harris said. "Close the door on your way out."

FIVE

WHEN PATTERSON RETURNED to the small windowless office assigned to her for the investigation, Bauer was sitting reclined with his feet up on the closer of the two desks, hands behind his head.

He watched her enter with a bemused expression. "Should I pack up my possessions and sling my hook?"

"You don't have any possessions," Patterson said, looking at the empty desk. "And get your feet off the furniture. You're an FBI agent, not a street lout."

Bauer dropped his feet to the floor and sat up straight. "See, I'm already learning something from the great Patterson Blake."

"What's that supposed to mean?"

"It means your reputation precedes you. You're a bit of a celebrity around the water cooler. Rumor has it you single-handedly took down not one but two serial killers in the last few weeks."

"That isn't what happened," Patterson said. The legend of her recent exploits appeared to have been blown way out of proportion. She looked around. "Where's that admin woman,

Vanessa?"

"She took the opportunity to flee. You weren't very nice to her."

"Yeah. Well…" Patterson rounded the desks and took a seat opposite Bauer. "I'll apologize to her later."

"I'm sure she'd appreciate that." Bauer watched Patterson through narrowed eyes. "How about we forget the last half hour and start over?"

"I'd appreciate that." Now that she'd calmed down, Patterson felt a little foolish.

"Wonderful. I'll go first." Bauer rolled his chair back and stood up. He leaned over the desk and extended a hand. "Hi there. I'm Special Agent Marcus Bauer."

"Special Agent Patterson Blake," Patterson said, standing and shaking his hand.

"It's a pleasure to meet you."

"Likewise." Patterson retook her seat. "Just how much of a newbie are you, Special Agent Bauer?" She asked as Bauer settled back down into his own chair.

"Graduated Quantico about a month ago," Bauer said with more than a little pride in his voice. "They gave me ten days to pack up my crap back home and move it halfway across the country, and now, here I am. Truth be told, I was hoping to be assigned to the New York field office. Flagship outpost. But I ended up here instead."

"You're lucky to even get a big city assignment the first time out of the gate," Patterson said. "Most new agents end up out in the boondocks, at least for the first year or two."

"Yeah. That's what I've been told. I guess the Big Apple was a stretch. Still, working with an agent like you from the New York Field Office is the next best thing, huh?"

"Boy. You really have a hero-worship complex about me, don't you?" Patterson said.

"Nah. I'm just giving you a hard time."

"Guess I deserve that after trying to ditch you earlier."

"Water under the bridge." Bauer smiled. "So, where was your first assignment out of the academy?"

Patterson shifted uncomfortably in her seat. "New York Field Office."

"Wow. Okay, then. I guess you are a superstar." Bauer raised an eyebrow. "Your instructors must have thought you were some kind of impressive."

"I wouldn't go that far." Patterson felt her cheeks grow warm. This compliment felt genuine. "Can we change the subject?"

"Sure. How about you bring me up to speed on your sister's disappearance?"

"How much do you know, already?"

"The basics. Read over the old case file yesterday evening after the ASAC told me I would be partnered with you. I'd like to hear what you've found out since, though."

"Very well." Patterson gave Bauer the short version, hitting all the major bullet points. She told him how her father had kept postcards hidden from her. Postcards that kicked the whole thing into motion. She told him about her trip to meet Julie's old roommate in Chicago and how she followed her sister's trail to Oklahoma City and the Welcome Inn. She ended with her discovery of the letter from Julie and the registration cards with the cryptic comment written on them. *Sunrise at Tex-fest.* She also admitted she had no idea what the phrase meant.

Bauer listened intently, nodding once in a while but never interrupting. When she was done, he scratched his chin. "I don't get it. I was told you were working a deep cover operation, but this sounds more like a personal quest. There's something you're not telling me."

Patterson wasn't about to admit she'd been placed on administrative leave back in New York or that she broke the rules for her own ends in Oklahoma City. She certainly wasn't going to tell him that Marilyn Kahn's burning ambition was the only thing that saved her hide. Instead, she shut down that line of inquiry before it could even begin. "I've given you all the required information to help me with this case, Agent Bauer. That's all you need to know."

"Fair enough." Bauer didn't seem particularly perturbed. "Don't suppose I could look at those registration cards and that letter? A peek at the map you got from Stacy Jensen would be helpful, too."

"Sure." Patterson had made digital copies of everything using her phone camera before leaving Mary Quinn's house in Oklahoma City. "I can send them to you. What's your email address?"

Bauer rattled off his official FBI email and waited while Patterson sent the documents. When they came through on his phone a few moments later, he gave her a thumbs up. "Got them. Give me some time to digest all this stuff."

Patterson was about to answer him when there was a soft knock on the open office door. When she looked up, the administrative assistant had returned and was standing there.

"Is it safe to enter?" Vanessa asked, lingering in the doorway.

"If you mean, have I calmed down? Then the answer is yes." Patterson wished she could start her day over from scratch. "I owe you an apology. I know you were just doing your job."

"It's fine, really." Vanessa stepped into the room. "I've been on the receiving end of worse, I can assure you."

"I bet you have," Patterson replied. While the FBI had made great strides over the years, a boys' club atmosphere still permeated the organization.

"No comment," Vanessa said, deftly skirting further explanation. "Now that you're part of the team, we need to get you an ID badge. Otherwise, you won't get past the lobby tomorrow morning."

"I sense a visit to HR in my future," Patterson said.

"How very perceptive. It's located on the third floor. If you head up there, they will issue you a swipe card to get into the building. You can also use it for the staff parking lot."

Patterson shifted her gaze to Bauer. "You good here?"

Bauer motioned for her to leave. "I'll hold the fort, boss."

Boss. Patterson suppressed a grin. He was appealing to her ego, but she couldn't blame him. It wasn't easy being the lowest rung on the ladder. She headed for the door. "I'll be back soon."

"Take all the time you need. I'll bring myself up to speed on the investigation while you're gone."

Patterson nodded. Then she stepped out into the corridor and made her way toward the elevators.

SIX

IT TOOK Patterson an hour and a half to get her ID badge from HR. She spent most of that time sitting on another hard plastic chair while she waited for someone to deal with her. When she returned to the windowless office on the floor below, Bauer had set up shop at the closest desk and was now sitting with his head bent over a laptop.

"Where did you get that?" she asked, going to the other desk and sitting down.

"FBI issue. I went and got it from my old home up in cyber-crimes. That's where I've been all the last week. They had me chasing down IP addresses looking for some fool who tried to hack into the power grid. Turns out a bunch of computer science students over at the technical college were competing with each other to see who could break into the most secure system. Idiots."

"Sounds like a blast," Patterson said. She eyed the laptop. "What are you doing?"

"Working on the TexFest angle." Bauer pushed the laptop to one side so he could talk to Patterson. "I read through the stuff you emailed me. Then I got to thinking that cracking that handwritten message on the hotel registration card might move this thing in the right direction."

"Or take it down a dead end. Could be a waste of time that will lead us in the wrong direction. The registration card might have nothing to do with my sister or her disappearance. Just two random strangers who were staying in the same hotel as her. Likewise, with the other registration card. The one with the name Simon Bailey on it."

"I agree. But that little handwritten note intrigued me. Call it a hunch. See, TexFest sounds an awful lot like a music festival. Now, I never met your sister, but I'm betting most college-age girls love music festivals."

"I thought the same thing," Patterson said.

"Except I couldn't find anything about it online when I searched."

"Yeah. Me either. First thing I tried when I saw that registration card," Patterson said.

"I guessed as much, which is why I didn't bother spending too long down that particular rabbit hole. But what I did do was email a buddy of mine who grew up in these parts. We were at Quantico together and hung out a few times. I remember him saying he was from Dallas, so I figured it couldn't hurt to ask if he'd ever heard of it."

"And had he?"

"He hadn't just heard of it. He went to it. Got the tickets for his sixteenth birthday. Guess what year that was."

"2005?"

"Bingo. Turns out there's a reason the Internet doesn't remember TexFest. It was an unmitigated disaster and almost didn't go ahead at all, by all accounts. Several headliners canceled at the last minute, claiming the organizers stiffed them. And by headliners, I'm being generous. They only managed to attract a handful of national acts, none of whom showed up when the festival's money woes surfaced. The rest of the spots were filled by regional and local performers. Some of those bands were paid as little as fifty bucks to play. As you can imagine, people weren't rushing through the turnstiles. A week before the festival, they'd only sold thirty percent of the tickets, and it didn't get any better. Worse, they hadn't bothered to secure permits for the festival because they were using privately owned land on the outskirts of the city in a tiny township called Somerdale out past Lavon Lake, and didn't think it was necessary. Almost closed them down before they even began. It was supposed to be a three-day festival, but they ended up condensing it into two because of the permitting issues and lack of acts. Needless to say, TexFest had a short lifespan."

"How short?" Patterson asked.

"One and done. It never came back the next year."

"Your buddy told you all this?"

"Some of it. The rest I got from the editor of Somerdale's only newspaper, a free weekly called the Collins County Gazette. A real old-timer who goes by the name of Harry Cline. Been around almost as long as the paper, which dates back to the forties. Keeps it going out of sheer defiance. I can't imagine they have many readers left in this day and age."

"So TexFest was a badly organized music festival. Still doesn't tell us much."

"Which is why I asked him to poke around his archives. I figured the local rag would be interested in the festival even if nobody else was. Those kinds of papers are always looking for a way to fill column inches."

"What did he say?"

"Told me it would take a while. Their archive is basically stacks of old newspapers stored in boxes by year. The digital age has not reached the Collins County Gazette, and my hunch is it never will."

"How long is a while?" Patterson was eager to learn more

about the music festival, even though she wasn't sure how it would help her track Julie's movements all those years ago.

"Your guess is as good as mine," Bauer said with a shrug. "He has my cell number, so I guess we'll just have to wait."

Patterson wasn't good at waiting. But she couldn't fault Bauer's initiative, and he was right. It might open up a new line of investigation. But not unless there was something useful in those newspaper archives. In the meantime, there were other leads to chase down.

She took out her phone and opened up the digital image of her sister's letter. The one that never got sent to Stacy because someone at the Welcome Inn spilled coffee on the envelope, rendering the address unreadable. "What about Trent?"

"You mean the guy in the letter?"

"There must be a way to track him down."

"You want to track down a guy from sixteen years ago based on nothing but his first name?"

"We don't just have a first name. We have his registration card."

"Right. Steiger. And he was traveling with someone by the name of Mark Davis."

"See, that's a place to start." Patterson leaned back in her chair. "What do you think... want to do a little more sleuthing?"

SEVEN

THEY WORKED for two more hours hunting down Trent Steiger and his buddy, Mark Davis. Patterson hadn't brought her laptop from the motel, so she wheeled her chair around the desks and shared Bauer's laptop. They ran both names through the FBI's National Crime Information Center, or NCIC for short. This database was the leading repository of crime data in the country. It comprised almost twelve million active records on everything from identity theft and stolen cars to sex crimes and gang activity. There was even a section for missing persons that had a record for Julie. But of Trent Steiger and Mark Davis, there was nothing. The only hit they got was a criminal history for a violent offender who shared the same name as their Mark Davis but couldn't be the man they were looking for. Even if the age had fit—which it didn't since the entries went back to the eighties—the man was dead. Killed by a security guard during a botched bank robbery in 1996. The people Julie met in Oklahoma City and presumably rode down to Dallas with might as well have been ghosts.

By three in the afternoon, Patterson was feeling dejected

and worn down. They had not heard from the old guy at the Collins County Gazette, either, which added to her frustration. How long could it take to go through some dusty old newspapers? She also realized she had not yet eaten anything that day. In her haste to be on time at the field center, she'd skipped breakfast. Now, it appeared, she had also skipped lunch. She was hungry. As if to confirm this prognosis, her stomach growled. She glanced at Bauer to see if he'd heard, but if he had, the man was too much of a gentleman to say so.

Still, a few minutes later, he gave a weary sigh and broached the subject. "We've been at this all day. Want to step out and grab a bite to eat before we soldier on?"

"Sure," Patterson said. "But why don't we just call it an early dinner instead. I'm not so sure I want to come back here again today."

"Suits me." Bauer closed the laptop and slipped it into a slim leather carrying case. "You got anywhere in mind?"

"Nope." Patterson shook her head. The only two places she knew of were the sandwich shop with the stale bread and the diner recommended by the motel desk clerk with pot roast that gave you the trots. Neither sounded appealing. "I've only been in town for twenty-four hours. I was hoping you might have a suggestion."

"I haven't been here much longer. Two weeks. Hardly enough time to discover many hidden gems. But there is one place." Bauer stood up and hitched the carrying case over his shoulder. "You like pizza?"

"Chicago or New York style?" Patterson shot back.

"New York, of course." Bauer was already halfway out the door. "It's only a short drive. You can follow me."

"Okay." Patterson gave an appreciative smile. "Pizza it is!"

EIGHT

NAPOLITANO'S PIZZERIA occupied an old brick building on a corner lot downtown. It turned out to be a longer drive than Bauer let on. He took her onto the interstate and then off again several exits later. By the time they parked, Patterson had no idea where she was or how to get back to her motel.

"This place is so good I've eaten here six times since I arrived in Dallas," Bauer said as he held the door open for her to enter.

"Six times, huh?" Patterson studied their surroundings as she approached the counter. The dining room was small, with only four tables and a row of booths against the far wall, all of which had seen better days. There were black-and-white framed photos hanging on the walls that looked like they had been taken in various places around a small town in Italy. Some of the photos had shifted in their frames and were now sitting askew. Others were faded by the sun. The restaurant looked like it had been there a very long time. That meant the pizza must be good, just as Bauer said. Mediocre restaurants didn't last long in locations like this. The rent was just too high.

"Would have been more, but I can't eat pizza every day," Bauer said with a grin. He patted his flat stomach. "Have to watch my figure."

"You know, they have salad on the menu, too," Patterson said, looking up at the blackboard behind the counter.

"Right. Salad." Bauer pulled a face.

"Okay, then. No salad." Patterson suppressed a smirk. "What *will* you eat?"

"Pizza, obviously. Pies are big here. We can split one," Bauer said. "You like pepperoni?"

"Do I even need to answer that?" It was the only topping her father considered worthy of gracing a pizza and, as such he held it in almost religious reverence. Now it reminded her of childhood and the happy times before Julie disappeared and her family broke apart.

Bauer nodded and turned toward the counter where a skinny older man with thinning hair and a narrow face chiseled by the passing of years waited to take their order. Afterward, they grabbed two sodas from a cooler, then settled at a table to wait for their food.

An awkward silence hung between them. Patterson watched Bauer for a moment, wondering if he would initiate conversation, then spoke up herself when he didn't. "What did you do before the FBI?"

"I was a cop," Bauer said without further explanation.

Patterson thought he looked uncomfortable. She didn't know why. "Uniform?"

"Mostly. Detective for the last three years."

"And you left that for the Bureau?"

"Needed a change."

Patterson sensed the hesitancy in Bauer's answers. He had

been so chatty before. Cocky even. Now he was guarded. "Where did you work? What city?"

Bauer hesitated. He let out a long breath. "Los Angeles." Then, before Patterson could speak, he jumped back in. "And before you say anything, yes, I know that's where the missing persons report was filed for your sister. It was my department that investigated it."

"Before your time, though," Patterson said. Bauer was not old enough to have been on the force when Julie vanished. Even so, her chest tightened.

Bauer nodded. "It was. I joined in 2010, but I read the original LAPD report last night. I kind of feel a connection to the case. And not only because my old precinct couldn't help your family."

"What do you mean?" Patterson studied Bauer's face with a growing sense of foreboding.

"The lead detective back then was a man named Eddie Caruso."

"I know." Patterson had practically memorized the LAPD report. "What of it?"

"By the time I knew him, he'd been promoted to lieutenant." Now it was Bauer's turn to study her. "He was my supervisor until he retired about a year after I made detective."

"You knew the man who handled my sister's case?"

"We weren't close. Not socially. He was my boss. But I can tell you that he was a good detective. At least, from my perspective. He helped a lot of people."

"I'm sure he did." *But he couldn't help my sister or my family when they needed it the most*, Patterson thought.

"You realize Julie might never have made it as far as Los Angeles?" Bauer asked as if reading her mind. "That postcard, and the one from Vegas, could have been mailed as decoys to throw investigators off the trail. Misdirection. She might not even have been present when they were sent."

You mean she might have already been dead, Patterson thought, but she didn't say that either. Instead, she nodded. "I know."

"I'm sure Eddie Caruso did his best."

Patterson didn't reply. She felt her throat tighten, felt the old pain resurface. She tried her best not to shed a tear in front of this man. A moment later, the pizza arrived and saved her.

NINE

BACK IN HER motel room that evening, Patterson found herself at a loose end. After changing out of her work attire into sweats and a tee, she sat on the bed, opened her laptop, and typed TexFest into the browser's search bar. Then she thought better of it. There was no point going over old ground. She already knew there would be no useful information on the web. Her only hope of learning more rested on the editor at the Collins County Gazette, who had not yet gotten back to them.

Likewise, there was no point in searching for the names on the registration cards. She had done that already and although she got hits, the results were impossible to verify as belonging to anyone who had stayed at the Welcome Inn sixteen years before or had any connection to her sister. Not surprising since most of what she found was on people-finder websites looking to sell dubious background checks.

Frustrated, Patterson closed the laptop and pushed it aside. She grabbed the television remote from the nightstand and clicked it on. In fancier digs, the TV would default to an in-house channel, pushing whatever local businesses deigned to advertise and providing information about the hotel's amenities, like the bar and restaurant or room service. Here, it turned on to the last channel Patterson had watched. There was a reality show playing that appeared to be nothing more than a bunch of well-heeled older women squabbling with each other while drinking cocktails. She browsed through the remaining channels, noting the number that were blocked because the motel was too cheap to pay for a premium cable plan, and settled on an old rom-com. Patterson had seen the movie before but it didn't matter. She was barely paying attention, anyway.

Her thoughts were consumed with the day's events and the revelation that her new partner had worked with the man who investigated Julie's case in Los Angeles and said there was no evidence of foul play.

Despite Special Agent Bauer's belief that Detective Eddie Caruso was a good cop, Patterson couldn't help feeling that he jumped to conclusions without thoroughly examining the circumstances of Julie's disappearance. After all, the last post-cards to arrive back in New York, the ones her father had hidden from her all these years, should have been enough to raise the suspicions of any competent investigator. There was a noticeable difference in tone compared to the previous post-cards, and even though the handwriting was unquestionably Julie's, the temperament was not. The police should have at least entertained the idea that someone coerced her sister into writing those postcards instead of saying the family was chasing shadows. Even Bauer, who wasn't involved in the original investigation, had speculated that the postcards could have been sent as decoys.

But this was typical of busy police departments. With no solid evidence of a crime, they defaulted to an assumption that the victim had simply grown weary of their family and run away. Broken off contact. It wasn't even something most cops did consciously. They lost sight of the reason for their job and viewed closing cases and clearing the books as the goal, not following their noses. This was partly due to pressure from above. The powers that be wanted low crime statistics and high solve rates. After all, those who occupied high office relied on such things to keep their jobs. Who wanted to reelect a mayor or chief of police who hadn't made the streets safer for their citizenry? The lack of willingness to scratch below the surface of Julie's disappearance was a sad result of that attitude.

Patterson felt a familiar sense of regret surrounding what could have been if only someone had stepped outside of their preconceptions all those years ago. Would a more thorough investigation have led to Julie's discovery? Would she have been reunited with her sister instead of spending the last sixteen years with a cloud hanging over her head? The answers, as always, were elusive. Yet one thought now stuck in her head. Special Agent Bauer had hinted at an outcome she sometimes pondered herself in her darkest moments yet refused to accept. It might not have mattered if Julie's disappearance was taken seriously at the time, at least not in the truest sense because her sister might already have been dead when those postcards were sent. Murdered by the very person—most likely a man—who put them in the mail. Patterson knew the unfortunate statistics. If her sister had been taken, the odds of her surviving more than a few days were slim. Most abductors killed their victims within twenty-four hours of taking them, often in as little as three.

Yet even here, there was a slim hope. After all, the Bracken Island Killer, whom Patterson had helped put behind bars less than a week ago, kept his victims alive for many months and maybe even a year or more, albeit abusing them. There were also cases of much longer abduction. A couple in California kept their victim alive for eighteen years before being liberated. Another abduction in Pennsylvania lasted ten years. But these were the outliers. The vast majority of such crimes ended in homicide. Still, it was hard not to wonder if her sister was, by some miracle, still out there somewhere waiting to be rescued.

Patterson was still pondering this when the jangle of a phone ringing jolted her from her thoughts. She looked up, realizing the movie had long since ended to be replaced by an action flick she didn't recognize. Turning off the TV, Patterson reached for her phone and answered.

It was Bauer. "Hey, I know it's late. Hope I'm not disturbing you?"

"No. What have you got?" Patterson asked. "Or were you just calling to say goodnight?"

"The old-timer over at the Collins County Gazette finally got back to me. He found some old newspapers with articles about TexFest. Said we could come over to look at them tomorrow."

"Fantastic." Patterson felt her spirit lift. "I don't suppose he could email us the articles instead?"

"What do you think?" Bauer chuckled. "We're lucky he knows how to use a cell phone."

"Fine. Might be worth talking to him in person, anyway. Maybe he'll remember something that isn't in print."

"That's what I thought."

"I'll meet you at the office first thing, and we'll head over there just as soon as he can see us."

"No need. I took care of it," Bauer replied. "He's expecting us at 10 AM. I'll swing by the motel and pick you up at nine. It's on the way."

"Oh." Patterson was taken aback. "You made the arrangements already?"

"Thought it would save time. You good?"

"Sure." Patterson forced down a twinge of anger. This was

her case, and she was in charge. He should have checked before making an appointment for them. But Bauer was right. It would save time. She took a deep breath and tried to remain objective. The junior agent was only trying to help. "But make it eight-thirty and we'll pick up breakfast on the way."

"Sounds good." Bauer took a breath. "See you in the morning."

"Right." Patterson went to hang up, but then Bauer spoke again.

"And Agent Patterson, good night and sleep tight."

Patterson smiled at this. "Good night, to you too," she said, moments before the line disconnected. Then she put the phone down on the nightstand and settled back with a pillow behind her head. She wasn't sure what to make of Special Agent Bauer. On the one hand, he rankled her with his take-charge attitude and unassuming confidence, but at the same time, she couldn't help feeling attracted to his boyish good looks and puppy dog eyes. The man knew how to play up his assets. Then she remembered Grant back in New York and banished that line of thought from her head.

TEN

SPECIAL AGENT BAUER pulled up at 8:30 on the dot. He blew his horn to attract her attention from across the motel parking lot and waved through the rolled-down window. When she approached, he leaned out the window with an amiable smile. "Hop on in. We'll take my car."

"Actually, I figured I would drive," Patterson said, the nagging irritation at Bauer's attitude poking its head up again.

"Yeah. No offense Agent Blake, but the Bureau stiffed you with that car. What did they do, give you a drug dealer's impounded ride?"

"It was all they had available at the Chicago Field office. They were using it for undercover work rather than send it to auction." Patterson glanced toward her battered Toyota Corolla with faded lime green paint, oversized shiny chrome rims, and low-profile tires, then back to the gleaming new Dodge Charger that Bauer currently occupied. "My Bucar back in New York is much nicer," she said, using the FBI slang term for her Bureau issued vehicle.

"It would be hard to find one that was worse. And since

your New York car isn't here, I still think I should drive. That monstrosity of yours will make us look like a pair of gang bangers up to no good. Not an impression I want to make."

"Fine. You can drive if I get to pick where we stop for breakfast."

"Deal. But no gas station food."

"Yuck. What do you think I am, a monster?" Patterson walked around the back of the car and jumped into the passenger seat. "How far away is this newspaper office?"

"Maybe thirty minutes. Could be double that with rush hour traffic."

"Then what are you waiting for?" Patterson said, slapping the dashboard. "Drive already."

———

They stopped at a McDonald's near the interstate and ate in the car. Afterward, as they pulled back onto the highway, Patterson struck up a conversation.

"Yesterday afternoon, when you said you worked for the LAPD, you never mentioned why you left."

"Does it matter?" Bauer changed lanes and zipped around a slow-moving truck.

Patterson shrugged. "Just curious, that's all. If we're going to work together, it would help if I knew something about you."

"Why?" Bauer glanced toward her, then back to the road. "It's not like we're married. Besides, your posting in Dallas is temporary. A month from now, you won't even remember my name."

"That's not true." Patterson wondered why Special Agent Bauer was so defensive. She sensed there was a story he didn't want to tell. "But if you want to keep your past private, I can understand that."

"You should. And while we're on the subject, I know nothing about you, either."

"You know a lot about me," Patterson said. "You know I have an older sister, and that she's been missing for sixteen years. That I live in New York. If you read the FBI file on Julie, you probably also know that my parents broke up after she vanished and that my mom moved to Colorado."

"How about you tell me something that isn't in that case file?" Bauer said.

"Like what?"

"I don't know. You started this conversation," Bauer said, picking up his coffee cup and taking a swig with one hand while keeping the other on the wheel.

"Fair enough." Patterson thought for a moment. "When I was young, I wanted to be a ballerina."

Bauer snorted and almost choked on his coffee. "That's the best you can do? Doesn't every little girl want to be a ballerina?"

"Maybe. But that doesn't make it any less true. I pestered my parents for a month to let me take ballet lessons, then after they finally gave in, I went to one class and hated it."

"I'll bet they loved you for that."

"They never found out, because I didn't tell them. I came home from class that first Saturday and my mother was so excited. She asked me how I'd gotten on, and if I'd made any new friends. My parents didn't have a lot of money back then, but they'd scrounged enough together to buy me a pair of dance shoes. It was a big deal. I didn't have the heart to tell them how dreadful it was, so I lied and said it was great."

"What happened the following Saturday when you had to go back?"

"I did exactly that. I went back. It wasn't so bad the second week, and even if it never became a passion, it stopped being something I hated."

"How long did you take lessons?"

"Three years. I was never going to be a prima ballerina, but I didn't suck at it either. Not like some of the other girls. Then puberty hit and what little grace I possessed went out the window. It was like I had six legs and four arms all of a sudden."

"Ouch." Bauer pulled a face. "I hope your coordination has improved since, considering the gun you carry around now."

"I'm not going to shoot you by accident, if that's what you're worried about."

"Glad to hear it." Bauer grinned. "I guess if you put a bullet in me, I'll know you meant it."

"Keep picking on me, and you might find out." Patterson gave Bauer a sideways look. "Okay, mister. Your turn. Tell me something about yourself and make it good. I don't want to hear any lame stories about how you wanted to be an astronaut when you grew up."

"Oh, you mean like how you wanted to be a ballerina?"

"I told you something personal. Now spill it."

"I'd love to," Bauer said as he navigated them off the highway and onto a small Main Street. "But there isn't time right now."

"What are you talking about?" Patterson sensed that she might have been duped.

"We're here." Bauer pulled into a parking space in front of a two-floor red brick building with large windows and white painted trim. A sign above the door, stenciled in gold paint, read Collins County Gazette. Bauer glanced at the dashboard clock. "And not a minute too early. Ten o'clock exactly."

"You planned that." Patterson gave a frustrated huff.

"Hey, I can't help it if you talk too much." Bauer pushed his door open and climbed out, then leaned back into the car. "You coming, or what?"

ELEVEN

THE OFFICES of the Collins County Gazette looked as outdated as their cardboard box filing system. The first thing Patterson saw when she walked through the door was an old manual typewriter sitting on a well-worn oak desk. To the left of this was a second desk that housed a CRT computer monitor on what was surely one of the first desktop computers ever produced. A banker's chair sat empty behind the desk. Above them, a fan with metal blades rattled in lazy circles. The air carried a faint odor of mildew and cigarette smoke, the latter of which came from an ashtray next to the computer, full of cigarette butts.

Patterson raised an eyebrow. "I guess a healthy working environment isn't a top priority around here."

"Like I said, old school." Bauer's gaze drifted around the empty room. "You think there's a bell or something we should ding to get some attention?"

"There's no need for that," a hoarse voice said. "I'm here."

Patterson saw a pole-thin man with a lined face and wispy white hair emerge through a door at the back of the office.

"You must be Harry Cline," Bauer said, stepping forward to greet the old man.

"Since my mama named me." Cline shook hands with Bauer. "And you must be the FBI agents from Dallas."

Patterson nodded and introduced herself. "My partner said you had some old newspapers with articles on TexFest."

"Ayuh."

"That's not a Texas accent," Patterson said, recognizing the archaic northern colloquialism. "What's a Mainer like you doing so far south?"

"You caught that, huh?" Cline sniffed and cleared his throat. "Came here as a young lad to work for a big city paper. Portland felt a bit small, and Boston was too cold. Turned out, the big city paper didn't want me as much as I wanted it, so I ended up here instead."

"How long ago was that?" Bauer asked.

"Longer than the sum of both your ages, I'll wager," Cline answered. "And let's leave it at that."

"Mr. Cline, you would've been around when TexFest took place," Patterson said. "Do you remember it?"

"Not so much. Wasn't me that covered it. That job went to a younger reporter by the name of Jimmy Bell. He did all our entertainment stuff. Back then, the paper was doing better. People still wanted to advertise and such. We could afford to have a real staff and I was a real editor. Even had a secretary who did nothing but answer the phone and brew coffee." A wistful look came upon the old man as if he wished he could turn back the clock by forty years. Then he shook it off. "But no matter. You're not here to watch an old reporter reminisce about his salad days. You want to see those newspapers."

"Very much," Patterson replied.

"It's all tucked away in here." Cline walked behind the desk with the outdated computer sitting on it and bent over. A moment later he straightened with a bankers box, which he placed on the table. He removed the lid and pulled out three yellow newspapers, which he dropped on the desk next to the box. "Ran articles on consecutive weeks. Two before, and one after the festival."

Patterson stepped closer to the desk and picked up the first newspaper. She didn't see an article on the front page, so she started leafing through it.

"First two articles were in the entertainment section a week apart," Cline said. "Don't get your hopes up. They're not very long."

Patterson kept turning pages until she found the right section. Cline wasn't wrong. The TexFest piece took up only eight column inches and mostly talked about the headliners that would be playing, and where to purchase tickets. She folded the paper and placed it down, then started through the next one. The following week's article was no better, just more of the same, and she found nothing useful. Frustrated, she dropped the newspaper back on the table and looked at Bauer. "There's nothing here. These are just fluff pieces to fill space."

"Not so fast, young lady," Cline said. There was still one more newspaper, which he picked up and opened to the entertainment section. There, printed in big black letters, was a headline.

TexFest Fails to Bring the Music.

And underneath, in smaller type.

Three-day Festival Reduced to Two as Bands Cry Foul.

Patterson felt a surge of hope. This was what they came for. The newspaper, dated the Friday after TexFest, had found something worth writing about after all.

She took the paper from Cline and laid it down on the desk. Almost the entire page was dedicated to the festival, except for a quarter-page ad hawking a local music shop in the bottom left corner. She read the article with growing excitement. It was a sad chronicle of the music festival's demise but offered no clues regarding the cryptic message scrolled on the registration card from Oklahoma City. Except for one thing. The festival didn't start until noon each day, and unlike larger festivals that provided camping areas, this one didn't offer any accommodations, which meant no one was watching the *sunrise at TexFest*. This only raised more questions and left them no closer to deciphering the message than they had been before. Patterson wondered if they were just chasing shadows. After all, she wasn't even sure the registration card had anything to do with her sister.

Then Patterson turned the page and found a second article. And this one was more useful. It was an interview with a man named Otto Sharp. He spent most of the interview griping about all the people that had contributed to the festival's downfall, from the town council who forced him to obtain permits for the event—which he claimed was unnecessary red tape—to the bands that didn't show up because they hadn't been paid. The bitterness and anger practically oozed off the page and did nothing to address the real reasons the festival failed, but it did one thing. It gave Patterson the name of the festival's organizer. She turned to Bauer with renewed hope. "We have to find Otto Sharp."

TWELVE

JUST HOW DO you propose we find this Otto Sharp?"
Bauer asked after they left the offices of the Collins County
Gazette. "That music festival was sixteen years ago. He could
be anywhere by now. For all we know, he's dead."

"Let's hope not, because he's our only lead." Patterson
was already on her way back to the car. After jumping into the
passenger seat, she took out her cell phone. "I have an idea."

Bauer climbed into the driver's seat and gave her a
quizzical look. "You going to run his name through NCIC?"

"Not quite." Patterson was busy tapping away on the
phone. After a minute, she let out a satisfied grunt. "Found
him."

"You did?" Bauer sounded skeptical. "Just like that?"

"Yup." Patterson held the phone out for her partner to see.
"I figured a registered company must have organized
TexFest, like a corporation. It would be the only way to get
liability insurance and such."

Now Bauer looked impressed. "You searched for Otto
Sharp's name on the Texas Secretary of State's website."

"Right. Any corporation set up in Texas would have to be registered there. And they keep those records forever, even if the company is no longer operating." Patterson felt a surge of renewed hope. "And there it is. Sharp Musical Entertainment, LLC. Registered in 2005 and defunct by 2007. They only filed two years of annual reports before the company went into administrative dissolution."

"And our man Otto was the registered owner," Bauer said, looking at the screen.

"He sure was. What are the chances that there are two people with that name running entertainment businesses in Texas on those exact dates?"

"Pretty slim." Bauer scratched his chin. "But this still doesn't help us. The registered office address is a lawyer's office downtown, and we'd need a court order to access those records even if they still exist."

"I know. But that isn't the only business Otto Sharp has registered." Patterson scrolled down to a second listing. "Look, here."

"Sharp Enterprises, LLC. Registered three years ago with two members. Otto Sharp, and a man named Edward Rossman." Patterson pointed at the screen. "And look here. There's a DBA. He's doing business as High Note Bar and Grill."

"That's got to be the same guy. As you said, there can't be two men called Otto Sharp running around Dallas. It's too unusual a name."

"Which means we've found the man who put TexFest together. I think we should go talk to him, don't you?"

"Hell yes." Now Bauer was tapping away on his own phone. He looked up with a triumphant grin. "I have the address of that bar. It's in Cedar Crest."

"I don't know where that is," Patterson said.

"Me either," Bauer admitted, reaching for the GPS. "Been here two weeks, remember?"

"Of course." Patterson watched him enter the address into the infotainment system and a moment later, their route came up, taking them around the east side of Dallas and below downtown. She looked at the travel time estimate and groaned. "An hour away. Almost forty-nine miles."

"Dallas is a big place." Bauer shrugged. "What else are we going to do? Go back and sit in that broom closet SAC Harris assigned to us?"

"Good point." Patterson put her phone away and clicked her seatbelt. Then she turned to Bauer. "While we're driving, you can tell me more about yourself. You can't say there isn't time now."

THIRTEEN

THEY DROVE south for the next hour, picking up I-635 as it looped around the east side of Dallas. As they drove, Patterson waited for Bauer to make conversation, but he remained tightlipped. After ten minutes, she decided to nudge him. "You just going to sit there in silence for the entire journey?" She asked.

"I was thinking, that's all." Bauer changed lanes and sped past a line of slow traffic. "You've probably already come to this conclusion, but I don't think the message on that registration card should be taken literally. They weren't excited about seeing the sunrise at that music festival."

"You're right. I do have a hunch about the sunrise comment," Patterson said. "But why don't you go first?"

"Very well. What if sunrise was a band?"

"I guess we're on the same page." Patterson nodded. "It's the only other thing that makes sense. But that leads us to another question. Was that registration card filled out by members of a band called Sunrise, or were they excited to see a band with that name?"

"Impossible to know without more information."

"Right." Patterson had her phone out again. She spent a few minutes on the web, then shook her head. "If they were a band, they're long gone. There's no mention of them anywhere."

"Not surprising. Think how many people start bands every year in the United States. I bet half of them never even get a gig, let alone get mentioned on the web. Hell, even I was in a band for about fifteen minutes back in high school."

"Let me guess, lead singer." Patterson smirked.

"Not even close. Drummer." Now it was Bauer's turn to smirk. "Which is better than being a ballerina."

"Hey. Watch it."

"Sorry. Couldn't resist." Now Bauer turned serious again. "If Sunrise was a band, they must have been playing at the festival. Maybe this guy we're going to see, Otto Sharp, will be able to tell us something."

"Unless they were one of the acts that pulled out after he stiffed them."

"Then let's hope they showed up."

"More to the point, let's hope Otto Sharp is even at this bar when we get there."

"You know, we could've called ahead," Bauer said.

"I thought about that. But I'd rather not give him advanced warning of our arrival. It sounds like he was a pretty shady character back in 2005. He might be no less shady now. We don't want to give him an excuse to skip out before we get there."

"Never thought of that."

"That's why I'm the senior agent, and you're shadowing me."

"I was a detective back in LA, you know." Bauer shot her a quick glance. "I'm not completely green."

"We'll see about that," Patterson said. She glanced at the dashboard clock; saw they had only been driving for twenty minutes. With nothing else to do, she settled back and watched the city pass them by. She couldn't help but wonder how long Julie had spent here, and what else she might discover about her sister's last days. Ahead of them, Otto Sharp waited. She only hoped he knew something that would move the investigation forward.

FOURTEEN

THE HIGH NOTE BAR AND GRILL occupied one half of a rundown strip plaza on a busy road next to a snow cone place that advertised a hundred flavors of frozen delight. Across the road was a paint and body shop with a bunch of beaters parked outside, some of which looked like they hadn't moved in years. Further away, Patterson could see a liquor store and a rundown trailer park. Everything was spread out, with patches of brown grass in between the buildings. For being so close to Dallas, it felt very rural.

"This looks like a class joint," Bauer commented, eyeing a row of motorcycles parked outside, their chrome gleaming in the sun. A lone biker in a black leather jacket and chaps stood outside drinking a can of PPR. He eyed their Dodge Charger with suspicion. "Maybe I should go in alone."

"What, you think I can't handle a couple of bikers in a dive bar?"

"I never said that." Bauer looked uncomfortable. "I just meant that it could be a rowdy place. I've been in this type of joint before, back in my LAPD days. People of a certain caliber who ride motorcycles and hang out in bars have an aversion to cops. They might not welcome us with open arms."

"Doesn't mean I should stay in the car." Patterson glared at Bauer, wondering if he was trying to be a knight in shining armor, or was just sexist. "Do I have to remind you yet again, Special Agent Bauer, that I am the senior agent here, and you are supposed to be shadowing me, not the other way around?"

"Whoa. Easy there. I just thought it would be better if we handled this lightly. Someone might misconstrue a pair of armed Feds barging into a biker bar."

"Then we won't barge," Patterson said, unbuckling her seatbelt and pushing her door open. "We'll go in as dainty as can be and treat the occupants inside that building with all the decorum they deserve."

"Yes ma'am," Bauer said, opening his own door. "We'll do it your way."

"That's more like it," Patterson replied. "And the next time you throw a ma'am in my direction, I'm writing you up for insubordination."

"Just recognizing your position as senior agent," Bauer said in an even tone as they walked across the gravel parking lot.

"Sure, you are," Patterson said under her breath as they reached the entrance.

The biker standing outside straightened up and crumpled his empty beer can while observing them with narrowed eyes. Patterson tensed, expecting him to step in their path, but instead, he threw the can into a dumpster sitting next to a leaning wooden fence at the edge of the parking lot and folded his arms. As she passed by, Patterson noticed his tattoos, including the letters FTW inked in Gothic outline text on his right forearm, which she knew from a stint in a gang task force back in New York meant *Forever Two Wheels*. A skull with deep black eye sockets and a rictus grin occupied his left forearm, but she didn't see any visible tats related to a specific gang affiliation. This meant nothing, and they would need to be careful. She hurried past the biker and went inside with Bauer a step behind.

The interior of the bar was everything Patterson expected. Dark, dingy, and smoky. A pair of pool tables stood near the back wall, one of which was in use. Neon beer signs of all shapes and sizes adorned the walls. In between these, in glass cases, hung electric guitars with signatures scrawled on the pickguards. A black-and-white photo in a thin frame hung next to each, no doubt referencing the signer. A sticky floor and an odor of stale beer and old tobacco that hung in the air completed the dive bar ambiance.

Rock music belted from speakers near the ceiling, which would, Patterson decided, make it hard to hold a conversation. The place was not overly busy, but it wasn't dead either. She guessed there must be twenty or more bikers present, even though it was only lunchtime.

As they made their way through the saloon toward the bar, suspicious eyes turned in their direction. They were hardly dressed for the part. She was wearing black slacks and a cream blouse under a light jacket, while Bauer wore a charcoal suit and white cotton shirt. Thankfully, their guns were snug out of view in low-profile shoulder holsters.

"This is a barrel of laughs," Bauer said, just loud enough to be heard as they approached the bar.

"I thought you had experience with places like this," Patterson replied, raising her voice over the music.

"Doesn't mean I have to like them."

Bauer kept his arms at his sides, but Patterson knew he was on high alert and could draw his gun at a moment's notice should it become necessary, as could she. But with luck, that wouldn't be necessary. They weaved around a high-top table, ignoring the leather-clad biker with a straggly beard who muttered something in their direction as they passed by.

It was surely not a compliment.

Patterson kept her eyes rooted frontward and then they were at the bar.

The server, a girl in her twenties with stringy, straw blonde shoulder-length hair that was already showing its dark roots, approached them with a wary look, her eyes lingering on their outfits.

"You two get lost on your way to the country club?" She asked.

"Hardly," Patterson replied, slipping her credentials wallet out and opening it briefly for the bartender to see before returning it to her jacket pocket. "We're looking for a man named Otto Sharp."

"You got a warrant or something?" The girl cocked her head to one side.

Bauer leaned on the bar, careful to avoid a patch of spilled beer. "Did he do something that would call for us to have a warrant?"

"Beats me." The bartender shrugged. "I just work here."

"Then you do know Otto Sharp."

"Sure. Owns the place. He's my boss."

"What's your name?" Patterson asked.

"Dakota."

"Well, Dakota, why don't you run along and find your boss before we're forced to leave and come back later with a warrant that has *your* name on it."

"You can do that?" Dakota's mouth pinched closed. She studied the federal agents as if she were trying to decide if they really had the authority to arrest her for something so trivial as stalling them.

"Obstructing justice," Bauer chipped in, doing a fine job of selling the lie.

"Okay. Whatever. I'll go get him. Why would I care if a couple of Feds want to crack his skull?"

"That's the spirit," Patterson said.

But Dakota didn't need to fetch her boss, because at that moment a large man in his early fifties appeared through a door behind the bar. He wore jeans and a white tee stretched over a muscular frame. An oversize silver belt buckle depicting an eagle with spread wings sat snug below his flabby stomach. His salt-and-pepper hair, long and straight, was pulled back into a ponytail.

He observed the two federal agents in the same way a Chef de Cuisine might watch a cockroach run across his kitchen floor. Then he ushered the bartender away before speaking. "I'm Otto Sharp. Why are you in my bar?"

FIFTEEN

PATTERSON STUDIED the man before her for a moment before she spoke, summing him up. "Are you the same Otto Sharp who was responsible for a music festival in a place called Somerdale several years ago?"

"Who's asking?"

"The FBI," Patterson said, speaking over the music but keeping her voice low enough for the reply to stay between them. For the second time in as many minutes, she flashed her credits. "Now, were you the organizer of TexFest, or not?"

"TexFest," Sharp echoed. "I didn't think anyone even remembered that stupid festival. If you're here to pin some bogus charge on me, it won't work. Statute of limitations must've run out years ago."

"We're not here to charge you with a crime, Mr. Sharp," Patterson replied. "We just want to ask some questions."

"About the music festival?"

"Yes."

"Alright. But make it quick. If the pair of you hang around here much longer, all my customers will leave."

"Don't worry, I'll get straight to the point," Patterson

replied. "We want to know if you remember any of the bands that performed there."

"One band in particular," Bauer said. "They might have gone by the name Sunrise."

"How would I know a thing like that?" Sharp shook his head. "That festival was sixteen years ago, and half the damn bands didn't even show up."

"Then you don't remember if there was a group called Sunrise?" Patterson asked.

"No. I don't recall any band with that name."

"What about paperwork?" Bauer asked. "You must have some of that. Contracts. Flyers. Programs." His eyes flitted to the signed guitars on the walls. "You seem to like your memorabilia. I can't imagine you wouldn't keep stuff relating to your own festival."

"Yeah. I got some stuff. Haven't looked at it in years."

"Great." Patterson felt her hope rising. "Now seems like a good time to stroll down memory lane. Why don't you drag it out and we'll take a peek."

"Not gonna happen," Sharp said.

"And why would that be, Mr. Sharp?" Patterson asked.

"Because I put it all in my storage locker years ago, and I'm not going to leave the bar just so you guys can rummage through some old paperwork."

"You don't have any of that stuff on the premises?" Bauer looked around. "Surely you have storage around here. Place is big enough."

"Yeah. I didn't have the bar when I packed that stuff away. I left town for several years after the festival. Moved around for a while. When I came back, I couldn't see the point of moving it all again. The storage place is cheap."

"Why *did* you come back?" Patterson asked. "Doesn't sound like you'd had much luck here."

"Friend of mine wanted help with this place. He had a

bad back—slipped disc—couldn't do the work anymore. Lots of lifting, what with the kegs and all. In the end, he sold it to me outright."

"That friend would be Edward Rossman?"

"That's him."

"His name's still on the business registration."

Sharp shrugged. "Never took it off. Probably should. Haven't even seen the guy in two years. Took off down to Florida."

"I see," Patterson said. "Still doesn't help us with the storage unit."

"Can't help that."

"Maybe we can change your mind," Bauer said.

"Don't think so." Sharp sniffed and wiped his nose with the back of his hand. "Unless you got some sort of court order. But you don't, do you?"

"No. We don't." Patterson could feel the frustration building inside her. They were so close to finding the truth about that registration card. And now they had run into a roadblock that went by the name of Otto Sharp. Without talking to a judge, they had no leverage, and she knew there wasn't enough evidence to make their request official.

"That's what I thought." A slight smile touched Sharp's lips. "Looks like your shit out of luck."

"That remains to be seen," Bauer said. "You call yourself a bar and grill."

"So what?" Otto looked perplexed.

"That means you serve food."

"Served. Past tense. We used to sell hamburgers, wings, the usual stuff. It was a lot of expense, and we weren't making enough money on it, so now we just pour beer and liquor."

"But you're still licensed to serve food."

"I guess."

Bauer glanced around. "This place is full of smoke and smells like old socks."

"What's your point?" Otto narrowed his eyes.

"Just that the health inspector might take a keen interest in your establishment if we pointed him this way. After all, Cedar Crest has a smoke-free air ordinance. I can see at least three people smoking in here at this very moment. That's a certain violation even if you're just a bar, but if you have a food license too . . ."

"Are you trying to blackmail me?" Otto did his best to sound defiant, but the tremble in his voice betrayed him.

"No. I'm just pointing out that it's probably easier to do what we want than pay a bunch of hefty fines and risk your bar getting closed down while you take care of the issue."

Patterson stepped closer to the bar. "You might even lose your liquor license. That would put a serious crimp in your business."

"They're not going to take away my liquor license over a couple of people lighting up."

"You sure about that?" Bauer replied.

"I have signs." Otto pointed to a small no-smoking placard propped on the back of the bar. "It's not my fault if people ignore them."

"I beg to disagree." Bauer was holding his cell phone. He glanced down at it and unlocked the screen. "But let's make that call to the health department and ask them."

"Wait. There's no need for that."

"You'll get us those records from the storage unit?" Patterson asked.

"Sure. Anything to get you people out of my bar."

"See, that wasn't so hard, was it?" Patterson folded her arms and gave the flustered bar owner a satisfied look.

"Whatever." Otto shook his head. "The unit's over in

Forest Hill about half an hour from here. I can meet you there after the lunchtime rush. Say four o'clock?"

Bauer glanced at Patterson. "That work for you?"

Patterson nodded. "Sure." She turned her attention back to Otto. "But you'd better show up, or our next call will be the health department. We might even be tempted to run a check with local PD and see how many disturbances this place has. Judging by your clientele, I bet it's enough for code enforcement to issue a public nuisance citation."

"All right. You've made your point." Otto was scribbling an address on the back of a business card. He held it out to them. "This is the storage unit. I'll be there at four."

"Thank you." Patterson took the business card.

Otto glanced around nervously. Several bikers were looking in their direction. "You should probably leave now if you know what's good for you. The natives are getting restless."

"Suits me," Bauer said, turning toward the door. "I need a shower after standing in here this long."

"You and me both," Patterson agreed.

SIXTEEN

WHEN PATTERSON and Bauer stepped out of the bar's dark interior and into the sunshine, they saw a pair of stocky bikers in leather duds leaning against their car with folded arms. The shorter of the two, the man they had passed on the way in, now had another can of beer, even though neither agent had seen him make a trip to the bar. He sipped this and watched over the rim of the can as they approached.

"Can I help you, gentlemen?" Patterson asked.

"Just looking after your sweet wheels here," replied the second biker. He was more muscular than his companion, with a bald head that reflected the sun. Stubble darkened his chin. A denim jacket with the sleeves removed, known as a cut, no doubt sported a club patch on the rear, although Patterson could not see it. The three dots under his right eye, a lifestyle tattoo that represented mi Vida Loca, or my crazy life, further solidified his gang associations.

"Thanks. But I think our wheels are just fine on their own." Patterson stopped several feet from the bikers. She felt the reassuring push of the Glock service weapon against her ribs, readied herself to draw should it become necessary.

"Nah. This is a dangerous neighborhood. Gotta watch your back."

"Doesn't look very dangerous."

"Yeah, well, looks can be deceptive." The biker cracked his knuckles and then folded his thick arms.

Bauer stepped forward. "Well, we certainly appreciate you looking after our vehicle. Now if you wouldn't mind stepping aside, we will be on our way."

The shorter biker grinned and took a swig of his beer. "How about you stay and party a while first? Buy us a drink for being such upstanding citizens and watching over your automobile."

"I don't think so." Bauer kept his tone level but forceful.

"Aw. Come on. Don't be like that." The biker with the tattoo under his eye gave Patterson the once over. "Maybe we can have some fun with your friend here. Take her out back and show her a good time. I bet she'd like that." He licked his lips, mouth curling up into a leering smile.

"Or maybe we can slap a pair of cuffs on you," Patterson said, doing her best to hide the disgust she felt. "Drop you off at the nearest police station on a charge of threatening a federal law enforcement officer."

"Just trying to be friendly." The biker held his hands up. "But hey, if you want to be a stick in the mud…"

"Hey." A shout came from behind Bauer and Patterson.

They turned to see Otto Sharp striding across the parking lot. He didn't look happy.

As he drew close, he motioned to the bikers. "Angel. Frankie. Get your butts back inside the bar, pronto."

"We weren't doing nothing," the larger biker, Angel, protested. "Just hanging."

"I know exactly what you were doing." Otto jerked his thumb toward the bar. "You have ten seconds to get inside or there'll be hell to pay."

If the two men thought Otto was bluffing, they didn't show it. Instead, they pushed themselves away from the car and sauntered past the FBI agents. As they went, Angel muttered something under his breath in Spanish. It didn't sound complimentary.

Patterson stepped in his path. "You have something to say?"

"Well now, maybe I—"

Otto closed the gap between them and gripped the biker by his collar. "You got nothing to say."

"Whatever." Angel shook the bar owner off and pushed past him.

Otto watched them leave, then turned to the federal agents. "This is why you shouldn't have come here."

"We needed to speak with you," Patterson replied.

"Ever heard of a telephone?"

"Would you have talked to us?"

"Probably not."

"Which is why we drove over here," Patterson said. "You should be more careful who you let drink in this place."

"Those two?" Otto grunted. "They're harmless. Mostly. Just a couple of numbskulls who don't know when to keep their mouths shut."

"Right."

"If we're done here, I'd really like you off my premises." Otto glanced toward the car. "Even your ride screams cop."

"Don't worry, we're going." Patterson stepped around the bar owner. "See you at four."

"I can hardly wait." Otto started back toward his bar.

Patterson noticed Angel and Frankie lingering by the door. They met her gaze for a moment, then turned and slipped inside the rundown building.

"Can we go now?" Bauer asked.

"Sure," Patterson replied. When they were back inside the car, she turned to him. "You did good out there."

Bauer shrugged off the compliment. "Dealt with people like them before, back in LA. Antiauthority types. Guys who run with gangs. They're all the same." He started the engine. "We've got a while before we need to be at that storage unit. There's no point in driving back to the office. You want to get some lunch?"

"Sounds like a plan," Patterson replied. "Not around here, though."

"Heaven forbid." Bauer chuckled. "I know a place."

"Wouldn't be pizza, would it?" Patterson asked with a grin.

"You really think I'm that one-dimensional?"

"Are you?"

"Sometimes. But in this case, it's not pizza."

"Great." Patterson settled back into the seat. "Surprise me."

SEVENTEEN

THE STORAGE UNIT was on a dead-end road in a part of town not much better than the one in which Otto's bar was located. Bauer got them there with ten minutes to spare, and they sat outside the facility until Otto Sharp pulled up driving a dented and rusty old Toyota truck. He typed the code in and waited for the gates to open, then pulled through and led them toward the back of the complex near a graveled area where RVs and boats on trailers were parked up.

He stopped and exited his vehicle next to a unit in the middle of the block and removed the padlock, lifting the roll-up door.

When Patterson and Bauer approached, they saw a large ten-by-fifteen unit with metal racks lining the walls. These were stuffed with boxes of various shapes and sizes, plastic containers, and other assorted objects, some of which looked like they might be related to his bar business. The center of the storage unit was stacked high with larger crates and boxes, along with a loveseat, some faded outdoor furniture, and a pair of floor lamps. A narrow pathway barely wide enough to fit through had been left between the jumble of items piled into the center of the storage unit and the racks.

"Wow," Bauer exclaimed to the bar owner. "I hope you know what you're looking for because this place is jammed. It could take all day if we have to hunt through these boxes."

"I know where it is." Otto inserted himself between the stacks of boxes and the metal racks. He worked his way down toward the back of the unit, using the flashlight on his cell phone to light the way.

Patterson and Bauer stayed outside and waited while Otto searched, pulling containers and boxes down from the rack and setting them aside on the floor. He soon found a bankers box toward the back of a shelf and heaved it out with a grunt. Navigating his way back up the narrow pathway, he emerged back into the sunlight and placed the box on the hood of his truck.

"Everything you want should be in here," he said, blowing a thick layer of dust from the box lid.

Patterson saw the word TexFest scribbled on the front of the box in black permanent marker that had faded to brown.

Otto removed the lid and peered inside. The box was stuffed with paperwork. "All the contracts and agreements are in file folders marked by type. Bands, facilities, vendors, and suppliers. There are also promotional materials like posters and flyers and the original maps showing the layout of the festival grounds."

"Great. Can we look?" Bauer asked, stepping forward.

"You want to go through it here?" Otto scowled. "That will take hours and I've got a business to run."

"We appreciate your cooperation, Mr. Sharp," Patterson said. "And we'll keep it as quick as we can."

"Or you could just take the stuff with you and bring it back when you're done." Otto put the lid back on the box. "That way I don't have to stand here all evening watching you paw through a bunch of dirty old paperwork that I should've tossed out years ago."

"We're very pleased that you didn't," Bauer said. "Just to be clear, you're giving us permission to remove these items from your possession and examine them offsite."

"I want them back afterward."

"We'll be sure to return them," Patterson said.

"Sure. You can bring them back to the bar. I don't want to drive out here twice in a week if I don't need to." Otto hesitated, as if a thought had just occurred to him. He placed a protective hand on the box. "You're not investigating anything that could get me in trouble, right?"

"As you already pointed out, the statute of limitations has long expired on any nefarious dealings you might have engaged in back then. Unless you murdered someone, of course. You didn't do that, I assume?"

"Is that what you're investigating?" Otto blinked in surprise. "Do I look like a murderer?"

"We're not inclined to reveal the nature of our investigation," Patterson said. "And as for your second question, murderers come in all shapes and sizes. If they looked like killers, it would make our job a whole lot easier."

"Boy, wouldn't it, though?" Bauer chuckled. He gave Otto a reassuring look. "You have nothing to worry about. We're not investigating you for any crime, but the contents of that box may help us in a matter not directly related to you or the music festival. A person of interest in a cold case may have attended or been associated with a band that performed at TexFest."

"Well, in that case . . ." Otto looked visibly relieved.

"May we?" Patterson reached for the box.

"Oh. Go ahead." Otto lifted his arm and stepped back. He still looked unsettled, but didn't stop Patterson when she picked up the box and carried it to their car.

She deposited it on the back seat and turned back to Otto. "We'll go through everything as quickly as we can and get it back to you in the next few days."

"Sure. Sure." Otto nodded. He pulled the storage unit door back down and slid the latch across before securing the padlock again. "Call me before you bring the box back to arrange a suitable time. I don't need y'all coming into the bar again. No offense, but you're not very good for business."

"Believe me, we'd rather not step foot back inside that bar either," Bauer said. "I'll have to dry-clean this suit to get the smell of cigarette smoke out."

"So long as we understand each other." Otto pulled the truck door open. "We all done, here?"

"I think we have everything we need," Patterson said. "So long as you've handed over everything related to TexFest."

"If it ain't in that box, I don't have it anymore." Otto climbed into the truck and started the engine. Without another word, he slammed the door and pulled away.

Patterson watched the truck turn between two rows of storage units and drive out of sight. "Such a pleasant guy."

"Salt of the earth," Bauer replied with a touch of sarcasm in his voice. "You want to go back to the office and sift through this stuff?"

"Not particularly." Patterson shook her head. "It will be past five by the time we get there. I don't see the point."

"It can wait till tomorrow, then."

"Or I can take the box with me and have a look through it tonight in the motel room. It's not like I've got anything better to do." Patterson walked around to the Charger's passenger side and opened the door. "They don't even have any decent cable channels."

"You want me to stay and help?" Bauer asked, climbing into the driver's seat. He didn't sound enthusiastic.

"Unnecessary. If I find anything of relevance, I can always call you."

"Great." Bauer eased the car forward and headed toward the gates. "I had plans, anyway. Now I won't have to cancel."

"Do tell," Patterson said. "Hot date?"

"I think I'll plead the fifth on that one."

"Ooh. *It is* a date." Patterson grinned.

"No comment." Bauer pulled through the gates and turned right, heading back toward the interstate. "But you have fun tonight with your box of moldy old paperwork."

EIGHTEEN

BACK IN HER motel room later that evening, Patterson lifted the lid off the box and delved inside. The first thing she came across were old posters advertising the music festival. She examined one but didn't recognize any of the headliners. Wherever he found his musical acts, Otto Sharp was scraping the bottom of the barrel. There was no mention of a band named Sunrise, which she did not find surprising.

Moving on, she pulled out a stack of folders, some of which contained receipts, while others were stuffed with paperwork. She went through them until she found an inch-thick folder marked *band contracts*. She moved the box to the floor and put the pile of contracts on the table in front of her, then leafed through them one by one. Otto Sharp had hired a lot of performers to play at TexFest. A necessity considering it was supposed to have been a three-day festival and the layout map showed a main stage and two smaller stages. Some of these acts had not shown up, she knew, forcing the festival to drop one of its days. But there was no indication of which groups had actually performed. The only clue was a photocopy of the payment check pinned to the back of some contracts. Presumably, the bands Otto paid had played. Even so, it was hardly worth it for them. The checks were, she noted, for modest amounts ranging from fifty dollars on the low end to a maximum of three hundred. Clearly, TexFest was thrown together on a shoestring budget.

She flipped through each contract, discarding it when she saw nothing of relevance. This went on for over an hour, with the reject stack growing higher until she came to a dogeared contract held together with a paperclip two-thirds of the way down the pile.

With a rush of satisfaction, she read the band name on the paperwork. *Sunrise.* She turned to the second page where the contract was signed. Here she found a name written next to the signature in block capitals. Martin Wright. She recognized that name. He was listed on one of the registration cards along with Karissa Harper. The attached check for fifty dollars was made out to the same person. Her satisfaction turned to disappointment. This was confirmation of their hunch regarding the cryptic message, *Sunrise at Texfest*, but it still didn't provide any connection to Julie. The only name her sister had mentioned in the unmailed letter she wrote to Stacy was Trent Steiger.

Patterson was about to throw the contract down in frustration, but then she noticed another smaller piece of paper stapled behind the last sheet of the contract. It was a band bio, presumably provided for Otto Sharp to include in the festival program.

With renewed hope, Patterson read the bio and let out a whoop of joy when she saw the band members listed there.

Karissa Harper—Vocals.

Trent Steiger—Lead Guitar.

Mark Davis—Bass guitar.

Martin Wright—Drums.

The two registration cards were connected, after all.

What's more, Trent Steiger, who Julie had mentioned in her letter, was the lead guitar player. It was all fitting into place now. Julie had met the members of the band Sunrise in Oklahoma City while they were staying at the Welcome Inn. Maybe they were playing a gig there en route to Dallas. Either way, she left with them and rode down to Dallas in the band's van, presumably to attend the music festival. The fact that a check was issued meant the band must have played. This was the first shred of proof Patterson had that Julie actually made it to Dallas. The only name still unaccounted for was Simon Bailey, but she figured he might be just a random stranger who checked out on the same day. Not that it mattered. She was getting closer to the truth about Julie's trip to Dallas.

Patterson looked over the contract again, saw a telephone number and address listed in the contact section. What were the chances the number still worked? After sixteen years, it was a long shot, but Patterson figured it was worth a try. She typed the number into her cell phone and waited. It rang three times before there was an answer.

"Hello?" It was a female voice.

Patterson figured the phone number must be associated with Martin Wright, who signed the contract. She asked for him.

The woman hesitated, then replied. "I'm sorry. There's no one here by that name."

"Oh." Patterson felt a thud of disappointment. "What about Trent Steiger or Mark Davis?"

"I don't know either of those names." The woman sounded suspicious. "Who is this?"

Now Patterson introduced herself and said she was an FBI Special Agent looking for someone who was on the woman's number sixteen years ago. There was one name she hadn't tried yet. The girl, Karissa Harper.

But she didn't need to, because the woman settled the

matter on her own. "I've only had this number for a year. Got it when I moved to Dallas. I'm sorry, I can't help you."

Patterson thanked her and hung up with a sigh. It was another dead end. But she still had the address written on the contract. Was it possible that someone associated with the band still lived there? There was only one way to find out. Patterson glanced at the clock sitting on the nightstand.

It was 8 P.M.

Deciding she didn't want to wait until the next day, Patterson scooped up her car keys and headed out the door.

NINETEEN

THE ADDRESS LISTED on the band contract was a single-story brick house with an attached two-car garage and a small porch over the front door. A kid's bike lay on its side in the yard, which was more dirt than grass. There was a car sitting on the driveway in front of the garage, and Patterson could see a light shining through a window with drawn curtains at the front of the house. Someone was home, for sure.

She walked up the driveway and cut across the yard to the front door, removing her credentials at the same time. When she knocked, the curtain inched back to reveal the face of a woman in her forties. Patterson acknowledged her and held up the credential wallet, opening it so the homeowner could see her badge. The curtain dropped back in place and a moment later Patterson heard a deadbolt being drawn back before the door opened barely enough for the woman to peer out.

"Can I help you?" she asked, sounding puzzled.

"I hope so," Patterson said. "I'm looking for someone who

lived at this address sixteen years ago. His name is Martin Wright."

"I remember the Wrights. My husband and I purchased the house from them back in 2012. They seemed nice."

"Do you know where they went?" Patterson asked. Her only lead was slipping away. If she hit a brick wall now, she didn't know what to do next.

"I hardly think so. It was such a long time long ago, and I only met them a couple of times. Once when we viewed this house, and again at the closing."

"I see." Patterson thanked the woman for her time and turned to leave. When she was halfway down the driveway, the homeowner called out to her.

"Wait. I just thought of something."

Patterson stopped and looked back.

The woman was coming down the front steps. She pointed to the house next door. "You might want to try Mrs. Coulter before you leave. She's lived in this neighborhood forever. I think she was friends with the Wrights when they were here."

"Really?" Patterson's disappointment turned to renewed hope.

"I'm sure of it." The woman caught up with Patterson. "I'll take you over there and introduce you."

"Thank you," Patterson replied.

"It's my pleasure." The woman started toward her neighbor's house.

Patterson changed direction and followed her across the lawn and up to the front door.

Mrs. Coulter answered moments after they rang the bell. She looked surprised to see her neighbor standing there with a stranger. "Cheryl? Is everything okay? What's going on?"

"Everything's fine. This here is an FBI agent," Cheryl replied. "She's asking about the Wrights."

"Oh dear." Mrs. Coulter opened the door wider. "Are they in trouble?"

"Nothing like that," Patterson said, to ease the woman's fears. "They might have information regarding a cold case I'm investigating. Just a routine inquiry, but it's very important I speak to them."

"Goodness. I haven't spoken to them in ages. They sold the house because of a divorce and went their separate ways. Shame too. They were a nice family. Had two kids. A teenaged girl and a boy at college. I bumped into the wife, Lillian, at the grocery store a few years after they split up but haven't seen her since. I think she lives out of state now. Or at least, that's what I heard."

"I don't suppose you have any contact information?" Patterson asked.

"I don't. As I said, they were a nice enough couple, and I had coffee with Lillian once in a while when they lived here, but we weren't close friends."

"What about Rachel?" Cheryl asked. "I remember you saying she was friends with the girl."

"That's right. I think they still keep in touch."

"Who's Rachel?" Patterson asked.

"My daughter," Mrs. Coulter replied. "She and Claire are the same age. They used to ride their bikes to school together. Wait there a minute. I'll go call her."

"I'd appreciate that." Patterson watched the neighbor retreat inside the house. A couple of minutes passed, and then Mrs. Coulter returned and handed Patterson a slip of paper with a telephone number written on it.

"You're in luck. Rachel said they still text back and forth sometimes."

Patterson looked down at the number. It had a Dallas area code. "Does Claire Wright still live in the area?"

"Don't know. Didn't ask. I can phone Rachel back if you want and ask her."

"There's no need," Patterson said. "You've been a great help, Mrs. Coulter."

"Always ready to assist an officer of the law. My uncle was a cop back in the day. Dallas PD." Mrs. Coulter beamed with pride. "Of course, he's retired now."

"Is there anything else we can help you with?" Cheryl asked.

"No. This number will be fine." Patterson thanked the women again and left them chatting on the doorstep. She returned to her car and climbed in before taking her cell phone out, then dialed the number.

It rang four times. Patterson hoped it wouldn't go to voicemail. She was anxious to talk with the sister and get Martin Wright's contact details. Julie had traveled all the way to Dallas in the band's van. Martin Wright must have spent considerable time with her. He might be able to tell Patterson where her sister went next.

The phone was answered on the fifth ring. "Hello?"

"Am I speaking to Claire Wright?" Patterson asked.

"Yes. How can I help you?"

Patterson introduced herself without saying that she was a federal agent. She knew nothing about this woman and didn't want to scare her off. If it became necessary, she could always say she was an FBI agent, but right now Patterson went with a different tack. "Your brother, Martin Wright, was a friend of my sister many years ago. She came to Dallas with him and his friends in their van and went to TexFest."

"Wow. TexFest. I haven't thought about that in years. Martin played at the festival. He was in a band back in college."

"I know. Sunrise."

"That's right. What do you want with Martin?"

"He might have some information regarding my sister. I'm trying to track her down."

"I see." Claire went silent for a moment. "I'm afraid Martin isn't going to be much help to you."

"Why is that?" Patterson sensed that a bombshell was coming. She wasn't wrong.

"Because my brother isn't around anymore. He had some issues. Depression." Claire paused again. "He took his own life two years ago. Martin is dead."

TWENTY

MARTIN WRIGHT WAS DEAD. Patterson could hardly believe it. After tracking down the names on the registration card, figuring out that Sunrise was a band, and finally thinking she was going to get some new information regarding her sister, it was all for nothing.

Except Claire wasn't done yet. "What's your sister's name?" She asked.

"Julie," Patterson replied. "Julie Blake."

"I think I remember her. She came to the house with the band. Martin had graduated college and none of them had anywhere to stay because they were pretty much broke. There wasn't a spare bedroom in the house, so they took up residence in our garage. They slept on the floor in sleeping bags and used it as a practice room for the gig. My father was mad that he had to leave his car in the driveway the whole time they were there."

"Julie stayed with you, too?" Patterson asked, sensing she might still glean some useful information from this call. "You met her?"

"Sure. She was a few years older than me—I was still in

high school—but she was nice. I think she enjoyed having another girl around to talk to other than Karissa, who could be a bit moody. We went to the festival together and watched the band play."

This was fantastic. Patterson had found someone who met Julie while she was on her road trip. She wanted to know more. "Do you have time to talk? I'd love to pick your brain about my sister."

"Well . . . uh . . . I don't really have time tonight. I just went back to school for hairdressing and have an early start. I was about to take a shower and climb into bed. We can meet during my lunch hour tomorrow if you want. There's a coffee shop in the same strip plaza as the school."

"I'd love to," Patterson said.

"Great." Claire told Patterson the address. "One o'clock work?"

"Sure. I'll be there."

"Awesome. I don't really talk about Martin much anymore, or that time in my life. There's no one to listen. This will be nice." Claire paused a moment. "If you don't mind me asking, why are you looking for your sister? Did you lose touch with her?"

"Something like that." Patterson wondered how much she should tell Claire about her sister's disappearance. She didn't want to reveal herself as an FBI agent. At least, not yet. In the end, she decided only to keep it simple. "Julie's missing. Nobody's seen her in a long time. I'm trying to find her."

"Oh. That's awful. I'm not sure how much use I can be. It was so long ago. But I'll tell you everything I can remember."

"That's all I'm asking," Patterson said. "I appreciate you taking the time to meet with me."

"Not at all." Claire sounded distracted. "Look, I have to go. I'll see you tomorrow."

The phone line went dead.

Patterson sat in her car and peered through the windshield at the dark street beyond. Her gaze drifted across to the house where the Wright family lived before the parents divorced. She looked at the garage, imagining Julie there, sleeping among band equipment with the group of people she'd met in Oklahoma City. How long had her sister stayed here in this place? Where did she go afterward? She hoped those questions, and more would be answered the next day.

Patterson tore her gaze away from the house and started the car. There was nothing more she could do tonight, and it was a good forty-minute drive back to her motel. Feeling like she'd made a small connection with her long-lost sister, and hopeful about her meeting with Claire Wright the following afternoon, Patterson pulled away from the curb and headed back toward the interstate.

TWENTY-ONE

IT WAS nine in the morning when Patterson arrived at the small office she shared with Special Agent Bauer in the Dallas FBI building. When she entered, he was sitting at his desk, head bent over his laptop.

"Morning," he said, looking up. "You look tired."

"Little bit." She brought him up to speed about her activities the previous night.

You tracked down one of the band members without me?" Bauer asked, a hint of annoyance in his voice.

"I didn't want to wait until this morning." Patterson took a sip of the coffee she had picked up on the way to work. "It's not a big deal."

"We're supposed to be partners." Bauer glared at her across the top of his laptop. "How am I supposed to keep up on the case if you're going it alone after hours?"

"First, we're not partners. I'm the senior agent and you're shadowing me. Second, it's not our case, it's mine. I was working on it before I arrived in Dallas."

"And without me, you would never have tracked down

the editor of the Collins County Gazette. You wouldn't have found Otto Sharp. Which means you wouldn't have had a telephone number to call or address to go to last night." Bauer leaned back and folded his arms. "Regardless of what you might think, you need me. I'm good at my job."

"You've been on the job for two weeks."

"No. I've been an FBI agent for two weeks. I've been solving crimes for over a decade. Hell, I bet I've solved more murders than you have."

"This isn't a competition." Patterson wished SAC Harris hadn't saddled her with a newbie, especially one with an attitude. She wondered why he had. Could it be because she was Marilyn Kahn's inadvertent tool to ascend through the upper echelons of the FBI? Certainly, there didn't appear to be any love lost between her SAC back in New York and Harris. Was there a story there? If there was, she would probably never know. And it didn't matter. Bauer was here, and she had to deal with him. She sighed and decided it wasn't worth an argument. "Look, you were a big help, and I appreciate that. I wasn't trying to exclude you. You're right. Without you, I wouldn't have gotten the newspaper lead. But I didn't want to wait, and I'm sure you didn't want to be disturbed on your hot date."

"Yeah, well, it didn't turn out to be so much of a hot date after all." Bauer looked uncomfortable. "I would probably have done better tagging along with you to check out the Wright residence."

"Sorry." Patterson pulled a sympathetic face.

"Meh. It happens. What did you find out?"

Patterson told him about the Wrights getting divorced and moving. She also told him about her conversation with Mrs. Coulter, which led her to the daughter, Claire. Last, she mentioned that Martin Wright was dead.

"Yikes. That's a blow." Bauer made a tutting sound. "There goes that line of investigation."

"Not so much. Turns out that Claire Wright remembers Julie. My sister stayed in her garage when the band visited to play at the music festival. The two of them hung out together."

"Maybe she'll be able to fill in some blanks."

"That's what I'm hoping. I'm meeting her for lunch today at one o'clock."

"I notice you said that in the singular." Bauer didn't miss a beat. "Does that mean another solo excursion?"

"I think so. I don't want to overwhelm her. I haven't even told the woman I'm an FBI agent yet."

"Why not?" Bauer asked. He raised an eyebrow.

"Because I think she'll open up more if she believes I'm just a worried sister looking for her missing sibling."

"You sure that's the right approach?"

"If it becomes necessary, I'll tell her I'm a federal agent. But it's not like we'll need her to testify in court or anything. I can't imagine she knows what happened to my sister. She wasn't even aware Julie went missing. But she may be able to point us in the right direction."

"You said the brother killed himself." Bauer was leaning forward now. "You sure he didn't have something to do with Julie's disappearance? Could be a guilty conscience."

"He only died a couple of years ago."

"Doesn't matter. He could've been living with what happened all these years and it finally got to him. You did say he was depressed."

"If Martin Wright had something to do with my sister's disappearance, then he would also have to be the person who sent the postcards from Los Angeles and Las Vegas. I'll ask Claire if he traveled out that way in the months after TexFest."

"There's another possibility," Bauer said.

"That the whole band was involved?" Patterson said. This had occurred to her too. The idea had kept her up for hours the previous night. Was it even possible that four individuals, one of whom was also female, conspired to hurt her sister. It was a long shot. Crimes like that happened, but they were rare. More often it was a lone wolf. She said as much to Bauer.

"Still worth checking out. We know Julie was with them, and we know that Martin Wright took his own life. It's a valid hypothesis until we prove otherwise." Bauer drew in a long breath. "Which is why you should talk to Claire Wright as an FBI agent, not Julie's sister."

"No. We'll keep it informal for now," Patterson said. "If I think Claire has any concrete information related to my sister's disappearance, if I suspect she has knowledge of a crime, then we'll bring her in for a formal interview."

"All right. We'll do it your way." Bauer glanced down at his laptop. "While you're gone, I'll try to find out more regarding Martin Wright's death. Contact the Dallas County Medical Examiner and see if I can get the coroner's report. If it was a suicide, there should be a police report out there somewhere, too. I'll get PD to send over anything they have. It might not tell us exactly why Martin Wright took his own life, but it may tell us what his state of mind was in the weeks and months leading up to his death."

"That would be very helpful," Patterson said. She leaned back in her chair and rubbed her temples where a tension headache throbbed. Was it possible that her sister had hitched a ride with the wrong people? If so, it meant that Julie was dead. She had already faced this possibility once before while investigating the Bracken Island Killer, and even if the members of the band called *Sunrise* were not a cadre of crazed murderers, she would surely have to confront this grim reality again. She knew Julie was probably dead. The statistics on missing persons supported that somber conclusion. Yet deep down, Patterson couldn't help but maintain a flicker of hope that somehow, someway, Julie would defy the odds and come back to them alive and well.

TWENTY-TWO

PATTERSON ARRIVED at the coffee shop ten minutes early, ordered a cappuccino, and found a seat near the window where she could watch the comings and goings. She took her phone out and placed it on the table. Claire Wright had promised to call when she arrived at the coffee shop. It was the easiest way for the two women to identify each other.

Patterson sipped her coffee and waited.

The hour hand on the wall clock behind the service counter inched past one.

A woman in a red dress entered and looked around. For a moment Patterson thought this might be Claire Wright, but then a man in a business suit sitting at a table near the back waved to get her attention. The woman waved back and made a beeline for him.

Patterson watched the clock tick away another five minutes.

More people came and went, collecting takeout orders or finding empty seats, but still there was no sign of the woman Patterson had come here to meet.

Frustrated, she picked up her cell phone and dialed Claire's number.

The phone rang.

Patterson looked around the coffee shop to see if anyone was reaching for their handset. Maybe Claire Wright had forgotten to call and was sitting at another table waiting for her. But even though several people were browsing on their devices, no one appeared to be answering their phone. Then, as if to confirm that Claire was not in the coffee shop, the connection clicked over to voicemail.

Patterson hung up and sat there for a minute. Maybe Martin Wright's sister had gotten held up at the hairdressing school. If that were the case, it made sense that she wouldn't answer her phone. It might be in her bag or a locker. It was already quarter past one. Patterson decided to give it another fifteen minutes.

But when that time lapsed and there was still no Claire, Patterson started to wonder if she'd been stood up. She called Claire's number again, waited with growing frustration as the phone rang twice and then went to voicemail.

"Dammit." Patterson cursed, drawing a startled look from a mother sitting with her preteen child at the next table. Patterson apologized and stood up, throwing her empty cup in a trashcan by the door before stepping outside.

Claire had said she was attending a hairdressing school in the same plaza as the coffee shop. Patterson's gaze swept the storefronts, looking for something that might fit the bill, but she saw nothing. There was a tax preparer's office, a closed Italian restaurant with a sign in the window saying that it opened at five, a furniture store, and a payday loan place.

Now Patterson wondered if Claire had lied to her about going to school, although she could think of no reason the woman would.

Stepping back into the coffee shop, Patterson approached

the counter. She waited for the barista to notice her before flashing the badge she carried in a black leather credential wallet. "I was supposed to meet a woman here who attends a hairdressing school in this plaza. She didn't show up and I don't see anything that looks like a hairdressing school. You wouldn't happen to know if there is such a place?"

"You must mean Lulu's Hair Academy," the barista replied while simultaneously working the espresso machine. "We get people in here looking for it all the time. Mostly new students who can't find their way there. I guess because we're a coffee shop, they think we're also an information booth."

"Want to *tell me* where it is?" Patterson wanted directions, not a conversation on the woes of running a coffee shop, and she felt her badge should get them for her.

"Oh. Sure." The barista pointed behind her to some vague spot beyond the building's side wall. "You have to go all the way down almost to the end of the Plaza. There's a payday loan place there next to an Italian restaurant."

"I saw those."

"There's a covered walkway between them. It leads to a set of steps that take you up to the Plaza's second floor. That's where the hairdressing school is. They should put a sign there, really. I don't know why they don't."

"Thanks." Patterson reached into her pocket and removed her wallet. She pulled out a couple of ones and stuffed them into the tip jar.

"Much appreciated." The barista smiled.

"You're welcome." Patterson turned and headed back toward the door. When she reached the sidewalk, she glanced up at the Plaza's second floor. All she saw was a row of blank featureless windows. Following the barista's directions, she found the walkway and the steps. They led to an open second story catwalk at the rear of the building with several units occupied by nonretail businesses, including a lawyer's office with a sign in the window advertising ninety-nine-dollar divorces. Patterson felt a tug of sadness for the couples that needed such a service. People whose lives together started with such hope, only to end inside a grimy office in a rundown strip plaza.

Patterson moved on. The last three units on the second floor belonged to the same business. Lulu's Hair Academy. She stepped inside, finding herself in a small reception area with a counter on one side and a row of plastic seats on the other. Head shots of models with their hair in braids, perms, bridal updos, and chignons. An odor of ammonia hung in the air. There was no one at the counter, but there was a small silver call bell.

Patterson was about to ding it when a door behind her opened and a woman in her thirties entered. She had long, straight black hair that matched her black trousers and blouse.

The woman glared at Patterson. "It's about time you showed up. You're late."

"I beg your pardon?" Patterson said. "I think you might have me confused with someone else."

The woman's demeanor changed. "You're not Anna, my new hair model?"

"No." Patterson shook her head. "Not even close."

"Oh dear, I'm so sorry. I have a student back there with no one to practice on. I guess Anna isn't going to show up. That's the third time this month that a model has flaked on me." A hopeful look flashed across her face. "You don't want a free hairstyling, do you?"

"Not really."

"Shame. You have gorgeous hair. If you're not Anna, how can I help you?"

"I'm looking for one of your students." Patterson showed the woman her credentials.

"You're an FBI agent?" The woman's expression turned to one of alarm. "Is there an issue here?"

"No. I need to talk with a student named Claire Wright. We had a lunch appointment, and she didn't show up. When we spoke on the phone last night, she said she was taking a hairdressing course here."

"She is." The woman folded her arms. "But not today. She was supposed to be here at nine, but . . ."

"She didn't show up here either?" Patterson had a bad feeling about where this was going.

"Right. Students are supposed to phone us if they can't make it to class. It's one of our rules. But I haven't heard from Claire."

"If you do hear from her, would you mind calling me straight away?" Patterson handed the woman a business card with the FBI crest on one side and her cell phone number on the other.

"Sure. I can do that." The woman looked worried. "I hope Claire's okay."

"Yeah." A prickle ran up Patterson's spine. "Me too."

TWENTY-THREE

AT THREE-FIFTEEN IN THE AFTERNOON, Patterson made her way back inside the FBI's Dallas Field Office and went straight to the broom closet office temporarily assigned to her. She entered with a sour look on her face and took a seat opposite Bauer, who had his head bent over his laptop.

Bauer looked up. "You look like you lost a dollar and found a penny."

"What?" Patterson was only half listening. She was still thinking about the blown meeting and its ramifications.

Bauer rephrased his comment. "I assume the lunch date did not go as planned, given your demeanor."

"You could say that." Patterson threw her phone on the desk. "Claire Wright didn't show up. I waited for almost forty minutes."

"Did you try calling her?"

"Of course. First thing I did. Got her voicemail." Patterson rubbed the bridge of her nose and then met Bauer's gaze. "I hunted down that hair academy she was attending. Spoke to an employee there. Once we'd established that I wasn't a hair model, she told me Claire hadn't shown up there this morning. She didn't call in either."

"That doesn't sound good."

"Tell me about it. I was so close."

"They thought you were a hair model?" Bauer tried to suppress a grin. "Really?"

"You don't think I could be a model?"

"I think you can be anything you want like I'm sure your parents always told you," Bauer said, realizing he'd put his foot in the mud. Then, before Patterson could reply, he steered the conversation back to the task at hand. "I don't want to state the obvious, but is it possible Claire disappeared because you were asking questions about Julie?"

"You think she dropped out of sight because I called her last night?"

"It's something to consider." Bauer closed the laptop. "Maybe the band really did have something to do with Julie's disappearance, and Claire knew something about it. When you came sniffing around, calling her out of the blue like that, it spooked her."

"That thought has occurred to me," Patterson admitted. She'd spent most of the forty-minute drive back to the field office mulling over reasons for Claire's vanishing act. Maybe the woman was sick with the flu. Maybe she decided hairdressing school wasn't for her and quit without telling anyone. Hell, she might even have gotten called out of town because of a family emergency. But none of those explanations rang true, because Claire wasn't answering her phone. Bauer might be right. Her call the previous night had prompted Claire to go underground.

"So where do we go from here?" Bauer asked.

"First thing we do is put a BOLO out with the locals." BOLO was law-enforcement slang for *be on the lookout*. It was standard practice when a suspect was on the loose and was also sometimes used to find witnesses such as Claire. If either Dallas PD or the County Sheriff's Department had any contact with Claire Wright, the FBI would be informed immediately. It also put a few hundred sets of eyes on the case. "Might as well use all our resources."

Bauer nodded. "Good thinking. I'll get on it."

"I'd appreciate that." Patterson had found Dallas to be a big, fat frustration so far. Everywhere she turned, there was another brick wall. "Did you find anything on the brother, Martin?"

"Nothing that points to him being involved in any crimes, against your sister or otherwise." Bauer leaned on the closed laptop. "I'm still waiting for the coroner's report, but PD sent everything they still have over to me. They investigated the death, found it to be a straight suicide. There's no need to go into the details of how he did it but suffice to say it was all pretty standard for this kind of thing. Turns out Martin Wright had been in therapy for several years. Clinical depression. The report didn't say why he was depressed. For that, we would need access to his therapist and any records that person might have, and we won't get those without a court order. Patient confidentiality and all that."

"And it doesn't matter that Martin Wright is dead already."

"Exactly. I ran into this a few times back in LA when I was working Robbery-Homicide. You wouldn't believe how many murderers have therapists."

"I guess therapy didn't help them much."

"Just like it didn't in this case. Despite regular sessions, Martin Wright's shrink couldn't help him in the long run."

"And his shrink won't help us determine if Martin Wright had a guilty conscience, either," Patterson said. "We don't have enough evidence to go before a judge."

"Even if he *was* experiencing feelings of guilt, there's no guarantee he unloaded on his therapist. And even if he admitted involvement in your sister's disappearance, confessed to a serious past crime, his therapist would be bound by the aforementioned confidentiality not to repeat such a confession or alert the authorities."

"I'm aware of how the patient-therapist relationship works," Patterson said with a tinge of bitterness. "It's a crazy world we live in when a killer can hide behind his therapist."

"Except we don't know that Martin Wright is a killer," Bauer said. "There isn't even any concrete evidence of foul play in your sister's case."

"I'd say those two postcards from LA and Las Vegas are pretty good evidence."

"I agree. They are suspicious. But they aren't concrete. Even you admit it looks like your sister's handwriting."

"I know." Patterson felt like screaming. The Martin Wright angle was a long shot, and she knew it. They had no proof that anyone in the band was involved in Julie's disappearance. But Patterson couldn't help but think that Claire Wright vanished because she knew more than she said on the phone. Something she didn't want to tell Patterson. Or maybe she had a guilty conscience of her own. There was only one way to find out, and that was to locate her and bring Martin Wright's sister in for a formal interview. But that would not happen tonight, she was sure.

Patterson pushed her chair back and stood up. She felt drained. Hopeless. "I've had enough for one day."

"Really?" Bauer glanced at his watch. "It's only four o'clock. You knocking off early?"

"Something like that." Patterson was already on her way to the door. She turned back to Bauer. "Do you happen to know the name of that therapist?"

"The one Martin Wright was seeing?"

"Yes."

"Hang on." Bauer brought up the police report on his laptop screen. He scrolled through it and then stopped. "Here it is. Doctor Carson Franks."

"Thanks." Patterson made a note of the name in her phone.

"What are you planning to do?" Bauer asked.

"Nothing." Patterson turned to leave.

"You know, we already discussed the therapist angle. He won't talk."

"I know."

"But you're going to see him anyway."

Patterson didn't answer. Instead, she pushed the phone back in her pocket. "Don't forget to put out that BOLO."

"I won't."

"And if we get any hits, call me right away. Same goes for the coroner's report if it comes over before you leave."

"Sure thing," Bauer said, sounding exasperated. "See you in the morning?"

"Yeah. See you in the morning," Patterson replied, then left Bauer alone in the office and headed toward the elevators.

TWENTY-FOUR

SITTING in her car in the field office parking lot, Patterson took out her phone and browsed the web until she found what she was looking for. A telephone number for the psychiatric practice of Doctor Carson Franks. But when she called, it rang twice and went to an operator who informed her that the doctor had finished work for the day. They suggested she should call 911 if she had an emergency or could leave a message, which they promised he would return the next morning. Patterson didn't want to wait until the next day and said as much, identifying herself as an FBI agent. But it got her nowhere. She wasn't even talking to an employee of the doctor's office. This was an out-of-state messaging service that answered calls for physicians and other medical professionals all across the country. Even if they wanted, they couldn't connect her to the doctor.

Patterson knew it was useless to argue. Even if they had a number for Carson Franks, they wouldn't share it with a stranger over the phone even if that person did claim to be a federal agent. She thanked the woman on the other end of the line and hung up, then returned to the browser on her phone.

There was more than one way to get the doctor's private contact information.

A few minutes later, she had what she needed. His phone number was not listed on any of the people-finder and background check websites that had become ubiquitous with searching a person's name online. As a practicing psychiatrist, he had most likely removed his details from their databases long ago. Something Patterson thought everyone should do for their own privacy. Apart from the obvious concerns that many of the sites baited customers with a promise of salacious details about a person's criminal history, past bankruptcies, and other often false information, they also listed past addresses, family associations, and other details that a person might not want to be out there for all to see—for the low cost of a subscription to the finder service, of course.

But what she did find was his home address on a website that searched public voter records in Texas. The website returned a list of more than fifty possible candidates, all bearing similar names, mostly variations of the doctor's first name, such as Carlton, Clarence, or Cody. But it took less than a minute for her to browse the list and whittle it down to one entry in particular, and the only person named Carson Franks, who lived anywhere near the Dallas-Fort Worth metropolitan area.

This must be him.

She entered the address into the GPS on her phone and discovered that the doctor only lived twelve minutes away in a neighborhood called Preston Hollow. Patterson started her car and swung out of the parking lot.

———

Preston Hollow was located in the north part of Dallas above University Park and Highland Park. It was clearly one of the richest suburbs the city had to offer, with winding tree-lined roads and gated mansions that made Patterson think she was in another world entirely.

The residence that Carson Franks called home was not one of the biggest houses Patterson had driven by as she passed through the swanky neighborhood, but it was certainly no slouch. The house sat on grounds surrounded by high walls. A set of wrought-iron gates blocked a brick driveway leading up to the house and Patterson worried she might not be able to gain entry, but then she saw an intercom sitting on a pole next to the gates.

She brought the car to a stop and rolled the window down, then reached out and pressed the buzzer. A moment later, a man's voice responded.

"Hello? Who is this?"

"My name is Patterson Blake. I'm a Special Agent with the Federal Bureau of Investigation." Patterson replied. "Is this the residence of Doctor Carson Franks?"

"The FBI?" There was a brief crackling pause. "Why do I have feds at my gates?"

"Not the FBI. Just one FBI agent," Patterson replied. "And I would be grateful if you could give me a few minutes of your time."

"Do you have any idea what time it is?" Came the gruff response.

"Yes, I do." Patterson glanced at the clock on her car's dashboard. "It's a little after five."

"Exactly. My practice closes at three. Which means I'm done for the day. If you want to talk to me about a patient, phone my office tomorrow morning after eight and talk to my receptionist, Simone. She'll make an appointment for a more convenient time."

"I'm afraid this can't wait that long," Patterson said.

"You do realize this is my private home."

"I do, and I'm sorry to disturb you. If it were not an urgent matter, I would not do so." Patterson hesitated, then said, "It might even be life or death."

"Life or death?" Franks echoed.

"Yes." Patterson knew she was stretching the truth, but on the other hand, she had no idea why Claire Wright had not shown up to either the hair school or their meeting earlier that day. It was not much of a leap to conclude that Martin Wright's sister had gotten herself into some sort of trouble, even if Patterson did still think that the most likely explanation revolved around Julie. If Claire was protecting one or more of the band members—and that included her dead brother—Patterson needed to know. "I would really appreciate it if you would speak to me."

"You promise this won't take too long?"

"I do," Patterson replied, sensing that her plea was about to be rewarded.

And it was. A moment later, the doctor spoke again. "In that case, you'd better come on up to the house."

A few seconds after that, the wrought-iron gates trundled back to allow Patterson entry.

TWENTY-FIVE

THE HOUSE that Doctor Carson Franks lived in was even more impressive up close than it was from beyond the wrought-iron gates that kept everyone but invited visitors at bay. It sat amid lush and manicured grounds, with perfect green lawns and flowerbeds bursting with color. The brick-paved driveway looped around a bubbling fountain at the front of the residence.

The building itself was no less impressive. An Italianate three-story structure with hipped roofs, jutting eaves with wide cornices, corbels aplenty, and tall rectangular, arched windows. A Cupola dominated one side of the home, while a decorative porch finished the picture-perfect façade.

The field of psychiatry, Patterson thought as she came to a stop on the driveway in front of the house, had paid well for Doctor Carson Franks.

No sooner had she exited the vehicle than the wide double front doors opened, and a man in his early sixties appeared. His full head of neatly trimmed hair was pure silver. He wore black-framed glasses that perfectly accented his narrow, hawkish face.

As she approached the steps leading onto the porch, he stood and waited with arms at his sides, watching her with coal-black eyes.

"Well, this is a first," he said as she reached the door. "I've never had the feds track me down at home before. I'm not in some kind of trouble, am I?"

"Nothing of the sort," Patterson reassured him. "I have some questions about an old patient of yours."

The doctor observed her for a moment and then nodded. "You'd better come in."

He stepped aside to allow her inside and then followed behind, gently closing the doors and blocking out the sunlight.

The interior of the dwelling was surprisingly different from the building's classical exterior. Patterson found herself in an entry hall with polished light oak flooring, stark white walls, and concealed lighting. Modern art hung everywhere in metal frames that were just as modern.

Franks motioned for her to follow him and then led Patterson into an equally modern living room. There was no TV in the space, but there was a projector mounted discreetly on the ceiling. The screen, she noticed, dropped through a slot near the fireplace, allowing it to be hidden when not in use.

The doctor settled in a leather chair that looked like it had come from an upscale version of IKEA and motioned for her to sit on a couch that shared the same design aesthetic. For all the warmth and charm of the home's exterior and grounds, the interior felt clinical and detached. The perfect lair, Patterson thought, for a man who spent his career battling the damaged emotions of others and exorcising them.

Franks hadn't spoken since inviting her inside, but now he watched her with narrowed eyes and fingers curled around the arms of his chair, and finally addressed Patterson. "I must confess, I'm curious to know what you think I can tell you."

"Several years ago, you treated a man named Martin Wright," Patterson answered. "He was suffering from depression, according to his sister, Claire."

"That is correct," the doctor replied. "I remember Martin very well. He saw me on and off over many years."

Patterson glanced around, noticing yet more expensive art hanging on the living room walls. "His family weren't well-off and judging by our surroundings, your hourly rates are not cheap. I wonder how he afforded that?"

"How does anyone afford it?" Franks replied.

"His insurance paid."

"Which is why his therapy sessions were not consistent. As I already mentioned, he saw me on and off and only when he had coverage that would pay for it."

Patterson felt a flicker of revulsion. This man who engaged in a profession meant to help others would only do so if remuneration was easily forthcoming. He was willing to abandon a patient simply because that person could no longer pay what he wanted. This attitude was antithetical to everything Patterson believed. A doctor should be invested in helping their patients, first and foremost, even if it did not make them obscenely rich. She bit her lip and took a deep breath, then pushed the thoughts from her head and got down to business. "What can you tell me about Martin Wright and the treatment he was receiving?"

"Nothing." Franks folded his arms and kept his gaze fixed upon Patterson. "As I'm sure you must be aware, my relationship with Martin was one of physician and patient. As such, I am not at liberty to divulge any of the details of his treatment or state of mind."

"Martin is dead." Patterson knew this tack was a long shot.

"Indeed. And confidentiality survives death." The doctor cleared his throat and continued watching Patterson with an unwavering stare that made her uncomfortable. "You must already have realized that when you came here. You are a federal agent, after all, and must have come upon this type of situation in the past."

"I was aware," Patterson admitted.

"And yet you tracked me down at my home out of office hours and didn't even come bearing a court order allowing me to discuss Martin's situation with you."

"That's because I was hoping to appeal to your better nature. A life may depend upon it."

"My unwillingness to talk is nothing to do with the lack of a better nature. It has everything to do with the oath I took as a doctor and my respect for the privacy of those who come to see me."

"What if I were to tell you that Martin's sister, Claire, is missing and it might have something to do with her brother and the reason for his depression?" Patterson knew she was reaching. She had no evidence that Martin Wright's depression was in any way connected to her sister. It was just a half-formed theory. Nothing more.

"I would say that without a court order, it alters nothing."

Patterson nodded slowly. "How about we try this a different way? I'll ask you a series of yes-no-style questions regarding Martin and his sister, and if I'm right, you can refuse to answer my question. If I'm wrong, you can tell me so. In that manner, you won't be betraying the confidence of your deceased patient. After all, telling me I'm incorrect in a particular assumption is not the same thing as giving me information."

"That is true, although I think you're pushing the boundary of what I can legally tell you, and what I can't, without putting my license at risk."

"I can assure you that anything we discuss will not go any

further," Patterson said. "But you can respond to my questions in whatever manner you wish."

"Very well," the doctor said, a bemused smile touching his lips. "But I warn you, there's a distinct possibility that I will answer your questions only with silence."

"I'll take that risk," Patterson said. She started with an easy one. "You were treating Martin Wright for clinical depression, is that correct?"

"I can't answer that," Franks said.

Patterson took that as a yes. "Did you ever treat any other family members for the same issue?"

"No."

"Did you ever meet his sister, Claire?"

"No. Not that I'm aware of."

Great, thought Patterson. This was going to work. Although it would have been much easier just to let him talk while she listened. But beggars couldn't be choosers. "Were you treating Martin Wright in the months immediately before his suicide?"

"I can't answer that."

"Was he on prescription medication for his depression?"

"I can't answer that."

"Was there ever a time when he stopped taking his prescription medications?" Patterson asked.

Franks settled back into his chair. "I can't answer that."

Patterson nodded. "Did he ever mention anything that would lead you to believe he was suicidal in the months prior to his death?"

"No."

This was progress. "Had he ever discussed suicide with you previously?"

"No."

Now for the big question. "Did Martin Wright ever

discuss a crime with you? Something that would weigh on him, like, say, a rape or a murder?"

Franks looked taken aback. He hesitated and Patterson thought he was going to say that he couldn't answer that question, which would effectively be a yes. But he didn't. Instead, he licked his lips, then said a firm, "No."

Patterson felt her heart drop. She was counting on this to explain Claire Wright's sudden vanishing act. But she wasn't done yet. "Did he ever discuss committing a crime of any kind?"

This time, the answer came instantly. "No."

Patterson lapsed into silence. She wasn't sure where else to go with her questioning. But then she had one last idea. "What about an accident? Maybe he was feeling guilty about something that was out of his control?"

"No." Franks glanced toward the door. "I think this fishing expedition is just about over. There really is nothing I can tell you about Martin Wright, except that he discussed nothing to do with a crime during our sessions. If you want more than that, I suggest you get a court order."

"That won't be necessary," Patterson said, standing up. "You have been more than helpful."

"Excellent." Franks clapped his hands together. "Now, let me show you to the door."

TWENTY-SIX

PATTERSON HAD BEEN in a bad mood since Claire hadn't shown up for their meeting, and it did not improve on the drive back across town to her motel. The psychiatrist had told her what she wanted to know, in a roundabout way. But it didn't clear anything up. Just because Martin Wright hadn't discussed a crime with his shrink didn't mean he hadn't committed one. Certainly, the good doctor had done nothing to save the young man. Worse, Carson Franks had not ever even met Claire, so he could provide no information that might help locate her. It was just one more frustration to cap off an all-round frustrating day.

She parked in the closest parking space to her room and let herself in, throwing her laptop bag on the bed. She hadn't even used the laptop all day, and she didn't intend to start now. What she wanted was a moment of peace. To put the search for her sister on hold, just for a few hours.

She wasn't sure what her expectations had been when she began this. Did she think it would be easy to find her sister after so many years? Did she think Julie was out there waiting for Patterson to come and get her? If so, Patterson was getting a rude awakening now. Every stone she turned just led to more questions. Julie felt further away than ever.

Patterson took her jacket off and unclasped the tactical shoulder holster that held her Glock 19M service weapon— fully loaded and with one up the pipe.

For once, the motel had a safe. It was a wall unit in the closet. Patterson removed the gun from its holster and placed it in the safe, then closed the door and set the combination. The firearm would be fine there for the next few hours while Patterson worked off the black mood that descended upon her.

She shucked off her clothes and padded into the bathroom, where she took a quick shower. Dressed again in skinny jeans and a black scoop neck T-shirt, she booked an Uber and waited for it to arrive.

When her driver pulled into the parking lot ten minutes later, she picked up her purse and hurried outside, jumping into the back seat. She gave him a destination not far from the motel. A bar and restaurant she'd noticed on her way back to the motel earlier. It was hardly an upscale joint, but worlds apart from the filthy dive she and Bauer had visited looking for Otto Sharp the previous day. For one, there were no bikes outside. Just regular late-model SUVs and sedans. It was also smoke-free and served food. Not that Patterson was there primarily for the cuisine, even though she was hungry.

She stepped inside and looked around. The place had a rustic charm, with weathered wood planks lining the walls and industrial-style lighting. There were no neon signs advertising cheap domestic beers. Soft rock music weaved its way into the general hubbub of conversation and the clink of glasses. The air was heavy with the smell of barbecued meat and hamburgers.

Patterson approached the bar and found an empty stool. The bartender was a tall, thin man a couple of years older than herself with short dark hair and just enough stubble on his chin to be trendy without looking unshaven. When he noticed her, she asked what he'd recommend for a good red wine that wouldn't break the bank. Either a Cab or a Merlot.

He recommended a California Cabernet Sauvignon from the Paso Robles region. It was, he assured her, one of their more popular house wines.

"Sure, why not?" Patterson replied, watching him pour the wine. She made quick work of the glass and then ordered another.

"Hard day at work?" The bartender asked, flashing a smile full of brilliant white teeth.

"Like you wouldn't believe." Patterson sipped the second glass of wine. When the bartender asked if she wanted to order any food, she studied a laminated menu for a few moments, then ordered a cheeseburger. It was hardly good for her waist, but right now she didn't care. It was comfort food.

When the food came, she polished it off with gusto and then ordered a third glass of wine.

When she flagged the bartender down for a fourth glass, he looked at her with a raised eyebrow. "You sure about that?"

"Why wouldn't I be sure?" Patterson shot back.

The bartender shrugged. "Just trying to keep you from doing something you might regret later. But hey, not my business if you want a hangover tomorrow."

"Good." Patterson hit the bar with an open palm. She could feel the alcohol dulling her senses. It was the most she'd had to drink in a long time. "Another glass, if you please."

The bartender shrugged again and complied with the request.

By the time Patterson booked another Uber, an hour later,

she'd added a fifth glass to the equation and was feeling positively woozy. She paid her bill—careful to leave the bartender a generous tip for putting up with her—and staggered out to the parking lot where her chariot awaited. On the brief journey back, she rolled the window down and let the cool night air play over her face. Back at the motel, she staggered to her room and spent a minute fighting with the key card, which stubbornly refused to grant her access.

Once inside, she kicked the door closed with her heel, peeled her clothes off, and sank onto the bed in nothing but her underwear. That was the last thing she remembered until the next morning.

TWENTY-SEVEN

THE FIRST THING Patterson noticed when she woke up was a blinding light. She shifted on the bed, out of a shaft of sharp sunlight that pushed through a crack in the curtains directly onto her face. Her vision cleared, but not her recall of how she got back to the motel room, or why she was lying on the bed in her underwear with the motel room lights still on.

What she did remember made her groan. As did the headache that hammered the back of her skull. Her throat was dry, too. She threw her legs off the bed and stumbled to the bathroom, splashing water on her face. There were painkillers in her cosmetics bag. She pried the lid off and downed two of them with a gulp of water.

From somewhere out in the bedroom, her phone rang. The jangling noise made her headache worse, and she wondered how long the painkillers would take to kick in.

She returned to the bedroom and looked around for her phone, finding it still in her jeans, which were abandoned on the floor near the bed. She expected the call to be from Special Agent Bauer. A quick glance toward the clock on the nightstand had confirmed what she already suspected. She had overslept. It was already nine o'clock.

But the call wasn't from Bauer. It was from a local number she didn't recognize.

"Hello?" She answered the call, grimacing at the sound of her own voice, which was croaky and thin.

"Agent Blake?" A female asked.

"Yes?" She recognized the voice but couldn't place it. Not surprising, considering she couldn't yet think straight.

"This is Cindy Lorenz. We met yesterday at the hair school."

"Of course," Patterson said, realizing why she recognized the woman's voice.

"You came in asking about Claire Wright and left your card with me. Said I should contact you if I heard anything."

"That's right." Patterson sat on the edge of the bed, felt a glimmer of hope through the discomfort of her hangover. "Did Claire show up?"

"Not exactly. When I arrived to open up this morning around seven-thirty, her boyfriend was waiting for me. He was asking about Claire, wanted to know if I'd seen her the day before. If she'd attended class. I told him the same thing I told you."

"Really?" Patterson forced her mind to focus. Claire Wright hadn't mentioned having a boyfriend when they spoke on the phone two nights before. But then, why would she? It wasn't relevant to the conversation. "I don't suppose you got his name?"

"I have more than that. He had a bunch of flyers in his hand with a picture of Claire. I guess he was handing them out. He gave me one. It has his name and telephone number on it."

"Hang on a moment," Patterson said. She jumped up— wincing when the movement caused a jolt of pain inside her skull—and went to the desk where there was a pen and notepad with the motel name on it. "Okay. I'm ready. Can you give it to me?"

"Sure. His name is Ryan Gilder."

"And the phone number?"

Cindy Lorenz rattled off the number, which Patterson wrote down under the boyfriend's name.

"Thanks."

"You're welcome," Cindy said.

"Did he say anything else?" Patterson asked.

"No. I told him she hadn't shown up. I asked him if he'd spoken to the FBI yet since you were looking for her too. He didn't know what I was talking about. Quizzed me on it. Wanted to know what you'd said to me, so I told him. Then he left real quick. Said he had to keep looking. Poor guy. He must be so worried about her."

I bet, Patterson thought. She wondered what Ryan Gilder had been up to all the previous day. The hair school was a logical place to start looking, yet he hadn't made it there until this morning. Patterson wondered when Claire had actually gone missing. "Did he say where he was going next?"

"I didn't ask. Sorry."

"That's okay." Patterson looked at the name and phone number written on the motel notepad. It might not be the lunch appointment with Claire that she hoped would provide more information about her sister, but it was still a step forward. It gave her a direction to go in. "If he comes back, will you let me know?"

"Sure." Cindy spoke to someone, her voice muted, before she came back on the phone. "Look, I have to go. I have work to do."

"Okay." Patterson thanked her and hung up.

She put the phone down next to the notepad and dressed quickly. Next, she retrieved her gun from the wall safe. She was feeling better now. The pills were kicking in, and the headache had receded to a dull throb. With any luck, it would go away completely by the time she arrived at the field office.

She ran a brush through her hair, slipped the gun into her shoulder holster, and pushed her phone into her pocket. She ripped the top sheet from the notepad and slipped it into her pocket next to the phone. Then she grabbed her car keys and stepped outside.

She was only halfway to the car when her phone rang again. This time, *it was* Special Agent Bauer.

"Hey, where are you?" he asked.

"Running late," Patterson replied without bothering to mention her hangover. "Overslept."

"Really?" Bauer sounded surprised. "Well, get here as soon as you can. We have a hot lead."

"I have one of those, too," Patterson said. "Claire Wright has a boyfriend. He showed up at the hair school this morning looking for her. He was handing out flyers. Kind of strange, don't you think? Why wasn't he looking for her before now, given that she appears to have been missing for at least twenty-four hours?"

"Yeah. Definitely odd. What time was he at the hair school?"

"Around seven-thirty, apparently."

"Then listen to this. After you left yesterday, I put that BOLO out like you asked."

"Go on?" Patterson unlocked her car and climbed in. She started the engine.

"Well, we got a hit ten minutes ago. Dallas PD just notified us that Claire Wright's boyfriend, one Ryan Gilder, filed a missing persons report with them."

"Huh." Patterson pulled out of the motel parking lot and took the interstate toward Love Field in the Northwest part of the city, which also happened to be where the FBI field office was located. "Wonder when he did that?"

"This morning, apparently. They took the report and sent it straight over to us."

"Which means he was at the hair school handing out flyers *before* he went to the police. Does that sound odd to you?"

"Boy, does it. If my girlfriend went missing, the first folks I'd talk to would be the police."

"Me too." Patterson pushed the gas and sped up. "I'll be there in fifteen. Then I think we should go have a chat with Ryan Gilder. See what he has to say for himself."

TWENTY-EIGHT

BAUER MET Patterson in the parking lot when she arrived.

"Yikes. You look like crap," he said, eyeing her as Patterson climbed from her car.

"See, that's why your date the other night didn't go so well. Because you make comments like that."

"I'm just calling it as I see it." Bauer leaned against his Bureau car, with his arms folded. "What did you do, lose a fight with a liquor bottle?"

"It wasn't a liquor bottle." Patterson reached the car and walked around to the passenger side. "You can drive today."

"What, you're not going to put up a fight?"

"Don't have the energy." Patterson climbed in and waited for Bauer to do the same before she spoke again. "Just don't take the corners too fast. Not this morning."

"Gotcha." Bauer eased the car out of the parking space and headed for the exit. "We're not going far, anyway. Police headquarters. They're keeping Gilder until we arrive."

"Good."

Bauer looked sideways at Patterson. "FYI. The coroner sent over their report on Martin Wright."

"And?"

"Nothing that will help us, not that I thought there would be. There weren't even any traces of drugs, legal or otherwise, in his system. No alcohol at the time of his death, either."

"Figures."

"Sorry."

"Not your fault." Patterson sank back into the seat and closed her eyes. "Wake me when we get there."

―――――

Dallas police headquarters was a part brick, part glass six-story structure sitting downtown opposite a modern apartment building converted from an old warehouse into trendy lofts.

Bauer circled the building and pulled into the parking garage, taking the spot near the entrance marked official use only. They proceeded into the lobby. A large glass atrium flooded with light. Patterson was surprised to find that this was nothing more than a precursor to the real entrance, which comprised a screening room and security door behind a secondary glass wall.

She identified herself and Bauer as federal agents on official business and waited while the officers on duty confirmed their identities. This allowed them to keep their guns, although they were still required to put them through the x-ray machine along with their cell phones and other possessions. After passing through a metal detector and retrieving their belongings, they were allowed through the rotating security door, one at a time. Once inside, another officer in a stiff black, neatly pressed uniform escorted them straight to an interview room where a plainclothes officer met them.

He introduced himself as Detective Bob Costa and nodded toward the door. "Your man's in there."

"Voluntarily?" Patterson asked.

"Mostly. He was itching to leave. Claimed he had to go look for his girlfriend. Says she's gone missing before, but usually comes back. He has a whole stack of missing persons flyers. Looks like he printed them at home on an inkjet."

"Thank you for keeping him." Patterson took a step toward the door.

"If you don't mind me asking, why is the FBI interested in this?" Costa said. "Is there something Dallas PD should know about?"

"No." Patterson shook her head. "I'm investigating an unrelated matter and his girlfriend, Claire Wright, has information regarding that case, which is why I need to find her."

"Then you aren't investigating Mr. Gilder in connection with any crime?"

"Not at this moment." Patterson didn't want to go into detail regarding Julie's case with local PD. It would just muddy the waters. She had no idea if Claire's disappearance was even connected, although she still felt like it was a hell of a coincidence. But a hunch did not constitute proof.

Costa nodded thoughtfully. "Very well."

Patterson reached for the doorknob, then pulled back. "What's your take on this, Detective Costa?"

Costa shrugged. "Hard to say. She hasn't even been missing two full days yet and according to her boyfriend, she has a tendency to disappear when things get rough. Honestly, we get our fair share of missing persons reported across the city, and most of them usually show up within a few hours or days."

"I see. Have you corroborated Ryan Gilder's claim that Claire has done this before?"

"Not yet," Costa said. "We tried to contact her mother based on information provided by Mr. Gilder but haven't been able to talk to her yet."

"Why not?"

"She's on vacation with some guy she met according to Gilder. A ten-day Caribbean cruise. We've left her a message but who knows when she'll get it."

"Will you keep us informed?" Patterson asked. "I'd like to talk to her, too."

"Sure." Costa nodded.

"What about the father?" Bauer said.

"Dead. Took their divorce hard and started drinking. Drove his car into a ditch on the way home from a bar seven years ago."

"That's one unlucky family," Patterson said. "Father and son both dead."

"And both by their own hand," Costa added. "Even if one was technically an accident."

"Where do we go from here?" Bauer asked.

"We'll keep a lookout for Claire, but unless more information comes to light, there won't be an official investigation. We have no reason to believe a crime has been committed."

Patterson felt her chest tighten. This was the same spiel the LAPD had given her family all those years ago when Julie went missing. She was about to tell the detective that just because there was no proof of a crime, it didn't mean one hadn't been committed, when Bauer stepped in.

"I think we should go inside and talk to Mr. Gilder now," he said. "What do you think, Special Agent Blake?"

"Very well," Patterson said, biting her tongue. She twisted the doorknob and pushed the door open, then stepped inside with Bauer right behind. As she closed the door, Detective Costa turned and left without so much as a glance back.

Special Agent Bauer stepped around her and approached the desk.

Claire Wright's prospective spouse sat on the other side, leaning back in the chair with hands behind his head. Lying on the table in front of him was the stack of missing persons flyers. Patterson noted they did indeed look homemade and had been sloppily cut in half from larger letter-sized sheets of copy paper. He did not look happy.

"I should be out there looking for Claire," he said before either agent could utter a word. "She's not well."

"You've reported Claire missing," Patterson said. "There will be plenty of people keeping an eye out for her now."

"No, there won't." Gilder shook his head. "That detective said as much. He told me to come back in a few days if she doesn't show up in the meantime."

"Well, we *are* going to take it seriously," Patterson said. She pulled out a chair and sat down opposite Gilder. Bauer took a seat next to her. "Now, if you don't mind, we have a few questions, and then you can be on your way."

TWENTY-NINE

WHY DID you wait so long to report your girlfriend missing, Mr. Gilder?" Patterson asked. She leaned forward with her elbows on the table and studied Gilder's face. He was good looking, with dark brown eyes that matched his neatly trimmed hair. A shadow of stubble darkened his jawline. But she wasn't checking out his features. She was looking for tells, those little involuntary ticks that could tell you whether a person was being honest or deceitful. If they were confidant or nervous. This was standard training at the FBI Academy, and Patterson had learned well.

"I don't know. I guess I thought she would come back."

"When did she go missing?" Bauer asked.

"The night before last."

Patterson and Bauer exchanged a look.

"Would you care to elaborate on that?" Patterson asked. "Exactly what time did she go missing?"

"What difference does it make?"

"Just answer the question," Bauer said.

"Okay. Fine. It was late. Nine o'clock. Maybe nine-thirty. She had to get up early to be at that hairdressing school. Her car needed gas, and she didn't want to take the time to stop in the morning."

"You're telling us she went out sometime after nine to fill up with gas?"

Gilder nodded. "She's done it before. There's a gas station close to the house. Maybe a five-minute drive. I thought she'd be gone for fifteen minutes and then come back."

"But she didn't."

"No. That was the last time I saw her."

"And yet you did nothing?" Patterson was incredulous.

"Sure, I did something. I called her cell phone a couple of times, but it went to voicemail, so I got in my own car and drove down to the gas station. She wasn't there, so I went to a couple of other gas stations, but I couldn't find her."

"What make and model of car was Claire driving, Mr. Gilder?"

"I already told the other cops. They wrote it all down."

"Well, we'd like you to tell us anyway," Patterson said.

"Oh. Alright. It's a red Honda Civic."

"Year?"

"2012."

"Any distinguishing characteristics?"

"I don't know. There's a dent in the front passenger door. But other than that . . ."

"And your car?"

"I don't see how that is relevant."

"Just humor us."

"It's a white pickup. F150."

"Thank you," Patterson said. "How long have you been with Claire, Mr. Gilder?"

"About a year, why?"

"Just curious." She saw Bauer make a note of the information on his phone. "Getting back to your account of the night in question. After Claire didn't return home in a timely manner, you went out looking for her at local gas stations. . ."

"That's right. Until I realized she wasn't at any of them. I even asked the people in the stores, but no one remembered her."

"And after that, what did you do?"

"I went back home and sat up waiting for her. What else could I do? I didn't know where she was."

"And yesterday?"

"I figured she'd get it out of her system and come home after hairdressing school, so I went to work."

"You didn't go looking for her again?" Bauer asked.

"Or file a missing persons report right away?" Patterson added.

"As I said to the cops when I filed the report, she's disappeared like this for a few days before."

"And why would that be?"

"I don't know how much you know of Claire's family history, but there's a tendency toward depression. She's suffered from it all her life. Her brother was the same. He killed himself a couple of years ago."

"I know about that," Patterson said. "You're saying she goes walkabout when her depression kicks in?"

"If you want to call it that. She takes herself away, gets her head back on straight, then comes home again. But I thought that was all in the past. She's been better the last six months since the doctor changed her meds."

"So what changed?" Bauer asked.

"I don't know."

"Did she take anything with her when she left the house?" Patterson asked. "Anything that might hint that she was leaving, like an overnight bag?"

"She didn't walk out on me, if that's what you're insinuating. She wouldn't do that." Gilder pressed his lips together. "All she took was her phone and purse. And her car keys, of course. That's why I'm worried. Her meds are still at home. Without them, the depression will almost certainly kick in again."

"I see," Patterson said. "Going back to yesterday evening when she didn't come home from hairdressing school . . . Why didn't you do something, then?"

"I did. I made up these flyers and went looking for her again. Went to all her usual hangouts. Spoke to anyone I thought might know her whereabouts. I still couldn't find her. That's why I went to the school this morning. I wanted to see if she showed up there yesterday."

"And when you found out she hadn't, you came here."

"Yes."

"What do you do for work, Mr. Gilder?" Bauer asked.

"Why is that relevant?"

"Just curious, that's all."

"I flip houses. Been doing it for a few years. Buy them cheap, fix them up, and then sell them for a profit."

"Sounds like a lot of work," Patterson said.

"Oh yeah. Lot of work. But it pays the bills."

"I see. Does Claire help you with the house flipping business?" Patterson asked.

"No. She doesn't have any interest. Besides, I have a crew that works with me. I don't do it all on my own."

"And that's where you were all day yesterday?"

"Yes. I have a property south of downtown I've been working on. It's almost ready. I was there until six. You can check with my crew if you don't believe me."

"Why wouldn't we believe you?" Bauer raised an eyebrow.

"I know how you people are. Always suspicious." Gilder glanced between the two agents. "Speaking of which, why are you here? I mean, the cops aren't taking me seriously, so why would the FBI have an interest?"

"We believe Claire has information pertinent to another investigation," Patterson said.

"I see." Gilder swallowed, his Adam's apple bobbing up and down. "What kind of information?"

"The kind we don't want to discuss with anyone but her," Bauer replied. "You needn't worry. It's a routine inquiry, nothing more. She's not in trouble."

"Oh. I see." Gilder didn't seem particularly relieved. He rested a hand on the stack of flyers. "If you have no more questions, I'd like to go now."

"Sure." Patterson nodded. "But before you do, can you think of anyone Claire would stay with? Anyone she goes to visit when she's feeling overwhelmed?"

"No. She doesn't have many friends in the area, and I've already spoken to them all. Besides, she's never gone to any of them before."

"You're sure about that?"

"I'm sure." Gilder picked up the flyers. He pushed his chair back. "If we're all done here, I need to go look for Claire, because the cops sure as hell won't."

THIRTY

BACK IN THE CAR, Bauer turned to Patterson. "Well, that was interesting. What do you make of Ryan Gilder?"

"Not sure yet," Patterson admitted. "I didn't clock any particular tells that would lead me to believe he's lying about anything, but I also didn't see much to convince me he's telling the truth."

"We're not even sure a crime has been committed."

"Right. That too." Patterson looked out through the windshield at the gloomy parking garage. Most of the cars she saw were personal vehicles, probably belonging to the officers and admin staff manning the Dallas Police Department's headquarters, but some would be unmarked units, distinguishable from their civilian counterparts only by the blue and red strobe lights mounted inside the grill or front and rear windshields. Squad cars painted in black with white doors filled one row. "Maybe he's right, and Claire just took off to decompress."

"We only have his word that she suffers from depression."

"True. But we do know that the brother, Martin, had his own issues and was on medication. Claire herself told me that. Clinical depression can run in families. It's not out of the realm of possibility."

"It's also a handy scapegoat if something else happened and he wanted to cover it up. He knew about the brother's mental health problems and subsequent suicide. He mentioned it in the interview. So far as I'm concerned, Gilder's story doesn't make a whole bunch of sense."

"Agreed. If she wanted to get away for a while, be on her own, why wouldn't she just say that instead of telling him she was going for gas?" Patterson let out a slow breath. "Also, why wouldn't she take a bag with her?"

"Or at least a change of clothes."

"Unless she didn't intend to be gone overnight."

"Or she didn't have time to pack a suitcase," Bauer said. "The answer might lay more in what Gilder didn't tell us than what he did."

"Like if they had an argument?"

"She wouldn't be the first person to storm out after a row."

"Why not just tell us if that's the case? I mean, we've all been there. If she left because she was angry, but then didn't come back as expected, that would go a long way to convincing the police to start a search."

"He might not want to admit that they argued." Patterson speculated.

"Maybe it had nothing to do with Ryan Gilder at all and he's just what he seems to be, a worried partner." Bauer looked sideways at Patterson. "Claire Wright went missing the same night she talked to you on the phone."

"I'm aware of that." Patterson wracked her brain to think if there was any sign that her call rattled Claire. Nothing jumped out. But that meant nothing. They had already discussed this and decided the timing of Claire's disappearance was one hell of a coincidence. Ryan Gilder had confirmed that Claire vanished immediately after talking to Patterson, even though he hadn't mentioned the phone call. Maybe he didn't hear it, or that particular detail slipped his mind. Regardless, the facts could not be ignored.

Bauer thought the same thing. "We should revisit the theory that your inquiries about Julie prompted Claire's sudden departure."

"I agree." Patterson was mad at herself. She should have been more careful. Instead of tipping her hand and mentioning Julie, she should have just gotten Claire's address and gone straight over there to talk with her in person. It was a rookie mistake, but there was no fixing it now. All Patterson could do was move on and hope it didn't turn out to be a disastrous one. "So we have a couple of open theories based on our gut reaction after speaking with Ryan Gilder. One, that he's hiding something regarding his girlfriend's disappearance, and knows more than he's saying."

"Which could be an argument or some other circumstance he's keeping to himself," Bauer said.

"Two—that my call spooked Claire and set in motion some chain of events that led to her disappearance."

Bauer nodded. "Which is plausible if we entertain the idea that Claire Wright knew something bad about Julie's disappearance. That she either witnessed or was involved in it all those years ago."

"Or maybe she witnessed nothing and only found out about it from her brother later. Keep in mind that we don't know the movements of either Julie or the band during and after TexFest. That was one of the pieces of information I was hoping to fill in when I met her."

"If Claire wasn't personally involved, why not just tell you what she knew?" Bauer looked thoughtful. "Her brother is dead. Nothing she says now would result in any sort of liability for him."

"Except to tarnish his memory," Patterson said. "Unless she's still covering for the rest of the band."

"Maybe." Bauer started the engine. "But so far, we have no proof to support one theory above the other. And there's also a third possibility. That something entirely different happened to her unrelated to either scenario and that Ryan Gilder is exactly what he appears to be, a worried man who doesn't know what happened to his girlfriend or why."

"Agreed. Which is why we need to establish some baseline facts regarding what happened two nights ago." Patterson put her seatbelt on. "Tell me, Special Agent Bauer, if this came across your desk back when you were with the LAPD, where would you start?"

Bauer cleared his throat. "First thing I would do is check the nuts and bolts of Ryan Gilder's story. Shake the tree and see what falls out, starting with the gas station. If Claire Wright really went to fill up her tank so that she wouldn't have to stop and do it the next morning, there should be a record of that."

"Very good. Exactly what I was thinking our next move should be. We have Gilder's home address from the missing persons report. All we need to do is find the closest gas station and work outward from there. These places keep security footage—it's pretty much required by their insurance—and we know the approximate time she would have been there."

"Checking now." Bauer was already on his phone, browsing the area around Ryan Gilder's address. After a minute passed, he hooked the phone up to the infotainment system and set directions. "Got it. Closest gas station to Gilder's house. We'll be there in twenty."

THIRTY-ONE

THE CLOSEST GAS station to the address shared by Claire Wright and Ryan Gilder sat on a busy intersection at the edge of the suburbs in North Dallas. Patterson already had her credentials in hand when they entered the convenience store.

When she showed them to the clerk, a gangly twenty-something with flaccid greasy black hair and a pockmarked face, he shrank back as if she had just pulled a gun on him.

"Don't panic, we're not here for you," Bauer said.

Patterson put the wallet away. "We need to see your security footage from two nights ago."

"Security footage?" The kid repeated as if he didn't quite understand Patterson's statement.

"That's right. We can give you the approximate timestamps."

"That doesn't sound like something I'd be allowed to do."

Bauer gave an exasperated sigh. "Son, we're federal agents. You really want to dance with us?"

"Huh?"

"What my partner means is that you should probably be

helpful and let us see those recordings," Patterson said. "We're trying to verify the movements of a young woman who's gone missing, and we want to see if she stopped here to fill up with gas."

"I don't have the authority to let people see stuff like that," the clerk said, shifting his weight nervously from one foot to the other. "I'd have to ask my boss."

"Would you mind doing that?" Patterson's headache was coming back, and her patience was wearing thin. "We'll wait."

The clerk looked surprised. "You want me to do it right now?"

"That was implied by the request," Bauer said with admirable restraint.

"Oh. Okay. He's not here, so I'll have to call him." The kid took a step toward a phone hanging on the wall behind the counter. "He only comes in to collect the receipts at the end of my shift. He has a bunch of other gas stations, so he goes between them, but he's always complaining about how much driving he has to do. He told me he's thinking of retiring—"

"We don't care." Patterson resisted the urge to jump over the counter and bang the clerk's head against the wall. "Just make the call."

The young clerk hesitated a moment, then scurried over to the phone, picked up the receiver, and dialed.

While they waited, Patterson wandered through the store to a bank of coolers where she liberated a bottle of water. On the way back, she grabbed a small tub of painkillers. She put both on the counter and fished a ten-dollar bill out of her pocket.

"Still suffering, huh?" Bauer asked as the clerk finished his call and turned back toward them.

"Just being proactive," Patterson said. She pushed the ten-spot across the counter. "That's for the pills and water."

While the clerk made change, she twisted the top off the pills and swallowed two, then followed it up with a hearty gulp of the water.

The clerk handed her back a one-dollar bill and a couple of quarters.

"Jesus." Patterson picked up the cash and put it back in her pocket. "It's like being robbed."

The clerk watched her with wordless indifference.

Bauer glared at the young man. "Well? What did your boss say?"

"He said you can see the recordings." The clerk came around the counter and started toward a door on the other side of the store marked private. "The terminal is in here."

Patterson and Bauer followed and waited while the kid unlocked the door with a key from a set hanging on his belt and let them inside. She looked around. The small space, no bigger than ten by ten, appeared to be a cross between a storeroom and janitor's closet. A broom sat in a bucket half-full of dirty brown water. There were shelves packed with boxed merchandise, mostly automotive stuff like windshield cleaner and oil, or electronics like car chargers. She didn't see any of the snack items or drinks that were stuffed on most of the shelves in the convenience store.

"We store all the food items out back in another room," the clerk said, as if reading her mind. "Have to keep them separate."

"Can we get on with this?" Bauer folded his arms.

"I'm getting there." The kid crossed to a desk wedged between two metal racks. There was a tower system on the desk. He woke the monitor and typed a password in, then browsed to an application marked StoreSurveilPro.

When it opened, Patterson saw a row of feeds from what looked like different cameras underneath the main viewing window.

The kid glanced back at them. "All the recordings are stored in the cloud. You can search by date and time, and it will bring up all the relevant feeds."

"Show me," Bauer said.

The kid brought up a search box beside the main viewing window. "Just type everything you want in here and hit enter." His eyes flicked back toward the door. "I have to get back behind the counter. I'm not supposed to leave the store unattended."

"Go," Patterson said. "I'm sure we can figure it out."

The clerk paused, as if deciding if he should leave strangers alone in the storeroom, then he hurried from the room.

Bauer took a seat in front of the computer and began typing. A moment later, he looked up. "Got it. All the recordings for the night in question."

"That was quick," Patterson said.

"Not my first rodeo when it comes to security footage." Bauer's attention was already back on the screen. "We should review the recordings for the ninety minutes after you spoke to Claire Wright."

"Make it two hours." Patterson leaned in to see the screen. "Is there a view showing the forecourt?"

Bauer clicked through several feeds until he found an exterior view showing the pumps. "I'm going to play this at eight times speed, otherwise we'll be here all day."

"Sure. Just make sure to keep an eye out for a red Honda Civic with a dented door."

Bauer nodded and played the recording.

It took them half an hour to review the footage even sped up eight times. They were forced to stop frequently and run the video back to check out a red car they thought might be Claire's. But each time it turned out to be the wrong make or model. The closest they came was a burgundy-colored Honda

Civic that pulled into the gas station around an hour after Patterson spoke to Claire, but the driver was male, and when they checked the plate against the information provided on the missing persons report, a copy of which Bauer had on his phone, it didn't match. When they were done, Patterson suggested they view an extra half hour of footage just to make sure. Also, she wanted to see if Ryan Gilder showed up looking for his other half, as he claimed to have done. Sure enough, just as they reached the end of their search a white F150 pulled in. They watched as Gilder exited the vehicle and looked around, then went into the store. He emerged a few minutes later, still alone, but carrying a bottle of water. He climbed into the truck and pulled off, disappearing from view as he drove out of the camera's field of view. This verified one part of his story, at least. He did go to the gas station. But of Claire, there was no sign.

Frustrated, they ran through the feed from a different camera mounted on the other side of the forecourt, but to no avail. If Claire Wright had gone out for gas on the night she went missing, as her boyfriend Ryan Gilder claimed, she hadn't come here.

THIRTY-TWO

BACK IN THE CAR, Patterson used her phone to find the closest gas stations to their current location. When the list came up, she showed it to Bauer. "There are three more gas stations within a five-mile radius of Claire Wright's residence. All further away than this one."

"It's going to take hours to check the surveillance footage at all of those," Bauer said.

"We don't have much choice."

"You know, if she didn't come here, it's unlikely she went to any of the others," Bauer said, even as he pulled the address of the next closest gas station up on his own phone and asked for directions. "Why would she drive further than she needed to?"

"I don't know," Patterson replied, "but we have to cross them off our list."

"Can't we ask local PD to check them for us?"

"You heard the detective. He isn't convinced Claire Wright is officially missing. He thinks she'll just show up on her own at some point." Patterson resisted the urge to voice her opinion of that perspective. It helped nothing. "Anyway, I like to do things myself. That way, I know it will get done right."

"Very well." Bauer gave a resigned sigh and backed out of the parking space they occupied in front of the gas station's convenience store. "Off to the next one we go."

———

They ate up another ninety minutes between the drive over and checking the surveillance footage at the next gas station. When their search proved fruitless, they moved on and wasted another hour checking the third location. By the time they arrived at gas station number four, the furthest of their targets, Patterson's spirits were sagging. She held little hope that Claire Wright's red Honda Civic would show up there, and she was correct. The red Honda was nowhere to be seen. Ryan Gilder's white Ford F150 didn't show up either, even though they'd found him in the footage at the previous gas stations. But unlike the first tape they viewed, Gilder didn't bother to get out of the truck the final two times. Instead, he cruised around the forecourt, circling before driving off again. It certainly looked like he was searching for his girlfriend.

"That's it, I'm done," Patterson said, yawning. They were sitting in a small office at the back of the gas station. An odor of burned coffee and cleaning fluids hung in the air. "This is a waste of time. Claire Wright didn't leave the house to fill her car with gas."

"Or if she did, it wasn't at any of the gas stations close to home." Now Bauer yawned. "We could check further afield?"

"There's no point. The bigger our search radius, the more time-consuming the hunt becomes for diminishing returns. I find it hard to believe that Claire Wright would drive past open gas stations. We can search the surveillance video of every other gas station in the city, but I bet we won't find her."

"Which means that either she lied to her boyfriend, or he lied to us."

"Agreed. We saw what time he showed up at that first gas station. It was after eleven. A couple of hours must've passed before he went looking for her. Maybe he wasn't there to search for Claire so much as to secure an alibi for himself."

"You think he drove around those gas stations to support the story he intended to tell?"

"I think it's a possibility."

"There's also another possibility," Bauer said. "What if Claire really did leave the house that night to get gas, but she never made it as far as the gas station?"

Patterson nodded. "I've considered that, too. The problem is we have no way of knowing one way or the other. And she was driving her car, so the only way someone could have gotten to her in between her house and the gas station was if she stopped along the way. It is unlikely that a woman driving alone at night would do that."

"Unless she had good reason."

"And that reason would be?" Patterson asked.

"I don't know. I'm just speculating." Bauer was silent for a moment. "Maybe she got a flat tire."

"Then she would just call her boyfriend. She was only a few minutes from their house, and we know that she took her cell phone because Gilder said he tried to call her before he went looking."

"Okay. How about this? She got pulled over by someone who then took her."

"You mean like a cop?"

"A fake cop. It's been known to happen. I worked a case back in LA where a guy put strobes on his car and pulled people over before handing them fake traffic tickets. In that instance, he was just a wacko trying to stop people speeding, but plenty of people have posed as cops for more nefarious purposes."

"Like the Hillside Strangler in your old stomping ground of Los Angeles," Patterson said. The two men responsible for the Hillside Strangler murders had used fake badges to pose as undercover cops in order to lure victims into their car.

"Yes. And he wasn't the only one, either. What about Ted Bundy? When he wasn't getting women to drop their guard by pretending to be on crutches, he would pose as a cop. There are others, too, and plenty of theories about serial killers masquerading as cops to pull women over on desolate highways before abducting them."

"Except this wasn't on some lonely back road. It was the suburbs of Dallas. It's a long shot."

"Then maybe we should bring Ryan Gilder in and have another chat with him, see if he sticks to his story."

"I have a feeling he won't come willingly," Patterson said. "And we don't have enough evidence to arrest him. Hell, we don't even have proof of a crime. For now, I say we keep looking and hope that Claire Wright just wanted to get away for a while."

"You think that's what happened?" Bauer asked. "Is that what your inner voice is telling you?"

"Honestly, no. I don't think she just ran off because she was depressed and wanted to get away. I got no sense of that when I spoke to her. There's more to this. I just don't know what." Patterson pushed her chair back and stood up. "One thing still keeps nagging at me."

"What?" Bauer stood and turned to her.

"The fact that she went missing so quickly after I spoke to her about Julie. What if Gilder is telling the truth, and he doesn't know what happened to Claire? What if all of this is tied to my sister's disappearance?"

"Which brings us back to our theory of the band having something to do with Julie going missing, and Claire knowing about it."

Patterson nodded. "That would be a good reason for her to pull a vanishing act."

"Except she could have lied and said she knew nothing about Julie. Why go on the run?"

"I don't know." Patterson shrugged. "Maybe she thought I knew something and was fishing for evidence."

"She didn't know you're an FBI agent, remember?"

"So far as we know. If she were keeping tabs, it wouldn't be very hard to figure out that I joined the Bureau. There were even a couple of newspaper articles written about me and how I joined the FBI because of my sister's disappearance back when I graduated. I'm sure those are online."

"Which brings us back to our clutch of hypotheses, none of which are any more or less likely than another," Bauer said. "Your phone call might have precipitated some kind of reaction from Claire, resulting in her disappearance. Or maybe Ryan Gilder did something to her. Then again, she could have left to get gas but never made it because something bad happened . . ."

"Or she really did just have a sudden bout of depression and she's holed up somewhere working through it," Patterson said, finishing the list.

"The question is, which one do we think is the most likely?"

Patterson shook her head. "Your guess is as good as mine."

"Then where do we go from here?"

Patterson glanced at her phone. It was past five o'clock, and all they'd eaten all day was a gas station hot dog at the second place they visited. "I don't know about you, but I'd like to get some dinner."

"Sounds good." Bauer hesitated. "You mean together, right? You're not ditching me?"

Patterson started toward the door. "No. I'm not ditching you. We can talk some more about the case while we eat."

"Or we could just enjoy some dinner without talking shop."

"You know that's not going to happen," Patterson said, stepping outside. "Right?"

Bauer sighed as he followed her. "Yeah. I know."

THIRTY-THREE

THEY WENT to dinner at the same pizza restaurant that Special Agent Bauer had taken her to on the first day they met. Since it was a Friday night, the place was busier, and they had to wait in line to order their food and then fight for a table. While waiting for the food, they discussed the various scenarios regarding Claire Wright's disappearance, but by the end of it they were no closer to figuring out which one was more likely than another. Their only hope was the BOLO, which was still active. It had already led them to Ryan Gilder when he filed a missing persons report for his girlfriend. Maybe Claire would resurface, and it would lead them to her, too. But Patterson wasn't going to hold her breath. Which meant they would keep looking and investigating every angle.

After dinner, Bauer drove Patterson back to the motel. She had booked five nights because she didn't know how long she would need to be in Dallas. As it stood, she was due to check out tomorrow. With the investigation about to stretch into its sixth day, she would need to extend her reservation.

She bid farewell to Special Agent Bauer and watched him

drive away before heading into the motel office. The same greasy-haired desk clerk was there, only instead of having his nose buried in a copy of guns and ammo, his eyes were glued to a small television mounted on the wall. A family-sized bag of chips was open on his lap, the contents of which he was shoveling into his mouth. When she entered, he put the chips aside, lifted a battered remote held together with tape, and turned the volume down.

"Back again, huh?" The clerk licked his lips, his tongue making a lazy circle around his mouth. "How are you liking the room?"

"It's passable," Patterson replied. "I need to extend my booking."

"Well, now. Shouldn't be a problem." The clerk sat up, his belly bulging out over his pants. "How many nights?"

Patterson didn't know how long it would take to finish her business in Dallas, and she didn't want to pay for nights she couldn't use. She thought about it for a moment, then decided to hedge her bets. "Make it another five nights, and if I need to extend again, I'll come back."

"Sure thing. That will be three-eighty with tax."

"You've got to be kidding." Patterson made a quick mental calculation. "I only paid sixty bucks a night last time. It should only be three hundred."

"Not for Saturday night. Rate goes up on the weekend."

"You're not even half full," Patterson protested. "Don't you think that's a little extreme?"

"Look, lady, do you want the room for five more nights or not?" The clerk stared at her with cool indifference. "Your choice."

"All right. Fine." Patterson fished a credit card from her wallet and slid it across the counter.

The clerk took it and ran it through his machine, then handed it back to her. He tapped away at his computer, then asked for her key card. A moment later, he handed it back. "All done. You're good till Thursday."

"Thanks," Patterson said through gritted teeth. She took the key card and turned to leave. As she stepped out of the office, the clerk called after her.

"You have a nice evening now, you hear?"

"Yeah." Patterson let the door slam behind her and stomped across the parking lot to her room. By the time she stepped inside, Patterson had calmed down a little. Who cared if the clerk had jacked the rate up on her? She was going to expense the room to Marilyn Kahn and the New York Field Office, anyway. And it wasn't like she was exactly living in the lap of luxury. This had been one of the cheapest motels she could find, mostly because the Bureau's per diem was lousy.

She took her jacket off and draped it over a chair, then unbuckled her holster with a sigh of relief. She slipped her shoes off and sat on the edge of the bed.

At that moment, the phone rang.

She fished it from her pocket and saw a familiar name on the caller ID. J Grant.

It was Jonathan, the Assistant Special Agent in Charge in New York. He was her direct boss, and also her lover. Things had been tense between them over the past few weeks, ever since she was suspended because she lost focus during a raid in upstate New York and almost ended up on the receiving end of a serial killer's pitchfork. This trip to find Julie had started on her own dime, only to be hijacked by Kahn, the New York SAC, after Patterson's success in Oklahoma City, to further her own career.

Patterson's finger hovered over the green answer button. She hesitated, not really in the mood to talk, but then she pulled herself together and answered.

"Hey." Jonathan Grant's baritone voice filled her ear.

"Haven't heard from you since the day you arrived in Dallas."

"Sorry about that." Patterson had been so caught up with the case, and dealing with her new partner, that she hadn't gotten around to calling again after leaving a message with Grant's secretary. "I've been busy."

"Too busy to spare your boyfriend five minutes?" There was a sour note in Grant's voice.

"I should've called. I really am sorry."

"Whatever. How's the search for Julie going?"

"Are you asking as my boyfriend, or are you getting a progress report for Marilyn Kahn?"

"Marilyn Kahn doesn't need progress reports from me. She can just phone Walter Harris at the Dallas office and get them direct from the horse's mouth." Grant paused. "I'm asking as your boyfriend."

"Good." Patterson felt a sudden tug of longing. "I miss you."

"Me too." There was an uncomfortable pause before Grant spoke again. "If you're too tired to talk, I can call you back another time."

"No. I'm fine."

"So, you want to tell me about your week?"

"Sure." Patterson took a deep breath and told Grant everything that had happened. She told him about the newspaper office and tracking down Otto Sharp, the organizer of TexFest. She filled him in on finding Claire Wright only to have her vanish before they could meet up, and the subsequent search which led them to her boyfriend, Ryan Gilder.

Grant listened in silence until she finished. "Sounds like you've got a real puzzle on your hands."

"Honestly, it's more than a little frustrating. I was so close to talking with Claire Wright. I'm sure she knows something about Julie."

"And you think that's why she vanished?"

"I don't know what to think." Patterson felt the frustration bubbling up again. She took a deep breath. "Can we talk about something else?"

"What would you like to talk about?"

"Anything but work. Make me laugh."

"Hmm. I think I can do that," Grant said. And then he did.

THIRTY-FOUR

IT WAS LATE—OR rather, it was early. Around one in the morning. The room was dark. Patterson was in bed. She and Grant had talked for more than two hours in the end, veering away from her sister's case to happier times. Like their first months together and the long road to a relationship that began when she was a rookie agent shadowing him in the same way Special Agent Bauer was now shadowing Patterson. After hanging up, she had sent a quick text message to her father, which she did often to make sure he was doing okay on his own back in New York, then watched TV for an hour before retiring for the night.

Now, an hour later, she snapped awake, her senses on high alert. Something had roused her from slumber, but she didn't know what.

The air conditioner hummed and clunked under the window, struggling with the humid night air. A door slammed, the sound distant and faint. From still further away, came the rumble of vehicles on the interstate.

Nothing out of the ordinary for a seedy motel on the edge of the city.

She sat up, her eyes sweeping the dark room.

The breath caught in her throat when she saw a bulky figure sitting in the chair next to the TV unit. But then she realized it was nothing more than her clothes discarded the night before. In its desire to find meaning out of randomness, her tired brain had interpreted them as a person.

Her gaze drifted toward the door.

Still locked—the privacy flip latch engaged.

Then her attention moved to the window, and she realized what had roused her.

There, standing on the other side of the window, visible in the gap where the drawn curtains didn't quite come together, was the partial silhouette of a person. And this time it was not her sleepy mind conjuring phantoms out of nothing.

A shiver coursed through her, and she shrank back, overcome by the distinct sensation that the figure was looking into the room. Looking *at her*.

For a long moment Patterson did nothing.

She didn't want to alert the person on the other side of the window that she had spotted them.

Her gun was within easy reach on the nightstand next to her.

Without turning on the bedroom light she swung her legs off the bed and slid the Glock close. She stood and scooped the gun up in a quick fluid movement, shielding it with her body as she padded to the bathroom. As far as the figure on the other side of the curtains was concerned, she had just woken up with a need to pee. Or so she hoped.

Stepping into the bathroom, she gathered herself together and thought about her next move. She felt vulnerable dressed only in a loose tee and pajama shorts, but she couldn't get dressed without tipping off her watcher and she didn't want to do that until it was absolutely necessary.

Patterson lingered in the bathroom doorway, took a deep

breath, then stepped back out. But instead of returning to the bed, she veered off at the last moment and headed for the motel room door, lifting the gun as she went.

Patterson glanced toward the window but from this angle, she could not see the crack between the curtains, or the stranger lingering beyond. But she would see him soon enough—somehow she sensed it was a male—on the business end of her Glock when she pulled the door open and surprised him.

In a quick but stealthy movement, Patterson eased the privacy latch back and gripped the door handle. She breathed deeply and centered herself, then pulled the door open and stepped onto the second-floor catwalk beyond, pivoting toward the window.

To her surprise, nobody was there.

Patterson swiveled around, half expecting to see the silhouetted figure bearing down on her from behind, but the catwalk was silent and empty in this direction too.

Patterson was alone.

She lowered the gun and made her way along the catwalk, checking in both directions. Below her, the parking lot was quiet with no sign of movement. Given the late hour, this was not surprising. Even so, Patterson stood for a while, looking out over the dark landscape. And that was when she saw it. A motorcycle sitting with its light off at the edge of the parking lot, near the road. A dark figure sat astride the vehicle; face hidden by the visor of a crash helmet. She could make out the faint idle of its engine.

Patterson observed it for a few seconds, wondering if the rider would have had the time to make their escape, mount the bike, and retreat to the far side of the parking lot before she exited the room. If they left the moment she stirred, it was possible. But this didn't mean the rider had anything to do with the figure she saw lingering outside her window. It could just be a weary traveler who pulled off the highway to rest awhile. There was only one way to find out.

Patterson turned toward the set of steps leading down to the motel's parking lot. But then, as if sensing her intentions, the motorcycle's engine revved, and the machine started to move. The rider made a quick turn out onto the service road fronting the motel and accelerated away into the darkness until all Patterson could see was the red glow of its taillight as the vehicle sped up the onramp and joined the interstate. This too, soon faded, lost in the sporadic flow of eastbound early-morning traffic.

Was this confirmation that the rider was just a solitary traveler resting up for a few minutes before continuing on their way? Maybe. But Patterson didn't think so. She hadn't imagined the silhouetted figure—of that, she was sure. She gazed out across the parking lot to the spot where the motorcycle had sat moments before, and a shiver coursed through her. The person on that bike had been peering into her room. Watching Patterson while she slept. The only question was why?

THIRTY-FIVE

PATTERSON RETURNED to her room and locked the door, engaging the deadbolt and pulling the privacy latch across. The room was dark and even though Patterson knew no one had snuck inside while she was on the catwalk, she couldn't shake the feeling of being watched by an unseen intruder until she turned on the lamp and looked around. Next, she went to the window and tugged at the curtains, trying to close them tight. But no matter what she did, there was always a slight gap. In the end, she rummaged through her overnight bag and found an oversized claw hair clip, which she used to hold the seams of the curtain together. It was a clumsy solution, but effective.

She retreated to the bed and placed the Glock back on the nightstand before climbing between the sheets.

She felt uneasy. Someone had been watching her, but the question was, why?

Had she struck a nerve in her quest to find out what happened to her sister? First Claire Wright vanished within hours of agreeing to talk with Patterson about Julie, and now someone was skulking around and peering in her motel room window. Patterson suspected the two events were related, which frightened and gave her hope, both at the same time. There was nothing she could do to unravel the mystery tonight, though. She also didn't think sleep would come easily, so she spent the next forty-five minutes browsing the web on her phone and reading until her eyelids felt heavy. She put the phone on the nightstand and turned off the lamp. But on her way back to bed, Patterson clicked on the bathroom light and pulled the door almost closed to bathe the motel room in a dim glow. Enough darkness to let her sleep, but enough light to make her feel safe.

That done, Patterson climbed back into bed and rolled over onto her side, facing the window. If the motorcycle riding mystery person returned, her gun was within easy reach, but she didn't think they would. Not tonight. They had come too close to getting caught.

She closed her eyes and forced her mind to be still, and soon fell into an uneasy slumber.

———

She was awoken sometime later by a shrill ringing sound that forced its way into her dreams and pulled her back to the real world. Startled, she realized it was her cell phone.

It was also still dark outside.

Patterson groaned and rolled over. It felt like she'd only been asleep for no more than a few minutes, but in reality it had been more like four hours. Dawn was still more than an hour away.

She reached out and fumbled on the nightstand for her phone, almost letting it fall to the floor in the process and barely saving the handset before it slipped through her fingers.

She rubbed the sleep from her eyes and sat up, then answered without even looking at the screen.

"Hello?" she said, her voice croaky and thin.

"Patterson. It's me," Special Agent Bauer replied. "Hope I'm not waking you."

"It's five-thirty in the morning. Of course you're waking me." Patterson reached for the lamp sitting on her nightstand and turned it on. "What's going on?"

"I just got an early morning wake-up call from Dallas PD. We have another hit on that BOLO. This time from a patrolman out on the northwest side of the city."

"Tell me." Patterson was already climbing out of bed. She dreaded what Bauer might say next. "Is it Claire Wright? Did they find her body? Is she dead?"

"Nothing like that."

Patterson felt a wash of relief. "What then?"

"Her car. Patrol officer saw it sitting on its own in a grocery store parking lot and pulled in to check it out. Thought someone might need assistance, but the car was empty and locked tight. When he ran the plate, it came back registered to our missing woman."

"Any sign of foul play?"

"Don't know yet. I'm heading over now."

"Great. I'll meet you there. Text me the location."

"Will do," Bauer said, before hanging up.

A few seconds later, Patterson's phone vibrated when his text came in. The car was located half an hour away across town. Patterson wished that just once something was close to her motel. It felt like she had been running in different directions all over the city ever since arriving in Dallas.

She yawned and gave the bed a wistful glance, then headed to the bathroom to get ready. Ten minutes later, Patterson was striding across the parking lot to her car. Five minutes after that, she was on the road.

THIRTY-SIX

PATTERSON MADE it to Claire Wright's car before Bauer, even though she stopped at a gas station and picked up a large cup of strong coffee on the way. She didn't want to spare the time, but it was that or risk falling asleep at the wheel.

Claire Wright's Honda was parked in a bay toward the middle of the grocery store parking lot. The strip mall contained a number of smaller stores, too, including a pack and ship center, nail salon, and a Chinese restaurant. The last unit was occupied by a bar called Charlies Tap Room.

A Dallas Police Department cruiser sat behind the car, lights flashing. Ryan Gilder's white F150 was parked on the other side of the red Honda Civic. He was deep in conversation with the police officers.

Dallas PD must have informed him of their discovery.

Worse, they allowed him to show up.

This rankled her. If Claire Wright's disappearance turned out to be the result of foul play—like if they discovered her lifeless body dumped somewhere—Gilder would be a natural suspect. His presence contaminated any evidence they might pull from her vehicle. For example, if they pulled prints and it turned out he was the last one to touch the driver's side door handle, that would now mean nothing.

She cursed under her breath and sat there for a moment while her anger subsided, then turned the engine off and opened her door. As she climbed out, Special Agent Bauer's gleaming Dodge charger pulled up behind her own less salubrious ride.

He exited his own vehicle and walked toward her. His eyes fell to the half-finished cup of coffee in her hand. "Dang. Wish I'd thought of that."

"You dodged a bullet," Patterson said. The coffee was burned and stewed. "Tastes like dirt."

"As long as it has caffeine, I'm good."

"Here." Patterson offered him the cup. "Take it."

"Thanks," Bauer said as they started toward the abandoned car. He took a sip and grimaced. "Crap. You weren't wrong about this coffee."

"Tried to warn you." Patterson rounded the police cruiser.

The uniformed officers stood with their arms folded and shoulders slumped. When they saw Patterson and Bauer, they snapped to attention.

"You must be the Feds we were told to wait for," the closest of the two said. His name tag identified him as officer Mark Kent.

Patterson flashed her ID and introduced herself.

Bauer followed suit. He looked at Ryan Gilder with narrowed eyes. "What's he doing here?"

Gilder scowled and glared at Bauer. "These police officers were nice enough to inform me that Claire's car had been found."

"Before you notified us?" Patterson asked, incredulous.

"Not our decision," said officer Kent with a shrug. "We

called it in to dispatch when the BOLO came up. They told us to hang around for you guys, so we did."

"Still doesn't explain why *he's* here," Patterson said, nodding toward Gilder.

The other officer, wearing a name badge that identified him as Dean Costanza, chimed in. "Again, not our call. We don't have any reason to impound it, and the vehicle can't stay here."

"A woman is missing," Patterson said. "You don't think that gives you just cause?"

"Just following orders. We spoke to a detective with the Missing Persons Squad, and they told us it was nothing more than a domestic. The woman has a history of going off the radar."

"You found her car abandoned in a parking lot."

Officer Costanza glanced toward the Honda. "We checked it over. Doors are locked. There's no sign of damage. It's not illegal to park up and walk away from your car."

"This is ridiculous." Patterson took a slow walk around the parked vehicle, but it was just as the officer claimed. There was no damage or indication of a struggle. The car was parked neatly within the lines. She pulled on a pair of latex gloves and checked the driver's side door, but it didn't open.

On the other side of the car, Bauer checked the passenger side. "Locked."

"Just like we told you," Officer Kent said, sounding irritated.

Patterson ignored the patrolman. She peered in the window but saw nothing out of place. To Gilder, she said, "Can you open the car?"

"Sure." Gilder nodded. "I brought the spare keys."

"Do it," Patterson instructed him.

Gilder fished a set of keys from his pocket. He used a key fob to unlock the doors.

"Do you give us consent to search the vehicle?" Patterson asked him.

Gilder hesitated a moment, then nodded. "Go ahead. You won't find anything more than I did."

"You've already accessed the vehicle?"

Gilder nodded again.

Patterson turned her attention to the cops. "Why did you let him do that?"

Costanza looked uncomfortable. "We had no authority to stop him. This isn't a crime scene."

"Dammit." Patterson shook her head. If Gilder had already gone through the vehicle, it was unlikely there would be much evidence remaining, and any that was there would be contaminated. "Did he remove anything from the vehicle?"

"Just a purse and cell phone," officer Kent replied. "They were on the passenger seat. We asked him to check the purse, but nothing appeared to have been taken."

"Which is further proof there was no crime," Costanza said. "Nothing was stolen."

Patterson was speechless. She looked at Bauer, who just raised his eyebrows.

"Can I make arrangements to have the car removed now?" Gilder asked. "I don't want it to end up towed."

"Aren't you even a wee bit concerned about your girl-friend?" Patterson asked him. "She's been missing for almost three days."

"Of course I'm concerned. The last time she disappeared, Claire didn't come back for almost a week," Gilder said. "And when she did show up, her breath reeked of alcohol."

"Then why didn't you report her missing earlier?" Patterson asked.

"Because I thought she would come home." Gilder paused. "I hoped so, at least. She didn't take her meds with her, and she suffers from depression. When it became obvious she was on another bender, I made up flyers and went to the police. I don't want her to do something stupid."

"Like what?"

Gilder shrugged. "Like get drunk again. End up passed out in the gutter . . . or worse."

Patterson nodded. "Can I look at her purse and phone?"

"Why?"

"Because we only have your word that she's done this before."

Gilder thought for a moment before replying. "Be my guest."

"Would you mind getting them for us?"

Gilder went to his car and opened the trunk. He took out a small red purse. There was a cell phone tucked into the front pocket. He held them out. "Have at it."

Patterson took the purse, still wearing the gloves, and put it on the hood of Claire Wright's car. She removed the cell phone and searched through the purse but found nothing of interest. Just the usual items any women would carry. Lipstick. Sanitary products. Gum. Next, she turned her attention to the phone, but the screen was locked.

"What's the passcode?" She asked Gilder.

"Don't know." Gilder met her gaze, then glanced down at the phone.

"You don't know your girlfriend's passcode?" Bauer said, stepping forward. "I find that hard to believe."

"Can't help that. She changed it a few weeks ago, and I forget what it is."

"That's convenient," Patterson said.

"It's also the truth."

"Something doesn't add up," Patterson said, watching Gilder. "You're not at all concerned that your girlfriend didn't take her purse or phone with her?"

"As I said, she's done this before. She's lived in Dallas all her life. She probably found a friend's couch to crash on." Gilder stepped forward, picked up the purse, and then held out his hand. "If you're done with that phone, I'd like it back."

THIRTY-SEVEN

THAT WAS CERTAINLY AN INTERESTING ENCOUNTER," Bauer said as they walked back toward their cars. Dawn was breaking now. The eastern sky was ablaze with yellow and red tones as the rising sun banished the night.

"Interesting is one way to describe it," Patterson replied.

"How do you want to play it from here?"

"Not sure." If she hadn't possessed prior personal experience of the police shrugging off a missing persons case simply because there was no evidence of foul play, she would have found the attitude toward Claire Wright's disappearance baffling. But it was a sad fact that police departments across the country had to prioritize their time, and she also knew that the majority of incidents resolved themselves naturally when the missing person resurfaced. With limited resources, investigators prioritized cases that involved minors, such as abductions and familial kidnappings, and ones that presented evidence of foul play. Claire Wright's circumstances did not yet rise to that level and disappearing voluntarily was not a crime. Still, Patterson was troubled. "I don't believe for a second that Ryan Gilder doesn't know the passcode to his girlfriend's phone."

"Maybe he's telling the truth, and she changed it recently," Bauer said. When he saw the look on Patterson's face, he held his hands up. "Just playing devil's advocate."

"We also only have his word that she suffered from depression."

"True. But her family history points toward it. Don't forget about the brother."

"I'm not." Patterson stopped at her car. "This whole situation feels wrong to me. Ryan Gilder feels wrong. But then again, I can't discount the coincidence of Claire Wright vanishing the day she was supposed to meet me to talk about Julie."

"You still think she knew something about your sister's disappearance that she didn't want to tell you?"

"I think it's a distinct possibility. If something happened to my sister when she was traveling with the band, and Claire knew about it . . ."

"Then she might be protecting the other band members or her brother's memory."

"Precisely. And I don't think it's a coincidence that someone was outside my room last night."

"Wait. What?" Bauer's eyebrows shot up. "Who was outside your room?"

"I don't know. I woke up in the night with the strange feeling that I was being watched. Someone was standing out on the catwalk, looking in through a gap in the curtains. I couldn't see their features, but I'm pretty sure it was a man."

"Maybe someone just stepped out to have a smoke," Bauer said. "It's not like you're the only person staying in the motel."

"I thought about that. But I don't think so." Patterson had replayed the incident over in her mind the previous night as she lay in bed and also as she drove over to meet Bauer at Claire Wright's car that morning. "I can't describe it, but there was an air of menace about him. Plus, he was directly outside my window. Also, I didn't smell any smoke or see any cigarette butts when I went outside."

"You went out to confront him?"

"Don't worry. I was armed."

"You should have called me."

"And said what? That somebody was outside in a public place, and it made me feel weird?" Patterson folded her arms. "Besides, he would have been gone by the time you got there."

"So what happened?"

"Nothing. When I opened the door, there was no one around. The catwalk was empty."

"Which means it could have been another guest." Bauer unlocked his car and opened the driver's door. He leaned on it. "Maybe it was just your imagination running wild. You've been so immersed in this search for your sister. Maybe you're just seeing shadows."

"I wasn't seeing shadows. There was a motorcycle in the parking lot. I swear the rider was looking at me."

"Okay. Did you see his face?"

"He was wearing a helmet with a visor." Patterson yawned. She felt dog tired. "Look, I don't know why, but I'm sure someone was skulking around outside my room last night. You have to trust me on this. I feel it in my gut."

"And you think it's tied into Julie and the disappearance of Claire Wright?"

"I think I'm getting close to something. Yes. Maybe I've spooked someone."

"Which brings me back to my original question. What's your next move?"

"First thing I want is a couple of hours' shuteye. I'm

IS SHE REALLY GONE   175

exhausted. I've barely gotten any decent sleep since I arrived in Dallas."

"You're going back to the motel?"

Patterson nodded. "Unless you have any hot leads you haven't mentioned."

"Wish I did."

"In that case, I'm going to go back and sleep for a couple of hours. I'll meet you back at the field office at noon, and we'll regroup."

"Sure. While you do that, I think I'll ask one of the intelligence analysts on the fourth floor to dig into Ryan Gilder's past. I'd like to know who we're dealing with."

"Good luck with that." Patterson took the keys out and walked to the driver's side of her car. She leaned on the roof and faced Bauer. "I'd love to track down some of Claire Wright's friends and family, too. If what Gilder says is true, she might be staying with one of them. We should start with her social network profiles."

"Will do." Bauer nodded. "Will you be okay going back to the motel on your own?"

"I'm an FBI agent with a gun. I think I can manage a drive across town without getting into trouble."

"I didn't mean that. You said someone was hanging around earlier. I can follow you there before I go to the field office. Give you some moral backup if you still feel uneasy."

"Thanks for the offer, but I'll be just fine." Patterson opened the driver's door. "I'll see you at noon."

"Roger, that." Bauer tipped his head, then climbed into the Dodge Charger.

Patterson got behind the wheel of her own car and pulled the door closed. She sat there for a moment, even as Bauer pulled away. Claire Wright's car still sat in a parking space twenty feet distant. The cops were gone now, as was Ryan Gilder. Presumably, he would be back later to collect the vehicle. She wondered if he really didn't know the passcode to his girlfriend's phone or if there was something on the device that he didn't want Patterson to see. Not that it mattered. She couldn't take the phone without a court order, and she couldn't get one of those without proof of a crime. For now, she would have to wait and see how it all played out.

THIRTY-EIGHT

PATTERSON DROVE BACK ACROSS TOWN, still thinking about the interaction with Ryan Gilder. He didn't come across as trustworthy to her, but then again, she had been trained to sniff out deceit and trust nobody. Maybe he really was just a worried boyfriend, as he claimed. Until she had more information, it was impossible to know for sure.

She pulled into the parking lot and stopped in the bay near the flight of steps leading to the second floor. She climbed out and locked the car, then started up. But when she was halfway along the catwalk and almost to her room, she came to a halt.

Her door was standing ajar.

It was only open a crack, but Patterson knew that was not how she had left it. She always double-checked that the door was locked and secure after she left the room. It was second nature. Someone else had entered while she was gone.

She glanced around, noting the lack of a maid's cart. If her room was being cleaned, there would almost certainly be a cart standing outside the room, loaded with items like towels, toilet rolls, and fresh bed linens.

Patterson's instincts took over.

She reached inside her jacket and slipped out the sleek, black Glock 19M pistol from its holster. She held it in the low ready position with her arms straight, gun barrel pointed downward and advanced forward along the catwalk.

When she reached the door, Patterson paused. She listened, straining her ears to detect the slightest sound, but heard nothing from within the room. Maybe the intruder was already gone. But she could not make that assumption.

Ready to bring her gun to bear at a moment's notice, Patterson used her foot to nudge the door open.

It swung inward to reveal what appeared to be an empty bedroom. The curtains were drawn, and the lights were off, bathing the interior in a gloomy half-light.

She gave it another moment, her gaze wandering the seemingly innocuous space, looking for any sign of movement. Seeing none, she stepped across the threshold. Then, before she could react, the door swung forward and smacked into her with enough force to send Patterson stumbling backward onto the catwalk. She glimpsed a figure stepping from behind the door just as she hit the railing with a jolt, almost losing her gun.

The door flew back open and banged against the wall.

A figure wearing a crash helmet and heavy leather jacket lunged forward, head bent low. He was much too close and barreled into Patterson before she had a chance to raise the Glock and fire. The top of the crash helmet caught her hard under the left breast.

The sudden and unexpected impact sent Patterson tumbling sideways even as the breath exited her body in a mighty whoosh.

She fell hard on her rump, gasping for air. A bolt of tingling pain shot up her spine. Her elbow hit the ground, and this time she couldn't keep her grip on the gun. It clattered onto the concrete, useless, just as the figure turned toward her, reaching around to his back and drawing a deadly-looking handgun in a quick, fluid movement.

Defenseless, with her own gun lying a couple of feet away, Patterson weighed her chances of rolling sideways and snatching it up before a bullet found her skull.

They were not good, but still a better option than sitting on her ass and waiting to die.

"Don't do it," the gunman growled, his voice muffled by the helmet's closed visor. He called back into the room without letting his attention stray from Patterson. "Hurry it up in there. We need to leave. Now!"

"All done." A second man stepped out onto the catwalk. He was thickset and muscular, with bulging biceps concealed under a long-sleeved shirt. Instead of a crash helmet, he wore a baseball cap. A bandanna concealed his features so that all Patterson could see were a pair of dark eyes in the shadow of the cap's visor. He carried the bankers box that held the documents related to TexFest.

"You get everything?" The gunman asked.

"Everything I could find." Bandanna man edged past his buddy and started along the catwalk. "Let's get out of here before someone sees us and calls the cops."

The gunman nodded and started backing up, careful not to turn away from Patterson. He kept the pistol aimed at her. "Don't even try to move until we're gone."

Patterson said nothing. She was too busy studying her assailants, looking for any identifying features that might help her recognize them again later. But the pair had done a good job of concealing their identities. Even so, she was sure the helmeted gunman was the same man who had been skulking outside her room in the early hours of the morning.

The two men reached the stairs. Bandanna started down first, disappearing from view. Crash helmet stood a few moments longer, his gun still aimed squarely at Patterson. Then he lowered it and followed his friend.

Now Patterson scooped up her gun and climbed to her feet. She ran along the catwalk toward the steps leading down to the parking lot, wincing in pain as she went. The bottom of her ribs hurt like crazy where the crash helmet had connected. She hoped they were only bruised, not broken.

She reached the top of the steps and started down without hesitation, even as the throaty revs of a powerful engine echoed up through the stairwell.

Patterson took the steps two at a time, gripping the handrail for support and ignoring the pain that flared with each heavy footfall. She reached the bottom and ran toward the parking lot.

But she was a few moments too late.

A shiny red quad-cab truck was already speeding away toward the service road fronting the motel. It turned out without slowing down, tires squealing as they struggled to grip the road. Then it sped away even faster as her assailants made their escape.

THIRTY-NINE

PATTERSON HOLSTERED her pistol and sprinted toward her car. She jumped in and fired up the engine, then reversed from the parking space and swung the wheel hard, peeling out and giving chase. She turned onto the road and followed in the direction of the fleeing truck but could no longer see it.

"Where have you gone?" she muttered under her breath, scanning the road ahead as far as she could see, and also the ramp leading to the interstate. If they had gone there, she would never find them. They could be miles down the highway by now. But she was sure they hadn't taken the ramp. She had watched them speed away and would have noticed if they headed for the interstate. Which meant they were still close by because they couldn't drive too fast on local roads without drawing unwanted attention.

Patterson zipped past the ramp and continued along the access road. There were industrial units on both sides—mostly small businesses. There was an auto body shop, a manufacturer of kitchen countertops, and an electrical distributor. The tenants of other units were less obvious. Patterson peered between the warehouse buildings as she passed them, aware that they presented ideal spots for a truck to pull in and hide from view. But she saw no sign of the red quad-cab.

She continued on as the road curved to the left and met a larger four-lane thoroughfare. Once the truck hit that, all bets were off. It could turn in either direction and keep going or vanish up a host of side streets. She would never find it. But the truck hadn't turned. It was parked on a vacant and dusty corner lot to her right. The patch of land was nothing but dirt and scraggly bushes, with some trash strewn around for good measure. A faded real estate sign that now leaned at an angle had apparently done nothing to attract a buyer to this unkempt quarter-acre patch of the city.

Patterson steered onto the lot and stopped ten feet behind the truck. She exited her vehicle, drawing her Glock. She kept the open car door between herself and the truck, all too aware that at least one of the men who fled the motel was armed. His companion would almost certainly be packing, too.

She stayed there a moment, making sure the coast was clear, then approached the truck. She could see no one in the cab, which was soon confirmed when she opened the driver's door. Empty. She did a quick three-sixty of the vehicle and even checked the ground underneath, but the men who broke into her motel room were gone, and along with them, the box full of TexFest documents.

FORTY

THE TRUCK WAS REPORTED STOLEN an hour ago from a neighborhood in Fort Worth," Bauer said, hanging up his phone. He had arrived a few minutes before, after receiving a call from Patterson. When she told him about the intruders inside her room, and the scuffle out on the catwalk, his face had creased with concern. Then, when it became clear that Patterson was more focused on the abandoned truck than taking care of her bumps and bruises, he had called in the scene to Dallas PD. Now he stood behind the red quad-cab, still parked on the vacant lot, and pushed the phone back into his pocket. "The owner discovered it missing from their driveway when they got up this morning."

"Makes sense," Patterson said. "They didn't want to use their own vehicles in case it was seen at the motel."

"You said vehicles, plural."

"That's because they left separately on two wheels, not four." Patterson motioned for Bauer to follow her and then showed him two sets of tire tracks pushed into the soft earth near the edge of the lot. She had found them after realizing the perpetrators had abandoned the truck, and before calling Bauer.

"They fled on motorcycles," he said, looking at the tracks. "I assume you photographed these."

"Naturally." Patterson tapped her pocket and the phone within. "Not that it will do any good. There must be thousands of motorcycles in the city, and we'll never get a forensics team out here to analyze these tracks, anyway. Not for something as inconsequential as a motel room break-in."

"Except the motel room is occupied by an FBI agent, and they stole evidence," Bauer said. "Not to mention the fact that they assaulted then pointed a gun at a federal law enforcement officer."

"Maybe if they'd pulled the trigger, you'd be able to get those tire tracks analyzed," Patterson replied. "As it is, there are more important crimes for CSI to work on, like murders and rapes. You should know all about prioritizing crime scenes, given your background with the LAPD."

"Doesn't mean I have to like it." Bauer stepped away from the tracks, careful not to disturb them. He wandered the lot, then stopped near a low fence at the plot's boundary. He peered beyond it, then hoisted himself up and over, momentarily disappearing from view. A few seconds later his head bobbed up from behind the fence. "Over here."

Patterson hurried over to the fence. "What have you got?"

Bauer was standing at the back of an abandoned industrial building in a paved outdoor yard that was clogged with junk. Piles of twisted metal sat like rusting islands. Old washing machines and dryers in various states of disintegration were piled precariously against a concrete block wall topped by razor wire on the other side of the yard. There was even a toilet with a cracked bowl. Broken glass littered the ground. But what had caught the FBI agent's eye sat close to the fence where the occupants of the truck had thrown it.

An old Brown bankers box.

It was empty, with the discarded lid sitting nearby.

He reached down and picked it up. "I guess our thieves took the contents and threw the box over here because they couldn't balance it on a motorcycle."

"Looks like it," Patterson said. "I wonder what was so important in that box that they would risk breaking into the room of a federal agent?"

"And committing assault. Let's not forget that."

"I have a feeling the assault was circumstantial." Patterson's ribs still hurt. Circumstantial or not, the guy in the motorcycle helmet had clocked her a good one. "They didn't expect me to come back so soon."

"Saw their opportunity and took it."

"Yeah."

"You think they were there when you left this morning, watching you from the parking lot?"

"I don't think so." Patterson shook her head. "There was plenty of opportunity for them to break into my room and take whatever they needed before I went back there. I think it's more likely they weren't in the room very long, and I disturbed them."

Bauer lifted the box and lid over the fence, then climbed back over. He brushed his pants off. "This was planned. They knew which room you were in. Checked to make sure last night, which is why you saw someone looking in through your window. Then they stole a pickup. Probably put their bikes in the truck bed and drove it over here. After that, they used the truck to commit the crime and made their escape on the motorcycles."

"They just didn't anticipate me coming back to the motel room so soon. Probably thought I'd be gone all day."

"Question is, what was so damned important in that box?"

"I don't know," Patterson said. There was nothing of any real significance among the TexFest documents. It was mostly old band contracts, festival flyers, permit applications, and other assorted paperwork. She had spent hours going through it looking for a reference to the band called Sunrise that Julie had traveled to Dallas with and had come across nothing incriminating or illegal. What she did find had led her to Claire Wright, who was now missing. Given the events of the last hour, she couldn't help but wonder if she had missed something important. Something someone decided they wanted back before she saw it. "The only person who knew we had that box was the organizer of TexFest."

"Otto Sharp." Bauer raised an eyebrow. "You think this is his doing?"

"The man runs a bar frequented by bikers, at least some of whom have gang affiliations."

"True. And guys like that wouldn't think twice about taking a pop at law enforcement. We're not exactly their favorite people."

"Yeah. Look at what happened last time we were there."

"Exactly. For all we know, the guys that broke into your room are the same ones that hassled us when we left the bar," Bauer said. "Maybe Otto Sharp had second thoughts about letting us dig through that box."

"And there's only one reason I can think of for that," Patterson replied.

"Because he didn't want us getting close to Martin Wright, and by extension, his sister, Claire."

"Or one of the other band members."

"He might not even know that Martin Wright is dead." Bauer looked thoughtful. "You think he had something to do with Claire's disappearance?"

"It's as good an assumption as any other," Patterson said. "Which means we need to take a closer look at our failed impresario." She took a deep breath and grimaced as the motion caused a flare of pain in her ribs.

Bauer noticed. His brow furrowed with concern. "Before we do that, I think we need to get you looked at."

"I'm fine," Patterson said, although she knew her expression said otherwise. "It's just a bruise."

"I really think—"

"I don't have time to be out of action. I can work through the pain."

"You are one stubborn woman," Bauer said. "Anyone ever told you that?"

"Once or twice." Patterson started toward her car. "Let's see what we can find out about Otto Sharp."

"Not a chance. Not until we get you back to the motel room and get some ice on that, at least," Bauer said, as a Dallas PD cruiser pulled up and two officers climbed out. "The local boys can take care of the stolen pickup."

"You're not going to take no for an answer, are you?" Patterson asked.

"Not on your life." Bauer held the door open for her as she climbed behind the wheel. "You okay to drive?"

"I was okay thirty minutes ago. I'm sure I'll be fine now."

"Good." Bauer slapped the roof of the car with his palm. "See you back at the motel."

FORTY-ONE

COME ON, let's see how bad the damage is," Bauer said once they were back in Patterson's motel room.

"I feel fine," Patterson protested, even though she felt anything but.

"I don't believe you. Let's get some ice on the bruises." Bauer walked to the vanity at the back of the room and picked up the ice bucket sitting next to the sink, then made his way to the door. "I'll be back in a minute."

Patterson watched him leave before removing her jacket and shoulder holster, then unbuttoning her shirt. She slipped the garment off, then unbuckled her bra, removing that too. The skin under her left breast was already turning shades of purple and brown where her assailant's helmet had made contact. She probed the area tentatively, grimacing as she did so. It was bruised all right, but she didn't think any ribs were broken. Not that she was an expert.

Realizing that Special Agent Bauer would be back at any moment, Patterson pulled a sports bra from her overnight bag and pulled it on.

Less than a minute later, the ex-LAPD cop turned FBI

agent was back. He eyed her for a moment, his gaze resting on the ugly bruise, then walked past her to the bathroom. She heard him moving around, and the clink of ice. He returned carrying a towel wadded up into a ball.

"Here, put this on the bruise," he said.

"Thanks." Patterson took the makeshift ice pack and pressed it against her ribs, letting out a hiss of breath through clenched teeth as the freezing ice made contact. She sat on the edge of the bed and held the ice pack in place.

"You might want to get that x-rayed," Bauer said.

"It's a bruise. I'll live."

"Just making a suggestion." Bauer went to the window and looked out over the parking lot, his back to her. "Did you notice if anything else is missing?"

"I don't think so." Patterson glanced around. She noticed that the drawers in the bureau under the TV were cracked open a few inches. She knew they hadn't been that way when she left, which meant the intruders had been going through the room, searching for who knew what. Not that it mattered. She had put nothing in the drawers and certainly wouldn't have put anything of any value there, anyway.

Her attention turned to the closet and the wall safe within. She was relieved to find it still locked. She only used the safe for two items. Her Glock, which had been snug in its holster about her person, and her laptop when she didn't need it. When she typed in the code and opened the door the computer was still there. Either the intruders had missed the safe—which she found unlikely—or had lacked the time to crack it.

Her overnight bag was another matter. The zip was pulled back, which meant they had rifled through it. An invasion of privacy she tried her best not to think about.

The intruders had done a good job of searching the room, with the exception of the wall safe. Another few minutes, and they might have popped the door and gotten their hands on her laptop, too. Her arrival back at the motel room had probably prevented that from occurring. Instead, they grabbed the bankers box and tried to flee, attacking her in the process. That they hadn't immediately emptied it and searched the documents inside led her to the conclusion that either they weren't sure what they were looking for, or the box of documents itself was the primary target. Which meant they were probably there on someone else's orders. It also meant that she had ruffled some feathers with her investigation. The more she thought about it, the more she became convinced that Claire Wright's disappearance and the break-in were connected. The only question was, how? She looked up at Bauer. "I think we should pay another visit to Otto Sharp sooner rather than later. If he did send goons to retrieve that box, the quicker we get to him, the better."

"I thought you wanted to do some digging into his background first." Bauer turned back toward her. He took a seat at the small table near the window. The same table the now missing box had been sitting on not so long before. "See what we can find out about him."

"I do, but if he took the box to destroy evidence, then we need to get it back."

"And how do you propose to do that?" Bauer rubbed his chin. "We don't even have proof that Sharp is involved in any of this. Hell, we don't have any concrete suspects at all. At least none that would hold up if we went before a judge, which is what would have to happen if we want to get a search warrant."

"I know," Patterson snapped, a little too abruptly, then instantly felt bad about it. She mumbled an apology. "Sorry, my ribs hurt like hell, and I don't like it when people get the drop on me."

"Ice pack helping any?"

"I think so." Patterson managed a weak smile.

"You still want to talk to Otto Sharp, even without a search warrant?"

"Don't see that we've got much choice," Patterson said. But she knew that the odds of retrieving the box—assuming Otto Sharp even had it—were slim to none without a warrant. He would never voluntarily give them permission to search his premises if the documents were there, or even if they weren't, for that matter. Still, the least they could do was put the fear of God into him. The weird thing was that she'd already looked through the entire box and found nothing except the band contract that led her to Claire. If Otto had thought twice about cooperating and wanted to get the box back because of that contract, he would surely have realized it was too late. The box had been in Patterson's possession for more than forty-eight hours already. More than enough time to go through the entire thing. None of this made sense. But they didn't have any other leads, and she could think of no one else who would care about the box. She adjusted the ice pack and stood up. "How do you fancy a trip back to the High Note Bar and Grill?"

"Maybe you should give it another fifteen minutes with the ice pack first," Bauer said.

"I'm good to go," Patterson replied. She walked to the back of the room and put the ice pack in the sink. Leaving the sports bra on, she got dressed again and strapped on her shoulder holster, ignoring the throb of pain as she clipped it. She picked up her jacket and made for the door. "Come on. Otto Sharp won't interrogate himself. I'll even let you drive."

FORTY-TWO

THE HIGH NOTE BAR AND GRILL didn't look any better the second time they visited than it had the first. If anything, Patterson thought, it looked worse, because there were more bikes parked outside. From somewhere, she could hear the sounds of a raucous gathering. Loud music. Laughter. Drunken conversation. She guessed it was coming from the back of the building, where there must be a courtyard. They would have to be even more careful than the last time they visited.

"Well, this is delightful," Bauer said as they crossed the gravel parking lot toward the bar's front door. He eyed the rows of motorcycles. "Looks like the gang's all here, pardon the pun."

"It's Saturday. Party time," Patterson said as her gaze followed Bauer's toward the bikes. She guessed there must be at least five times more motorcycles here than their previous visit, mostly Harleys with a couple of Indians mixed in. Absent were any foreign makes, like Suzuki or Kawasaki. An outlaw biker wouldn't be caught dead on such a machine. Patriotism ran strong in the biker community, even if respect for law enforcement did not. She stepped past the rows of motorcycles but paused at the door. "We should watch each other's backs in there. I have a feeling we aren't going to be well received."

"Ya think?" Bauer snorted and reached for the door handle.

When they stepped inside, a dozen heads turned in their direction. By the time they reached the bar, two dozen more bikers were watching them. Thankfully, none of the assorted denizens inside the bar made a move toward them. At least, not yet.

Patterson recognized one of the two bartenders. Dakota, the girl they had spoken to the last time they visited.

She rolled her eyes when she saw them. "How stupid are you two?"

"I beg your pardon?" Bauer said.

"Coming back here unannounced, and on a Saturday, to boot. You looking to have your asses kicked?"

"No." Patterson had already been in one skirmish that day, and she had no desire to be in another. "We're looking for your boss, Otto Sharp."

"We have some more questions," Bauer added.

"Of course you do." Dakota's eyes flicked toward the door, then back to the agents. "You bring the cavalry along? You got more cops out there?"

"Just us." Patterson sensed they were walking a knife-edge. The mood in the bar had changed from raucous to hostile the minute they walked in.

"You really are stupid." Dakota chuckled. "But, hey. What do I care?"

Patterson folded her arms and glared at the gangly bartender. "Your boss?"

"All right, already." Dakota turned and sauntered back along the bar, then disappeared through a door near the end.

Patterson cast a surreptitious look over her shoulder, but so far none of the gathered bikers had made a move toward them. But she wasn't sure how long that would hold. "Hope she doesn't take forever. I'd rather not linger here any longer than necessary."

"Me either." Bauer stood with his hands deep in his pockets, but Patterson knew he was coiled tight, ready to react at a moment's notice. If things went south, the Glock concealed under his suit jacket would be in his hand within half a second.

Patterson's own gun would not be far behind, but she prayed it didn't come to that. If a brawl ensued and they were forced to defend themselves, they would have to call it in, and the paperwork alone would be a nightmare. Patterson was not a fan of paperwork.

She turned her attention back toward the bar, deciding that it was better not to look too interested in their surroundings.

A moment later, Dakota stuck her head out through the doorway and motioned to them. "Otto's in his office. He can talk to you there."

Bauer looked at Patterson and shrugged. "Guess he doesn't want to be seen talking to us again."

"Who cares? At least he *will* talk to us." Patterson made her way to the end of the bar and stepped through the hatch. She held it up for Bauer and together they followed Dakota into a short corridor with dirty walls and threadbare carpet. A door to their left, secured by a hefty padlock, was marked 'storeroom'. On their right was another door, this one unmarked. The corridor dead-ended in a fire door with 'emergency exit' written on it.

Dakota stopped outside of the unmarked door and pointed. "He's in there." Then she pushed past them and made her way back toward the bar. She was about to step out of the door when she glanced backward. "When you're finished, don't come back through the bar. Leave by the emergency exit. You'll be on the side of the building. Just turn left and it'll take you back to the parking lot."

"Thanks," Patterson said. And she meant it. She had no desire to walk back through the dingy, smoke-filled bar. It amazed her that anyone wanted to spend their free time in such a place, even bikers. But then again, a lot of things she came across on this job didn't make sense to her. Some people had low standards and did crazy things. Sometimes even stuff that would land them in prison. Like breaking into the motel room of an FBI agent and stealing evidence.

She waited for Dakota to close the door leading to the bar and then knocked on the office door.

A gruff voice bade them to enter.

Patterson pushed the door open and stepped into the office with Bauer right behind. It was a cramped space barely big enough for the desk that sat within. There were no windows. A rickety-looking particleboard shelf unit stood in the corner stacked with paperwork. Music festival posters in cheap frames adorned the walls. Most of them were years old and from a variety of cities, including Las Vegas, Phoenix, and Reno. TexFest was conspicuous by its absence.

The man himself sat behind a cluttered desk. The only other chair, pushed into the corner of the room, was made of hard plastic.

Otto looked up at them with a look of distinct irritation. "I thought I told the pair of you not to come back here."

"I'm sorry, do we take orders from you?" Bauer asked. "Because I don't recall seeing your name on the FBI's chain of command."

"Whatever." Otto glared at the two agents with narrowed eyes. "Just tell me what you want and then get the hell out. You're stinking up my bar."

FORTY-THREE

WHERE IS IT?" Patterson placed her palms on the desk and leaned toward Otto Sharp.

"Where is what?" Otto looked genuinely confused. "I have no idea what you're talking about."

"Don't play dumb with me," Patterson said. "The box. Where is it?"

"Are you talking about that old bankers box full of TexFest stuff?" Otto shook his head. "I gave it to you already."

"And then you took it back."

"What the hell are you talking about? I didn't take anything back. I haven't seen either of you since we met at the storage unit."

"Who did you send?" Patterson was like a dog holding onto a bone. She refused to let go. "Was it those two meat-heads who hassled us the other day out by our car? What were their names?" Patterson paused a moment. Thinking. "Angel and Frankie. That's it. Is that who you had follow me and ransack my room?"

"Lady, you're freaking nuts."

"Really? Because your goons assaulted a federal agent. If they were following your orders, then by extension you are just as guilty. Do you know what the penalty is for that?"

"I know that I don't have to sit here and listen to you accuse me of crap I didn't do." Otto half rose out of his chair.

"Sit the hell down." Patterson was losing her patience.

Otto looked like he'd been slapped in the face. He sank back into the chair. "This is harassment."

"If you want to see harassment, I can do that," Patterson said, drawing her jacket back to show her gun.

"Are you threatening me?" Otto looked from Patterson to Bauer, no doubt hoping the ex-LAPD cop would come to his rescue.

"I just want the truth," Patterson said. Every moment they were wasting time talking to Otto Sharp, there was more chance the contents of the box would end up destroyed. He probably had someone out back right at that moment, burning or shredding it.

"I told you the truth," Otto said in a measured voice laced with indignation. He met Patterson's gaze. "Last time I saw that box was at the storage unit. If someone took it, I had nothing to do with that."

"Great. Then you won't mind if we search this place."

"Hell yes, I mind if you search my bar. You want to do that, you'd better have a search warrant." Otto leaned back in his chair. "But you don't have one of those, do you?"

Now Bauer jumped in. "We were hoping you'd be a civic-minded individual and grant us permission to look around without the need to go to that trouble."

"That's what I thought." Otto's gaze shifted from Patterson to Bauer. "If you had a search warrant, we wouldn't even be having this conversation."

"So, are you going to let us search?" Bauer asked. "If you have nothing to hide, it's not a big deal."

"I already told you, the answer is no." Otto pressed his lips into a thin line. "And for your information, I have nothing to hide. I'm a businessman operating a legitimate business."

"Right." Patterson folded her arms. "You'll excuse me for not believing you because I've seen the clientele who frequents your establishment."

"Just because I cater to a certain demographic doesn't make me a criminal."

"Then let us conduct a search," Patterson said. "Or better yet, just give us back the box with everything intact, and we'll call it quits."

"I already told you, I don't have it."

"And I already told you, I don't believe—"

"Special Agent Patterson?" Bauer stepped forward and touched Patterson's arm. "I think we should confer."

"What?" Patterson shot the trainee agent a vexed look.

Bauer jerked his head toward the door. "Can I have a quick word with you outside?"

"Fine." Patterson looked back at Otto. "You. Stay there. Don't move a muscle."

Otto raised his hands and shook his head. "Whatever you say."

Patterson turned to the door and pulled it open, then stepped out into the short corridor. After Bauer joined her and closed the office door, she spun toward him. "Never undermine my authority in front of the suspect again."

"I wasn't undermining your authority," Bauer said in a calm voice. "I felt it was necessary to have a little tête-à-tête. We're clearly not getting anywhere with Sharp. Even if he led a Boy Scout troop and helped old ladies across the road in his spare time, he wouldn't let us search this place on principle."

"I know that." Patterson sighed. "I was hoping that if we ruffled his feathers, he'd make a mistake."

"That doesn't seem to be working," Bauer said. "I didn't see any tells. No obvious signs of deception."

"That just makes him a good poker player."

"Or it means he's telling the truth and really doesn't know where the box is."

"Do you believe that?" Patterson asked.

"I don't trust him, for sure. That doesn't mean he took the box."

"Okay. Tell me this. If Otto Sharp didn't send those thugs to my room, then who did?"

Bauer shrugged. "Look, I'm not saying that Otto isn't behind this morning's events. I'm just pointing out that he won't admit it, and we can't force him to let us search his bar. Even if he showed signs of deception, which he didn't, we have no solid proof of his involvement in anything. Actually, quite the opposite. He was the one who gave us the box in the first place. We're at an impasse."

"I agree," Patterson said grudgingly. She rubbed her temples. "We need to try another approach. Dig up the dirt on Otto Sharp and see what skeletons might be lurking in his closet."

"If any."

"Oh, he's got skeletons. The only question is, do any of them relate to my sister or Claire Wright?"

"So, we're back to your original idea of looking into Sharp's background."

"It looks that way." Patterson was frustrated. If she'd hoped to ride roughshod over Otto Sharp and bend him to her will, she'd miscalculated. He was clearly adept at handling confrontation. Not letting it fluster him. A skill he'd probably acquired from years running a bar full of miscreants and roughnecks. His disdain for law enforcement didn't help. "Let's hope something pops out."

"Uh-huh." Bauer nodded. "Does that mean we can get out of here now?"

Patterson stepped past Bauer and opened the office door. She fixed Otto with a withering stare. "We're done, for now."

"Are you sure you wouldn't like to threaten me some more?" Otto retorted. "I was having so much fun."

"Don't get too cocky," Patterson said. "We'll be back soon enough." Then she spun on her heel and walked down the corridor. She pushed open the emergency exit door and stepped out into the bright sunlight, with Bauer at her rear.

FORTY-FOUR

BAUER DROVE them back toward downtown and the Dallas Field Office. But instead of going straight there, he took a detour to Parkland Memorial and insisted that Patterson get herself checked out.

Patterson had protested, but Special Agent Bauer gave no quarter and all but threw her out of the car, so in the end, she relented and stomped off toward the ER, leaving Bauer parked in an official use spot near the entrance. A perk of riding with federal plates.

Unfortunately, the special treatment ended there. Despite showing the nurse behind the desk her badge, Patterson was forced to wait more than an hour to get seen. After that, they poked and prodded her, took x-rays, and eventually confirmed what she already knew. There were no cracked ribs, and she was just bruised. By the time she returned to the car, which was still parked in the official use spot, Patterson's mood was dark.

Bauer's attention was focused on his phone, and he didn't look up when Patterson slid into the passenger seat next to him.

Patterson waited a few seconds, then said: "In case you hadn't noticed, I'm back."

"I can see that," Bauer replied, finally looking her way. "They get you all fixed up?"

"They didn't do much of anything except shoot some x-rays and give me these," Patterson said, holding up an orange pill bottle with a white lid.

"Painkillers?"

"Yup." Patterson pushed the bottle into her pocket.

"Did you take one already?" Bauer asked, watching her.

"No. They might make me drowsy, and I've got work to do."

"I see." The look on Bauer's face told her he was less than pleased. "Ribs still in one piece?"

"Everything is where it's supposed to be, and there's no permanent damage." Patterson nodded toward the phone. "What are you up to while I was wasting my time in there?"

"Getting work done. I ran a background check on Otto Sharp. Or rather, I had the field office do it."

"And?"

"Zip. He's either clean or good at covering his ass."

"There has to be something." Patterson pulled the seatbelt across her chest, holding it away from her bruised ribs with her other hand as she clicked it, then gently lowered the strap. "He must have some secrets, given the circles he moves in. We need to find them."

"Well, we're not going to do it through official channels. There are no arrests in the system. Or at least, if he has, there is no record available."

"Sharp told us he moved around after TexFest. Did you run him through NCIC to see if he got in trouble somewhere else in the country?"

"I might be new to the job, but I'm not *that* new. Of course I did. Nothing."

"Just asking." Patterson felt the pill bottle press against her hip. Her ribs were throbbing. She briefly entertained the idea of taking a pill and damn the consequences, but she resisted. She needed to keep a clear head. "So that leaves us at another dead end."

"Maybe." Bauer put his phone away and started the engine. "Or maybe not."

"What do you mean?" Patterson tried to ignore the pain even though it had grown worse since she climbed into the car. The dull ache under her left breast flared each time she took a breath. Again, her mind wandered to the pills. Again, she pushed the temptation aside.

"Back when I was in the LAPD, we had a gang task force. We used confidential informants to get intel all the time."

"Okay."

"So, I got to thinking that Dallas probably has some informants of their own. Maybe even in one of the biker gangs that hang out at Otto's bar."

"Smart thinking." Patterson was finding Special Agent Bauer to be more valuable than she had initially expected. He was resourceful—a good investigator. Once again, she wondered why he left the LAPD so soon after making detective to join the Bureau. "Do they have an informant in any of the motorcycle gangs hereabouts?"

"I don't know yet. I shot the inquiry down the line. Now we'll see what comes back to us."

"Let's hope it doesn't take too long."

"Amen to that. I feel like we're running in circles." Bauer reversed out of the parking space and headed for the exit. As he pulled out onto the road, he spoke again. "That truck from this morning was clean, by the way."

"The pickup?"

"Dallas PD towed it in and had forensics give it a quick once over but didn't find any trace evidence."

"Perps were both wearing gloves. They were careful."

"At least the forensics guys gave it a go. Apparently, DPD views assaulting a federal agent as a bigger deal than you give them credit for."

"Did they analyze the tire tracks left by the motorcycles at the place where they dumped the truck?"

"No. They didn't do that," Bauer admitted.

"There you go. And I bet that forensics examination constituted dusting for prints and not much more."

"Hey, it's better than nothing. The pickup truck's owner isn't too happy, though. His ride's been impounded as evidence until this mess is sorted out."

"At least the truck was recovered with no damage. He should be thankful for that. He's lucky they didn't torch it, just in case."

"Yeah. Probably thought a burning vehicle in the middle of the city would attract attention too quickly."

"Probably." Patterson glanced out the window and noticed that they were heading across town in the wrong direction for the field office. She looked at Bauer. "Where are you going?"

"Back to your motel."

"Hell no. We've still got work to do."

"I've still got work to do. You need to get some rest. You only went back to the motel this morning to get a few hours of shuteye, and you ended up in a brawl with armed robbers instead. You've been on the go ever since."

"I'm fine," Patterson protested.

"You're not fine. I can tell that those ribs are bothering you. It's late in the day, anyway. We're not going to achieve much more until we hear from the gang unit, and that could take hours or even days."

"That's not the point."

"I'm taking you back to the motel, and that's all there is to it." Bauer kept his eyes fixed on the road ahead. "If you feel so inclined, you can report me for insubordination later. But here and now, you're going to rest up and let those bruises heal." Now he cast her a quick glance. "You going to keep arguing?"

"No," Patterson replied. Because deep down, all she wanted to do was swallow a couple of painkillers and close her eyes for a few hours.

FORTY-FIVE

PATTERSON CLOSED her eyes for more than a few hours. In fact, it was more like four. After arriving back at the motel room, she had taken a quick tour to make sure no one was lurking within and then locked the door. Feeling secure now, she took the pills out of her pocket and downed two with a couple of swigs from a bottle of water. After that, she changed into sweats and a tee then flopped down on the bed. That was the last thing she remembered until she woke up several hours later.

The room was dark now. It was nine o'clock. She was also hungry. Patterson turned on the lamp next to the bed and rose as the last vestiges of sleep fell away.

She heard an engine revving from somewhere outside, the noise crass and loud. She went to the window, pulled the curtain back, and then peered out. At first, she didn't see the vehicle making all the racket, but then a Mustang GT with oversized rims and low-profile tires came into view before making its way toward the road. It was nothing to worry about, just some yahoo showing off with their muscle car.

She turned from the window and went over to the bureau

upon which the TV sat. There was a sign in a plastic stand advertising an online food delivery service. They probably gave the motel a small kickback every time anyone ordered. She went to her laptop and pulled the website up. There were several delivery options, including a couple of pizza places, a Chinese restaurant, McDonald's, and Subway. After deliberating for a few moments, she chose the Chinese food and ordered sweet-and-sour chicken with a side of pork fried rice, even though it wasn't exactly healthy.

While she waited for her meal to arrive, Patterson browsed the web to see what she could find out about Otto Sharp, but as expected, she came up empty. The man didn't even appear to have a social media presence. All she found was an old website for the High Note Bar and Grill that was hopelessly outdated and had probably been created before Otto even became involved with the business. She wondered if he even realized it was online.

She was still thinking about this when the food came. She went to the door and peered through the peephole to confirm that it was the delivery driver, then opened it and tipped him five bucks after he handed her the food.

She pushed the laptop aside and ate at the small table next to the motel room window. The food was passable at best. She only ate half before deciding it wasn't worth the calories. After pushing it aside, she returned to the computer and focused on Claire Wright. Earlier that day, after discovering the red Honda Civic, she'd asked Bauer to hunt through the missing woman's online footprint. She was eager to track down any friends or acquaintances of Claire's. That hadn't happened because Patterson arrived back at the motel to find intruders in her room, the consequences of which derailed the rest of their day.

Now Patterson figured she might as well make up for lost time. She typed Claire's name into her browser's search bar and soon found Facebook and Pinterest pages. Patterson started with Facebook. There were only a few posts visible, either because Claire wasn't much into social media or because most of them were hidden. Strangely, the last post on Claire Wright's wall was more than three years ago.

When she browsed the woman's Pinterest account, she found the same thing. No posts or updates for several years.

Returning to Facebook, Patterson turned her focus to Claire's friends, who only numbered twenty-six. A meager amount compared to most people's social network pages. She started through them, clicking on each friend's page as she went and noting their location. The majority were not local, and Patterson recognized none of the names, which meant that Claire had not kept in touch with any of her brother's old band members, at least on the social networks. By the time she was finished, Patterson had compiled a list of six people around Dallas who Claire knew. Four females and two males. Each was a potential source of information that could lead them to the missing woman. And they shouldn't be too hard to track down, given the Bureau's resources. But that was a job for tomorrow. The pills Patterson had taken earlier had all but worn off now, and her ribs were aching again. A dull yet insistent throb that made it hard to focus. Without more pain meds, it would only get worse.

Patterson closed the laptop and slid it back into its slim-line soft-sided bag. She went to the safe and locked the computer inside. She felt sure that the men who had ransacked her room earlier that day would not return, especially with her there, but she felt safer stashing it, anyway. In some ways, she hoped the men would return because she would be waiting with her Glock this time. She was still miffed that they had gotten the drop on her earlier and had replayed the scene over in her head more than once, looking for ways she could have changed the outcome. Now she pushed the thought away, realizing it would do no good to keep obsessing about her failure.

For the second time that night, she went to the window and pulled the curtains open a crack, looking out onto the catwalk, and the parking lot beyond. If anyone was still watching her, they were keeping themselves well concealed. She let the curtains fall closed again and used the oversized hair clip from the night before to secure the slight gap that remained and ensure no one could look in. That done, she went to the bathroom and pried the top off the pill bottle, swallowing two more pills along with a chug of water. She lifted the tee and examined the angry bruise under her left breast in the bathroom mirror. It had turned a deeper shade of purple now, rimmed by yellow at the edges. She dropped the T-shirt back in place and padded into the bedroom, crossing to the bed. But not before taking the Glock out of its holster and placing the gun on the nightstand within easy reach. Then she slipped between the covers, turned the lights off, and lay awake waiting for the painkillers to do their job.

FORTY-SIX

HOW ARE THE RIBS FEELING TODAY?" Bauer asked when Patterson strode into the small office they shared at the FBI's Dallas Field Office the next morning. He was sitting with his laptop closed, cradling a cup of Starbucks coffee.

"Better than they felt yesterday," Patterson replied. And it was true, but that didn't mean she felt fine. It still hurt if she drew too deep a breath, and when she'd gotten a tickle in her throat and coughed during the night, it was like someone had stabbed her in the side with a red-hot poker. She looked wistfully at the coffee. "I don't suppose there's a second one of those lying around somewhere?"

"Uh-huh." Bauer pointed toward Patterson's desk.

She looked sideways and spotted a Starbucks cup sitting there with the plastic lid still attached. "Oh my God. You're a lifesaver."

"Figured you'd want one," Bauer said before taking another sip of his own coffee. "It's been there for fifteen minutes, so I can't guarantee it will still be piping hot."

"I don't care." Patterson descended on the coffee and

pried the lid off. She ripped the top from a sugar packet and dumped it in, then stirred the liquid before taking a large gulp. "I need caffeine."

"I hear you." Bauer waited for her to sit down and set up her laptop, which she had been carrying under one arm, before he spoke again. "I heard back from DPD's gang task force this morning."

"Do they have a confidential informant we can speak to?" Patterson asked.

"They told me there's a guy in one of the motorcycle gangs that hangs out at the High Note. He feeds them information once in a while."

"He knows Otto Sharp?"

"Yup. This might be what we're looking for."

"And he's agreed to meet with us?"

"That's what they said." Bauer looked across the desk at Patterson. "But he won't come near a police station for obvious reasons. He's a one-percenter."

"Meaning he's a member of a motorcycle club that leans toward criminal enterprises," Patterson said.

"Which makes talking to the cops a dangerous proposition," Bauer replied. "These gangs are into all sorts of bad things. Prostitution and trafficking. Extortion. Weapons. Dealing drugs. If they even suspect a member of passing information to the police, that person will be in a world of pain."

"Or dead."

"Right." Bauer nodded. "We had a CI back in LA. The guy was in one of the big gangs. He turned up one day with a bullet through the back of his skull. But before they did that, they hogtied and beat him. They even blacked out his gang tats."

"Blacked out?" Patterson asked.

"Tattooed a black square over them. Then they added the word 'snitch' underneath."

"Damn." Patterson had been warned to handle informants with care back when she was working a gang task force in New York. She knew how vicious gang members could be when one of their own turned on them. Even so, Bauer's graphic first-hand account of retaliation against a CI was shocking. The fact that they had put a bullet in his head rather than just beat and expel him from the gang meant he must have given the cops some juicy information. His death was a warning to others. Don't tell tales.

The informant that she and Bauer were about to meet risked a similar fate if caught. It was bad enough to provide the local cops with information. Meeting with the FBI was worse. Many gangs operated nationally. They didn't want their secrets leaked to the feds, who had the power to pursue them across state lines and shut down their criminal operations, or at least make it harder for them to continue.

"Where are we meeting him?" Patterson asked.

"Behind the Hotel Leon downtown. There's a service alley that leads to the kitchen for the hotel's restaurant. It's out of sight and not the kind of place he's likely to run into anyone who knows him."

"Smart. What time?"

"Noon."

It was ten o'clock. They had two hours before the meeting. Patterson looked at Bauer across the desk, her gaze sweeping across his pressed shirt and black suit. He looked like a fed. Her own black slacks and white blouse were no better. "We need to change into something more appropriate. We can't assume one of his associates won't spot him. If we meet him looking like this and they'll know right away that we're law enforcement."

"Good idea," Bauer said. "We can take your car, too. No one's going to look twice at that pile of scrap."

"Hey. It's not that bad."

"Yes, it is. Trust me." Bauer stood up. "But to go undercover and meet a gang informant, it's perfect. You can drive me to my apartment to change into something more suitable, and then we'll swing by your motel before we head downtown."

"Sounds like a plan," Patterson said, pushing her chair back. She picked up her laptop and dropped her now empty coffee cup into a trashcan next to the desk. "We can pick up another drink on the way, too. I've had nowhere near enough caffeine yet today."

"Amen to that," Bauer said as they stepped out into the corridor.

FORTY-SEVEN

TWO HOURS LATER, Patterson and Bauer arrived at the Hotel Leon and found a parking spot down the road away from prying eyes. They were casually dressed now. Bauer was decked out in a pair of worn stone-washed jeans and a faded black tee. His outfit was completed by a pair of boots that made Patterson laugh when she saw them. For her part, Patterson wore skinny jeans and a tank top that covered the bruising on her ribs. Her shoulder-length dark blonde hair, which she often pulled back into a tidy ponytail, hung free and loose. Her service weapon sat snug at the front of her hip in an IWB, or inside the waistband, holster. What she didn't do was to conceal the gun in the small of her back where it could crush her spine if she ended up in an altercation and fell on it. Bauer carried his weapon in a holster on the outside of his pants and let his tee fall over it for concealment. Neither she nor Bauer looked like cops as they sauntered down the street and turned into the alley behind the hotel.

"I don't see anyone," Patterson said, her gaze sweeping the row of dumpsters that lined the alley wall. Further away was a pile of empty plastic trays sitting on a metal cart. The type used for delivering bread and other baked goods. Aluminum beer kegs, no doubt also empty, stood in a precarious stack near a door that probably led into the hotel kitchen. There were also a couple of old chairs sitting there, surrounded by cigarette butts and a couple of crushed soda cans. The kitchen staff's unofficial break room.

"We're a few minutes early," Bauer said. "Maybe he's not here yet."

"Or maybe he changed his mind." Patterson wrinkled her nose as a sudden gust of wind blew down the alley, snatching the odor of rotting food from the dumpsters. Then, from between the two furthest dumpsters, she saw movement.

A figure dressed in ripped jeans, and a leather waistcoat stepped out into the alley. Someone Patterson recognized only too well.

"Angel," Bauer said, also recognizing one of the two bikers who hassled them when they were returning to their car the first time they visited the High Note Bar and Grill.

The man nodded and moved closer to them. His eyes darted first one way and then the other, as if he expected more cops to show up. Or maybe members of his own gang who knew what he was doing.

"You're the confidential informant?" Patterson asked, incredulous.

"What of it?" Angel said, stopping close enough that he didn't have to raise his voice, but not too close.

"You and your friend were about ready to rip our heads off back at the bar."

"What did you want me to do? Give you a hug." Angel scowled. "If I'm gonna be an informant, I gotta make it look like I hate cops more than anyone else. It's . . . what do you guys call it . . . my cover."

"Makes sense," Bauer said.

Patterson glanced sideways at him. "How do we know he wasn't one of the guys that almost broke my ribs?"

Bauer shrugged and fixed Angel with narrowed eyes. "Were you?"

"Was I what?" Angel looked confused.

Patterson stepped closer to the biker. "A couple of goons broke into my room yesterday morning and almost put me in the hospital when I discovered them. They pointed a gun at me and stole a box full of evidence. Were you one of those guys?" Patterson paused, then said, "Think carefully. My ribs still hurt like a bitch and if I find out you've lied to me, I might just tell your buddies what you're up to in your spare time."

"I don't have to put up with this crap." Angel put his hands in the air. "I came here voluntarily to answer your questions. I'm putting my life at risk in doing so. Maybe I should just walk away now."

"How about we all just calm down," Bauer said, stepping between Patterson and the biker.

"I don't enjoy being threatened." Angel glared at Patterson.

"Answer the question, and we can move past this," Bauer said. "Were you at her motel yesterday morning?"

"No. And I don't know who was. But it wasn't anyone I ride with. I can tell you that much."

"Thank you." Bauer to Patterson. "Satisfied?"

"That depends if he can tell us what we want to know," Patterson replied. She turned her attention back to Angel. "How long have you been drinking at the High Note?"

"Dunno. A while, I guess." Angel scratched his chin. "All the clubs in town drink there."

"You mean motorcycle clubs?"

Angel nodded.

"And you guys all get along with each other?" Patterson

knew there was rivalry between the different biker gangs. Sometimes it spilled into open bloodletting.

"We get on well enough." Angel glanced between the two agents. "Is this what you wanted to talk to me about? How friendly we are with each other?"

"We want to talk about the bar owner," Bauer said. "Otto Sharp. How much you know about him?"

"Is he in trouble?" Angel looked nervous.

"We want to know about his past," Patterson said, ignoring the question. "Does he ever speak about what he did before the bar?"

"Sometimes. He likes to brag about the shit he's done."

"Keep talking." Patterson didn't want to get her hopes up, but she sensed Angel might be able to give them useful information after all.

"Where do you want me to start?"

"How about after TexFest. You know about the music festival, right?"

"Sure." Angel pushed his hands into his pockets. "He doesn't talk about that so much. I guess it didn't work out too well for him and he left town."

"You know where he went?"

"After the festival?"

"Yes."

"Went out west to find work. Spent a couple of years backstage at concerts. Guess he was better at lugging amps and guitars than he was running the whole show."

"Where did he go out west?" Patterson asked with a growing sense of foreboding. "Which cities?"

"Not cities." Angel cleared his throat. "Just the one city. Las Vegas."

FORTY-EIGHT

YOU'RE KIDDING ME," Patterson said, barely able to believe her ears. "Las Vegas?"

"Yeah." If Angel understood the significance of his words, he didn't show it. "What about it?"

Patterson looked at Bauer. "There was a postcard sent from Vegas."

Angel observed the two FBI agents with a puzzled expression. "What's so special about a postcard sent from Vegas?"

Patterson ignored him. "Los Angeles is only a four-hour drive from Vegas. Otto could get there, mail a second postcard, and be back in less than a day."

"You're making a real leap, here," Bauer said. "There's nothing to indicate that Otto Sharp had anything to do with your sister's disappearance."

"Except that he went straight to Vegas after TexFest and the last two postcards sent by my sister were from Vegas and Los Angeles."

"Okay." Bauer didn't look convinced. "That doesn't prove anything."

"It's enough to make him a suspect in my sister's disappearance," Patterson said. "And it hardly clears him of suspicion in my motel room break-in."

"It's all circumstantial," Bauer said.

"That's good enough for me." Patterson looked at Angel. "Do you know what Otto did after Las Vegas? Where he went next?"

"Said he got offered a roadie gig. Traveled with a couple of bands. Where he went after that, I don't know. You'll have to ask him."

"Maybe we will," Patterson said.

Angel looked nervous. "If you guys are done, can I go now? I'd rather not hang around any longer than necessary."

"Go on. Get out of here," Bauer said. "If we have any more questions, we'll be in contact."

"I'm hoping you don't have any more questions," Angel said. "Because this was a onetime deal. I can't guarantee I'm going to be so amenable if you come calling again."

"We'll take that chance."

"Yeah, right."

"We appreciate your help," Patterson said. "And don't worry, we won't reveal your involvement in our case."

Angel frowned. "You'd better not."

He turned to leave before Patterson stopped him. "Actually, I do have one more question."

Angel glanced back at her. "What?"

"If we assume you're telling the truth and it wasn't you and your friend Frankie at my motel room yesterday morning, who else would Otto Sharp use to do something like that?"

"Beats me," Angel said. "Could be any number of guys. He's paid people to do things for him in the past. Stuff he doesn't want to do himself."

"Illegal stuff?"

"I assume. I stay clear of it. Don't need the aggravation."

"You know if he's paid anyone to do anything recently?" Bauer asked.

Angel shook his head. "Not so far as I'm aware, but that doesn't mean he didn't. He likes to be discreet about these things."

"Understood." Patterson thanked the biker again and watched him leave. When they were alone, she turned to Bauer. "What if Otto Sharp sent people after Claire Wright? What if he was somehow involved in my sister's disappearance and realized she could expose him?"

"It's a possibility," Bauer conceded. "But that still doesn't explain why he would have given us the box of TexFest stuff if he knew the contents might lead us to her and implicate him in your sister's disappearance. He could've just told us he had nothing left relating to the festival and that would've been the end of it."

"Maybe it didn't occur to him until later."

"I don't know," replied Bauer. "There's really nothing linking Sharp to either Claire or Julie. The only contact he might have had with anyone your sister knew was Claire's brother Martin when he signed the contract to play at the festival, and he's already dead."

"Except for Las Vegas."

"Which, as we have already discussed, is a tenuous link at best."

"It's all we've got, and I want to pursue it." Patterson knew she was clutching at straws. Sometimes coincidences were just that. Coincidence. But not always. Once in a while, if you got lucky, you could unravel a whole ball of yarn by tugging at a stray thread. "I say we bring him in and have a chat in an interrogation room."

"On what grounds?" Bauer asked.

"I don't know," Patterson said. "Yet."

"We could just go back and talk to him at the bar again."

"I have a feeling he's done with us," Patterson said. "We won't get anything out of him there."

"What makes you think we'll get any further with him in an interrogation room?" Bauer raised an eyebrow. "He's hardly likely to admit involvement in your sister's disappearance, even if he is guilty. And we don't know that he is."

"I'm aware of that."

"Why don't we keep an eye on him instead, see what he does next. If he's worried about us sniffing around, he will make a mistake."

Patterson nodded. It was a good suggestion, and probably their only option, given the circumstances. "You think SAC Harris will give us permission to put someone on him?"

"Not in a million years. We have nothing to support an FBI stakeout."

"But we do have the information Angel gave us. He said that Otto Sharp sometimes pays the bikers to do stuff for him."

"Again, we can't prove that he sent those guys around to your motel room."

"That's true," Patterson said. "But if we tell Dallas PD's gang task force what Angel told us, and that we have reason to believe there's illegal activity going on at the bar, maybe they'll do us a favor and put someone on Sharp. If they catch him paying bikers to do his dirty work, they'll have to bring him in. Then we can talk to him."

"It's worth a try," Bauer said. "I'll pass the information along, and we'll see what happens." He glanced toward the dumpsters. "I'm getting a whiff of that trash every time the wind changes direction. Not sure how much more of it I can take. You want to get out of this alley?"

"Hell yes." Patterson followed Bauer out of the alley and onto the sidewalk in front of the hotel. There was no sign of Angel. He was long gone. They walked toward Patterson's car in silence, but as they reached it, her phone rang. Patterson pulled it from her pocket and looked at the screen.

Bauer glanced sideways toward her. "Well, who is it?"

Patterson held the phone out so he could see the screen. "It's Claire's boyfriend, Ryan Gilder."

"I wonder what he wants?" Bauer said with narrowed eyes.

Patterson shrugged. "There's only one way to find out."

FORTY-NINE

SPECIAL AGENT BLAKE?" Gilder said as soon as Patterson answered the phone.

Patterson put the phone on speaker so that Bauer could hear the conversation too before answering. "How can we help you, Mr. Gilder?"

"I hope you don't mind me calling. You gave me your card when we found Claire's car in that parking lot yesterday."

"It's fine," Patterson said. "What's on your mind?"

"I wanted to get an update. See if you had any new information about her."

"No. Nothing new." Patterson wasn't about to discuss the case with Gilder. He was one of her only suspects, along with Otto Sharp.

"Oh. I see." If Gilder sounded disappointed, he didn't show it. "Do you know if the Dallas Police Department is searching for her yet? That detective didn't seem inclined to do much when I filed the missing persons report and I haven't heard from them since."

"That's something you will have to ask them."

"Right. Right. Maybe I'll give them a call."

"Was that everything, Mr. Gilder?"

"Well, there is one more thing. You wanted to look at Claire's telephone yesterday."

"That's right. And if I recall, you refused to let us do that."

"Like I told you already, I didn't have the access code. I couldn't unlock the screen. Otherwise, I would have let you look right there and then."

"Sure you would," Bauer said, interjecting.

"Look, I really was telling the truth. But I've found the code now. Claire wrote it down on a password list she keeps on her laptop."

"That kind of defeats the purpose of having passwords," Patterson said. She wasn't sure she really believed Gilder's story. "There are better ways to store passwords."

"I've told her that so many times. If the laptop ever got stolen, they would have access to all her accounts."

"Getting back to the phone . . ."

"Right. I figured you might still want to look at it."

"We do," Bauer said. "Where are you at the moment?"

"I'm at my property south of downtown. Had to meet a contractor."

"Right. Because you flip houses."

"Yes. I haven't been here in a couple of days, but I still need to make a living. I've had this guy booked for weeks. Electrician. I couldn't miss the appointment."

"I wasn't judging you, Mr. Gilder." Patterson paused, thinking back to their first meeting. "I thought you had a crew of your own that you worked with?"

"I do. But not for electrical. My guys mainly do tear-out and construction. Carpentry. Drywall and the like."

"I see," Patterson said. "If you give us the address, we'll stop by there and pick up the phone right now."

"I don't have it on me here," Gilder said, a little too

quickly. "It's back at the house. I'll be finishing up here around four and then heading home. Why don't you swing by then and I'll give it to you?"

"After four?"

"Yes. Just give me enough time to drive back across town."

"Let's make it five, then," Patterson said.

"Sure. Five will work." Patterson waited for Gilder to hang up and then looked at Bauer. "Well, what did you make of that?"

"I think the likelihood that we'll find anything on that phone is next to nothing." They were back at Patterson's car now. Bauer waited by the passenger door while Patterson rounded the front of the vehicle and approached the driver's door. "He's had the phone in his possession for more than thirty hours. More than enough time to get rid of anything incriminating."

"My thoughts exactly," Patterson said, climbing into the driver's seat. "I still find it hard to believe he didn't know how to get into his girlfriend's phone. Hell, I know the code for my father's phone, and I don't even live with him."

"Yeah." Bauer slipped his seatbelt on. "Highly suspicious. You think he was covering his tracks?"

"Maybe." Patterson bit her bottom lip. "Everything he's done so far has been suspicious. It took him thirty-six hours to report Claire missing even though he already had flyers made up."

"Right. If I was worried enough to have missing person flyers made up, I would've already gone to the police. In fact, that would be the first place I'd go."

"Exactly. His actions are contradictory. When we spoke to him at police headquarters, he claimed Claire had gone missing before. That she was depressed and had been off her meds. He was filing a report while downplaying the situation at the same time."

"And he did a good enough job that the detective he spoke to didn't appear particularly concerned for Claire's safety," Bauer said.

"And what was he doing during the first twenty-four hours that she was gone?"

"Well, we know he drove around the gas stations looking for her." Bauer rubbed his chin. "Of course, he waited a while before he did that. Several hours had elapsed."

"Which means he could've been establishing an alibi," Patterson said.

"You thinking he did something to Claire, and he's been playing us this entire time?"

"The partner is always the first suspect in a case like this, as you well know." Patterson started the engine. "I think we should put a fire under the intelligence analysts on the fourth floor. I know they're busy, but the quicker we get background on Ryan Gilder, the better."

"I agree." Bauer nodded. "Question is, where does that leave us with Otto Sharp and his band of merry men at the High Note?"

"He's our suspect number two, and I'm not ready to walk away from him yet."

"You still think this could be about your sister?"

"Someone broke into my room and stole the TexFest stuff. I can't think of a reason anyone would do that unless we were getting close to a breakthrough on Julie's case."

"So that leaves us with three conflicting scenarios."

Patterson nodded. "The first is that Ryan Gilder had something to do with Claire's disappearance and it's not connected to Julie's case."

"The second is that Otto Sharp did something to Claire to keep her from talking to you, then broke into your room and took back the documents he'd already given you for some reason."

"Probably because he realized there was something incriminating in them."

And the third is that something else happened to Claire. Something that doesn't involve either man."

"Yes."

"Which could still be related to your sister," Bauer said.

"Right. Our theory that she went on the run to avoid speaking with me."

"Which means she could have arranged to have the documents stolen."

"Unlikely." Patterson shook her head. "She didn't even know I had them."

"I agree. It's a stretch."

"Yes. It is." Patterson put the car in gear and pulled out from the parking space. "Let's get Claire's phone and see what it can tell us. Maybe then we'll have a clearer idea how to proceed."

"Except that Gilder will have wiped any incriminating evidence there might be from that device before he hands it over."

"True," Patterson said with a thin smile. "But there's one thing he's not considering. Nothing is ever truly deleted. And the technicians in the FBI forensics lab are good. Really good."

FIFTY

AT FIVE O'CLOCK THAT EVENING, Patterson and Bauer pulled up to Ryan Gilder's place right on time. It was a small concrete block dwelling, probably built back in the sixties, with a one-car garage. A chain-link fence surrounded the front yard. Gilder's white pickup truck, the same one they had seen on gas station surveillance video searching for Claire a few days before, was parked in the driveway behind his girlfriend's Honda Civic. Patterson wondered when he had moved it from the parking lot where the car had been abandoned. In an ideal world, the Dallas Police Department would have impounded the vehicle pending an investigation, but until they had proof of a crime, this would not happen. So here it sat on Ryan Gilder's driveway as if nothing was wrong.

"For a guy who flips houses, this isn't a very salubrious neighborhood," Bauer noted as they opened the front gate and made their way up a cracked concrete pathway.

"Maybe he doesn't make much money on the flips," Patterson said. "I'm sure he's buying places like this. Cheap properties that he can tidy up and make a quick buck on."

"True. I just figured a guy who bought and sold houses for a job would live somewhere a little nicer."

"Maybe he likes to put his money back into the business," Patterson said. She looked around, searching for a bell but didn't see one, so she rapped on the front door with her knuckles.

Ten seconds later, the door opened inward to reveal Ryan Gilder. "Look at that, right on time."

"Can we come in," Patterson asked.

"Sure." Gilder turned and strolled back into the house, leaving them to step inside and close the door.

The interior was modern and fresh, with gray painted walls and light oak vinyl flooring throughout. The sound of a TV came from the living room, and when Patterson entered, she saw Gilder standing with his eyes fixed upon a local news station. He turned the TV off and set the remote down on a rustic wood coffee table.

"I've been watching the local news to see if they mention Claire. The more people that know she's missing, the better."

"And have they?" Patterson asked.

"No. Not so far."

"Did you call the station and tell them about her?" Bauer asked, his eyes shifting from Gilder to the stack of missing flyers sitting on the coffee table.

"Not yet," Gilder said. "I thought the police might appeal for information, but so far, they aren't taking her disappearance very seriously."

"We know," Patterson said. Given the circumstances of her own sister's disappearance and the LAPD's lack of interest, Patterson felt empathy with this man and had to remind herself that he was not just her boyfriend but also a suspect until proven otherwise. At least in her own mind. If any evidence of foul play came to light, he would be a prime suspect in the minds of the Dallas Police Department, too.

That's how these things work. Those closest to the victim were always suspected first.

"I tried to call that detective earlier—after we talked—but they said he wasn't there," Gilder said. "They took a message and promised he would get back to me, but . . ."

"I'm sure he's swamped," Patterson said, wondering why she was making excuses for the man. If she had her way, the Police Department would scour the city looking for Claire Wright. But the FBI had no say in the affairs of local police, so the best she could do was follow her instincts and pray they found the woman alive and well. "If he doesn't return your call this evening, try again tomorrow."

"Maybe." Gilder pushed his hands into his pockets, then withdrew them again as if he didn't know what to do with them. "Honestly, I'm so worried about her. She's gone away to clear her head in the past, but this feels different. What if something terrible has happened to her this time?"

"We don't know that," Patterson said, trying to reassure him. "If she's out there, we'll find her."

"Thank you. At least someone is taking this seriously."

"Which is why we need that cell phone," Bauer replied.

Patterson nodded in agreement. Gilder was doing a good job coming off as the concerned boyfriend. He was hitting all the right notes of concern, But Patterson was careful not to get sucked in. For all she knew, it was an act. There were things that didn't add up. Like why he had made flyers before he even reported his girlfriend missing, or why he waited days to phone her family. He was doing everything backward. Maybe it was because Claire had done this before, and he didn't want to create an unnecessary drama, or perhaps he wasn't thinking straight because of the worry. There was a third possibility, too. That he was involved in her disappearance, and this was all a cleverly orchestrated performance to throw them off. She waited for Gilder to get the cell phone. When he didn't move, she decided to nudge him. "The quicker you give us that phone, the faster we can check it for evidence."

"Oh, right." Gilder made a move toward the door, then turned and looked back at them. "Although I'm not sure what you'll find on it. I looked and saw nothing out of the ordinary. Not even a text message since before she went missing."

"I'm sure that's the case," Patterson replied. "But would like to go through it, anyway. We can check her contacts and the outgoing calls in the days before her disappearance. Maybe we'll find a friend who knows something."

"That makes sense." Gilder continued on his way, vanishing toward the back of the house. A moment later, he returned, clutching the phone. He held it out to Patterson. "There you go."

"Thank you." Before accepting the phone, Patterson pulled on a latex glove and removed a clear plastic evidence bag from her pocket. She dropped the device into the bag and sealed it, then tucked the bag, now containing the phone, back into her pocket. "What about her purse?"

"What about it?"

"We'd like to take that, too, if you don't mind." The purse had been in Claire's abandoned car along with her cell phone. She wanted forensics to give it the once over.

"You already looked inside," Gilder said. "Back at the car."

"I know. But there could be trace evidence we can't see." Patterson had half expected Gilder to question her request given his attitude at the car, and they couldn't force him to hand it over. "It might help us find her."

"Honestly, I really don't want to let it out of my sight right now. It reminds me of her. Brings me comfort."

Patterson nodded. "I understand."

"Is there anything else?" Gilder asked, his gaze shifting toward the door. He obviously wanted them to leave.

"Actually, there is one thing," Bauer said.

"What?"

"You told us Claire takes medication for depression. Can we see it?"

"Her medication?"

"Yes."

"It must be here," Patterson said. "According to you, she left it behind."

"She did." Gilder turned and left the room. He came back a moment later with an orange pill bottle. "See?"

Patterson took the bottle and examined it. The name on the label was Claire's, but she didn't recognize the medication. She took a photo of the label with her phone, then handed the meds back to Gilder. "Thank you."

"Is that all?" Gilder pushed the bottle into his pocket.

"For now," Patterson replied. "We'll get out of your hair."

Gilder nodded. "You'll call if there's any news?"

"Of course." Patterson moved toward the door with Bauer at her side. The phone weighed heavy in her pocket. "We'll let ourselves out."

FIFTY-ONE

THEY HAD TAKEN Bauer's car to see Ryan Gilder, so the ex-LAPD detective was driving as they headed back toward downtown. Patterson sat in the passenger seat and studied Claire Wright's phone through the clear plastic bag.

"You think he knows we can recover deleted data?" Bauer asked as they worked their way through a backup caused by a wreck on I-30.

"If he does, then we won't find anything on this phone because there was never anything there to begin with," Patterson replied. "But I'm betting he has no idea that our forensic analysts can pick this thing apart in a heartbeat. Even if he dumped it into a tub of water or smashed the phone with a hammer, it wouldn't make any difference. The data would still be there. It's incredibly hard to erase a digital footprint. He'd need some spy-level software to wipe this phone completely."

"Ryan Gilder doesn't strike me as a superspy."

"Me either."

"And the FBI might not have spy level tech either, but

they've got some pretty advanced stuff that will peel the hard drive on that phone like a banana."

"That's what I'm hoping." Patterson placed Claire's phone inside the glove box and took out her own phone. She searched the name of the drug on the pill bottle. "Those meds are for depression."

"That much of his story is true, then," Bauer said.

"Looks like it." Patterson lapsed into silence and watched the city roll by outside her window. The sky had turned black as thunderclouds rolled in, fueled by the day's heat. It was already spitting with rain, and she expected a full-blown storm by the time darkness fell.

"You alright over there?" Bauer asked after a few minutes.

"Why wouldn't I be?" Patterson pulled her gaze away from the window and looked at him.

"This must be hard on you. The uncertainty, I mean. Feeling like you're chasing a ghost."

"It's fine," Patterson said, even though Bauer touched a nerve. "And I'm not chasing a ghost." At least, she thought, I hope not.

"Sorry. Bad turn of phrase. I just meant that the stress of working a case with such close personal ties must be immense. I can't imagine what it would be like if my brother vanished, and I didn't know where he was for decades."

"You have a brother?" His response took Patterson by surprise. Bauer struck her as a loner. An only child. She didn't know why. It was just a feeling she got when she looked at him.

"Two of them, actually. Both older."

"They in law enforcement, too?"

"God, no. Elijah is in IT and lives in Cleveland. Kendrick wanted to be an artist, but then he discovered money and became an accountant. He works with the movie studios back in LA."

"Impressive."

"Not really. Hollywood is nowhere near as glamorous as people think and being an accountant in Hollywood is about as unglamorous as one can get."

"Still, must be useful come tax time. Having an accountant in the family."

"I wouldn't know. I've never made enough to need one," Bauer replied. They had left the interstate and were on a side street close to the field office now. He swung off the road, approached the gates leading to the parking lot, then used his Bureau-issued key card to raise the barrier and drove on through. He circled the parking lot until he found the lime green Toyota Corolla Patterson had borrowed from the Chicago Field Office, then pulled up next to it and parked. "Here we are, then. Your chariot awaits."

"Not quite yet," Patterson said, removing the phone from the glove box and holding it up. "I figured I'd run this straight up to forensics rather than wait until morning. That way, they can get started on it right away."

Bauer nodded. "You want me to come with?"

"No need." Patterson tugged on the door handle. "It won't take more than a few minutes, and then I'm going back to the motel."

"Sure." Bauer watched her climb out of the car before rolling the window down and looking up at her as she came around the vehicle and passed by. "Don't stay up half the night working, okay?"

"I have no idea what you're talking about," Patterson replied.

"Sure you don't." Bauer chuckled. "I see the dark rings around your eyes. The way you guzzle coffee in the morning. You never let up."

"Not on this case," Patterson said, the bagged cell phone

still in her hand. "Not while my sister is still out there somewhere."

"Yeah. You won't be any use to her if you burn out. And after sixteen years, it's not like she can't wait a little longer, especially since . . ." Bauer closed his mouth abruptly as if he were trying to stop the rest of the sentence before it escaped his lips.

"Especially since she's dead already?"

"That wasn't what I was going to say."

"I don't believe you. But that's okay. I've come to terms with the fact that Julie is probably dead. Doesn't mean I should stop looking for her."

"I agree," Bauer said. "But you don't have to do it all in one night. Take an evening off and get some sleep. You'll feel better for it."

"You a doctor now, too?"

"No. Just a concerned colleague who's seen his fair share of cops that couldn't leave the job behind when they went home at night."

Patterson nodded slowly. "I'll take it under advisement."

"You're not going to listen to me, are you?"

"Probably not." Patterson started across the parking lot in the direction of the field office building. As she went, she glanced over her shoulder. "See you in the morning, Special Agent Marcus Bauer. Bright and early."

"You want me to bring you a coffee?"

"What do you think?" Patterson shouted back at him, looking frontward again. "A strong one. Two shots of espresso and extra sugar."

Bauer never replied. She heard the throaty roar of the Dodge Charger's engine as he pulled away. While from the sky above came a rumble of thunder. Then the heavens opened, and the rain came down. Hard.

FIFTY-TWO

PATTERSON SPRINTED FOR THE LOBBY. It was a short distance, but far enough. By the time she got inside, her hair was matted to her scalp, and she was dripping onto the tile floor. Undeterred, she used her key card to pass through the security checkpoint, made her way across the lobby to the elevators, and rode up to the fourth floor, where the FBI's digital forensics lab was located.

When she entered, the room's only occupant—a white-coated analyst with unruly black hair and lean features—looked up from behind a long bench where he was hunkered down over a disassembled laptop. "Can I help you?"

Patterson introduced herself and held up the cell phone, which had been protected from the downpour by its plastic evidence bag. "Got some work for you."

"Doesn't everyone?" The analyst grinned. "If only bad people realized all the incriminating evidence they left lying around on their electronic devices and the Internet, they would go live off the grid somewhere."

"Then let's be thankful they're not that smart," Patterson

said, returning the grin. She looked down at herself. "Sorry, I'm making your floor wet. Got caught in a downpour."

"Meh. They clean the lab every night at seven. Someone will mop it up. My name is Elliot, by the way."

"Pleased to meet you, Elliot." Patterson approached the bench. The laptop he was working on looked like a truck had run it over. Its screen, which was smashed, had been removed and set to one side. The rest of the machine lay face down with its guts exposed. The hard drive had been lifted out and was connected to a cable running to a high-tech-looking desktop machine. Patterson lifted her gaze from the destroyed laptop to Elliot. "Looks like you have your work cut out."

"Nah. People always think that if they smash their electronics, it gets rid of evidence. Morons." He snorted. "I'll have this hard drive cloned and its data extracted quicker than you can say 'guess I just incriminated myself'."

Patterson held the cell phone up. "Speaking of extracting data . . ."

"A phone. Goodie. I love working on those." Elliott tapped the bench with his palm. "Put it down here."

This made Patterson laugh. "Elliott, you need to get out more."

"I'm happy right where I am," Elliott said. He slid a clipboard containing evidence forms across the bench toward her. "You need to fill this out. Chain of custody."

Patterson put the phone down on the bench and plucked a pen from a tub sitting next to the desktop computer. She filled out the form and handed the clipboard back. She touched the phone. "I need to know everything that's on this. I need the contacts, call logs, and text messages."

"Piece of cake."

"Any photos, too, if you can get them."

"Goes without saying." Elliott pulled the bagged phone toward him and studied it. "Doesn't look like it's damaged. That makes the job easier. I assume you need it yesterday?"

"Will that be a problem?" Patterson asked.

Elliott jerked a thumb toward a row of plastic trays on another bench containing various electronic devices sealed in their own evidence bags. "See that? It's all the jobs ahead of yours."

"Guess yesterday is out of the question, then." Patterson was expecting this. The FBI crime labs were always over-worked, often processing evidence for other agencies ranging from local and state law enforcement to the DEA and even fire department arson investigators. But sometimes, just once in a while, she could sweet-talk them into doing her a favor. She figured it was worth a try in this instance. "I really do need this fast-tracked if you could do it. I know it's a lot to ask, but a life may be on the line. A missing woman."

"If that's the case, why don't you just ask the ASAC to make it a priority? Then I can put it ahead of everything else."

Patterson had thought of going to the Assistant Special Agent in Charge already but didn't think it would work. The local police still weren't investigating Claire Wright's disap-pearance as suspicious and hadn't formally asked the FBI for assistance. The main reason Patterson was being so dogged in her pursuit of the woman was personal. She wanted to find Julie and thought that Claire might have information. And even though her motel room had been broken into and she had been attacked, there was nothing linking that incident to Claire other than her own speculation. If she wanted the contents of that phone in any reasonable time frame, she would have to think fast. "The SAC and ASAC have both left for the day. I'd rather not disturb them at home. I can wait until tomorrow, but if something happens in the meantime . . ."

"I've seen plenty of agents call the ASAC at home." Elliott leaned back in his chair and put his hands behind his head. "You don't want to ask the powers that be, because you don't think they will approve the fast track."

"All right, you got me." Patterson's hope was fading. With nothing left to do, she decided to tell the truth. "Truthfully, there's more at stake than just finding this woman. The case I'm working is personal. I'm looking for my sister who went missing sixteen years ago and I think the owner of this phone may have vital information."

"I'm sorry to hear that." Elliott leaned forward again.

"I wasn't lying when I said that a life may be in danger. Claire Wright, the woman I'm looking for, may either be on the run because of what she knows about my sister or might have been snatched by persons unknown for that same reason."

"You really believe that?"

"I do." Patterson nodded.

Elliott touched the shattered laptop. "Look. Once I get into this hard drive, it's going to take a couple of hours to extract all the data. Theoretically, I could move on to the next job in line while that's happening. Or I could fudge the truth and say that the extraction needs close monitoring. The cell phone hack won't be a very complicated task so I could do that while I'm keeping an eye on the data being transferred from the laptop."

"Oh, my goodness," Patterson said with relief. "That would be incredible."

"I'm a sucker for a sob story," Elliott said. "Just don't go telling anyone that I did this, okay?"

"My lips are sealed." Patterson hesitated, then asked, "How long do you think it will take?"

"It won't be immediate." Elliott scratched his chin. "The phone is in one piece, so that's half the battle. If you just wanted to see the files stored on the phone, I could just do a file system acquisition. That process will give us access to everything stored on the phone, including hidden and root files. But you're after deleted files, too, right?"

"Yes. Photos, incoming and outgoing call logs, and text messages."

"That's what I thought. For that, I'll have to do a physical acquisition, which is not so easy."

"Oh."

"Don't worry. I can still do it. I'll have to make a copy of the phone's storage and dump it into a separate file that I can dig into. The only way I wouldn't be able to recover something is if that section of the phone's flash memory has already been overwritten with new data, but recent stuff, like in the last month or two, almost never gets overwritten given the storage capacity of modern phones. Instead, the device just deindexes it."

"Which means?"

"It means the phone effectively forgets where the data is and doesn't bother with it anymore. But everything is still there, just waiting for a chap like me to come along and pluck it out."

"And you can do that now?"

"Well, not right at this moment. I do still have the laptop to deal with. And even if I didn't, it's not a two-minute job." Elliott pulled on a fresh set of gloves and opened the evidence bag. When he touched the phone, it sprang to life. "Good. The battery still has a charge. You know how to unlock it?"

Patterson nodded. "I have the code."

"Write it down on the evidence form."

Patterson obliged, then gave the forensic technician her business card. "Will you call me as soon as it's done?"

"You have my word," Elliott replied. His gaze slid from her still wet hair to her damp clothes. "Now why don't you get out of here and dry yourself off before you catch your death."

FIFTY-THREE

AS SOON AS Patterson returned to her motel room, she stripped off and headed to the bathroom for a shower. Twenty minutes later, clean and dry, she sat on the bed and called her father to see how he was doing and fill him in on her progress. He listened in silence, then apologized yet again for not showing her the last two postcards earlier. His voice sounded strained. There was a tremble when he spoke, and Patterson wondered if he was crying. She reminded herself that her quest to find Julie must've opened old wounds. Unpacked emotions he had kept at a distance for over a decade. She quickly changed the subject, and he perked up. By the time she hung up an hour later, he was back to his old self.

But not Patterson. Julie lay heavy on her mind. She took the old postcards from her bag and spread them on the comforter in front of her, as she often did when she wanted to feel close to her sister. She turned them over and read each one in succession. When she reached the last two, sent from Las Vegas and Los Angeles, she studied them longer than the rest, looking for any hidden meaning in the text, trying to read between the lines. But if Julie was sending a cryptic message, Patterson couldn't see it. Except for the impersonal nature of her opening and the unusual way she signed off, using her real name instead of Jelly—the nickname she had used on all the other postcards. It had been a running joke between the two sisters because their initials spelled out PB and J—Patterson Blake, and Julie.

Again, the thought of her sister being held captive and forced to write those messages wormed its way to the front of Patterson's mind—a shadowy figure threatening her sister with untold evil if she didn't do as she was told. And Julie, always clever, doing the only thing she could. Signing in a way she knew would arouse her family's suspicion. Except it hadn't worked. At least, not well enough. Because sixteen years ago, her father hadn't been able to convince anyone to take his concerns seriously. So now the grown-up Patterson found herself on the road and following Julie's footsteps. But this time, she had the might of the FBI behind her. And if Julie was still out there, Patterson swore to herself, she would find her.

There was so much that Patterson knew now that wasn't available to the police back then. The map Stacy had given her in Chicago. The un-mailed letter that remained hidden for so many years in a box of old registration cards back at the Welcome Inn—a sleazy hotel in Oklahoma City where Julie had stayed, and eventually, also Patterson. If those items had come to light earlier, would they have changed anything? Patterson didn't know. Judging by the police reaction to Claire Wright's disappearance, she suspected it wouldn't have made a difference.

But Patterson could make a difference now. If she could find Claire. To that end, she gathered up the postcards and put them away, then rose from the bed and sat at the small table in front of the window. The list of Claire's friends still

sat on her computer desktop. Five of them were local. She
had intended to track them down earlier in the day but had
gotten busy meeting the confidential informant Bauer had set
up. Then came Ryan Gilder's unexpected call, offering to turn
the cell phone over.

Now, though, with nothing better to do, Patterson went to
work tracking them down. She could have asked the analysts
on the fourth floor of the FBI's Dallas Field Office to do it, but
they were already looking into Ryan Gilder. And she had
pushed her luck with Elliott, the affable digital forensics
analyst who was currently unlocking the secrets of Claire
Wright's cell phone. This one was on her.

In the end, it only took Patterson a little over an hour to
research each of Claire's local friends and find out where they
lived, as well as their cell phone numbers. Unlike the psychiatrist she tracked down a couple of days before, Doctor Carson
Franks, none of them had taken steps to have their information removed from the people-finder websites. It amazed her
at how easy it was to cyber-stalk people in the digital age. It
was no wonder identity theft was on the rise, given the vast
amounts of personal information on the web.

Feeling pleased with herself, Patterson set about
contacting each of them. The first, a woman named Kara,
turned out to be nothing more than an acquaintance. A
person Claire had worked with at a previous job and with
whom there had been no contact outside of the occasional
social media like for more than three years. When she found
the second woman on the list, she got a recording saying the
number was out of service. This was a frequent problem with
people-finder websites. Their information was often out of
date or just plain wrong. She struck out again with the first
man on the list. He was nothing but an old work acquaintance. Then her luck changed.

Rebecca Bagley, the fourth woman on the list, knew Claire

Wright well. They were old school friends. But when Patterson asked if she'd seen or spoken to her recently, the answer was disappointing.

"I haven't," Rebecca said without hesitation. "I haven't heard from Claire for almost a year, ever since she took up with that guy."

"You mean Ryan Gilder?"

"Yes, that's him." There was a pause on the other end of the line as if Rebecca was weighing what to say next. "I only met him once a week after they got together, but to tell you the truth, I didn't like the man."

"Why?" Patterson asked.

"He rubbed me the wrong way, I guess. Claire fawned over him. She was giddy, like a teenager, and he just sucked it up."

"Really?" Patterson filed the comment away mentally. "Anything else you can tell me?"

"No. Sorry. I saw him once and that was it. Every time I phoned Claire after that, she sounded distracted. I invited her out a couple of times in the weeks that followed for a girl's night, but she turned me down. Eventually, she just stopped answering my calls. I figured she was too busy being in love to make time for me."

"I see." Patterson thanked the woman and hung up. She wasn't sure what to make of Rebecca Bagley's comments. Was Claire really just head over heels in love and too distracted to bother with her friends, or did Ryan Gilder have something to do with the sudden withdrawal from her social life?

There was one more local name on the friend list mined from Claire Wright's social media. Leonard Hemphill. His Facebook page identified him as an artist. His timeline was full of paintings and drawings, which Patterson thought were pretty good. She wondered if he was also a school friend, but his social media profile did not list his academic history.

Patterson dialed his number and waited while the phone rang. Then, after four rings, it went to voicemail. She left a message asking him to call her back before hanging up.

Her task completed, she sat back in the chair. It was almost ten. Bauer's words echoed in her head. He was right. She didn't have an off button. Ever since she started looking for Julie, the only time she relaxed was when she was sleeping. Now she decided to step away and force herself to decompress. She changed into a pair of pajamas, plumped up the pillows, settled down on the bed, and turned on the TV, forcing herself to avoid all the news channels. An hour later, after watching a couple of Big Bang Theory reruns, she switched the TV off, killed the lights, and sank down into bed after texting a quick good night to Jonathan Grant back in New York, as had become her custom. An hour later, just as she was falling into a disturbed sleep fueled by exhaustion, her phone rang.

FIFTY-FOUR

SPECIAL AGENT BLAKE?" A male voice on the other end of the line said when Patterson answered the phone.

"That's me," Patterson replied, rubbing the sleep from her eyes and sitting up straight in the bed.

"This is Elliott from the digital forensics lab. You came to see me earlier today to extract data from a cell phone tied to a missing persons case you're working on."

"Yes, of course." Patterson was still half asleep when she answered the phone and hadn't recognized the analyst's voice at first. "Did you find something?"

"I did, and I think it might be urgent, which is why I'm calling so late. I was about to head home for the night and thought you would want to know right away rather than wait until tomorrow."

"I appreciate that," Patterson said. "What did you find?"

"So, I did a physical acquisition like we discussed, and I've spent the last couple of hours reconstructing the data on the phone's flash memory. Most of it is fairly mundane. There's the usual spam and phishing texts. Some deleted text streams back and forth between herself and a person who is obviously her mother. There are a bunch of exchanges with a man named Ryan Gilder, too. I assume he's the boyfriend?"

"Correct."

"I thought so. When did this woman go missing?"

"Sometime between Wednesday evening and Thursday morning," Patterson replied.

"Okay. That makes sense."

"Why?"

"There are a bunch of unanswered texts from Ryan Gilder on Wednesday night starting around ten PM."

"What kind of texts?"

"The kind you'd send if you were worried someone hadn't come home when expected." Elliott paused a moment and Patterson heard rustling, then he came back on the line. "This is the first one. 'You should be back by now. I'm getting worried.'" He paused again. "There's more of the same. Eighteen messages over the next twenty-four hours. They get more frantic as time goes on. For example, 'You need to come home now. I'm so worried. Everything will be okay, I promise.'"

"Huh. Were any of those messages deleted?" If they were, Gilder would be the most obvious candidate since Claire had not replied to any of them.

"No. None of them."

"Is there any other information on the phone?"

"Oh, yes. That's why I'm calling now instead of waiting until tomorrow or just emailing the results to you." Elliott cleared his throat. "There was a deleted text exchange I believe is significant."

"Tell me," Patterson said, prickling with anticipation.

"The messages start around one-fifteen in the morning on Thursday. She's texting back and forth with a man named Leonard Hemphill."

"Hemphill?" This was the final name on the list of local

friends Patterson had pulled off Claire Wright's social media profile. She had phoned him only a couple of hours before and received no answer. "What do the messages say?"

"I think it would be better if you read them yourself. I've already sent everything to your Bureau email address."

"Thank you." Patterson was already swinging her legs off the bed. She made her way to the table in front of the window and opened her laptop, then signed on to the FBI's secure email server. There was an unread message from Elliott sitting there. She put the phone on speaker and placed it next to the laptop, then opened the message. Elliot had pasted the text exchange between Claire Wright and Leonard Hemphill into the message body. She hunched over the laptop and studied it.

Claire Wright
    Thursday 1:17 AM
    Hey. You up?
Leonard Hemphill
    Thursday 1:21 AM
    I am now.
Claire Wright
    Thursday 1:21 AM
    Didn't mean to wake you.
Leonard Hemphill
    Thursday 1:22 AM
    Just went to bed. LTNS.
Claire Wright
    Thursday 1:22 AM
    IK
Leonard Hemphill
    Thursday 1:22 AM
    It's late. RUOK?

Claire Wright
Thursday 1:22 AM
Come get me.
Leonard Hemphill
Thursday 1:23 AM
Now?
Claire Wright
Thursday 1:23 AM
PLZ?
Leonard Hemphill
Thursday 1:23 AM
K. Where are U ATM?
Claire Wright
Thursday 1:23 AM
A bar. DNK the address. Dropping a pin.
Leonard Hemphill
Thursday 1:23 AM
K. Be there ASAP.
Claire Wright
Thursday 1:23 AM
THKS.

Patterson read the text message exchange twice, her heart racing. This was proof positive that Claire Wright had driven herself to the strip mall parking lot where Dallas PD later found her car abandoned. A strip mall that contained not only a grocery store but also a bar. Claire's movements the night she went missing were clear to Patterson now. Instead of going for gas, as Ryan Gilder claimed she left to do, Claire drove to a bar miles away from her house and then texted another man to come and pick her up. Different scenarios raced through Patterson's mind. She could have fled to avoid answering questions about Julie and asked Leonard Hemphill to hide her. After all, she disappeared the same night Patterson called to ask about her sister.

But there was another possibility. A much more mundane one. She was having an affair with this man. Except that didn't explain why Claire hadn't resurfaced since.

Patterson realized Elliott was still waiting on the phone. She scrolled through the rest of the email and forwarded a copy to Bauer, then picked the handset up. "Is this everything you found?"

"Yes," came the reply. "If you need the actual phone, I've already checked it into the evidence locker."

"Thanks," Patterson said, telling Elliott how much she appreciated his help. She was already halfway across the room when he hung up. Dropping the phone on the bed, she dressed quickly, then picked up her car keys and headed for the door. There wasn't a moment to waste now that she knew where Claire had gone the night she vanished. With any luck, the woman was still at Leonard Hemphill's abode. But Patterson might have tipped her hand by calling him earlier. Maybe that was why he hadn't picked up. Because Claire recognized the phone number. She had to move fast. There was still a chance she could get the answers she so badly needed about Julie. But not if Claire Wright ran for a second time.

FIFTY-FIVE

PATTERSON CALLED Bauer from her car as she turned out of the motel parking lot.

"Why are you calling so late?" was his immediate response upon answering. "What's wrong?"

"I've found Claire Wright," Patterson replied. She should feel tired, but instead, she was running on pure adrenaline. "I know where she is. Or at least, I know where she was a couple of days ago."

"Where?"

"She had a friend pick her up from that bar in the plaza where we found her car. A man named Leonard Hemphill."

"And how do you know that?"

"Because I had the digital forensics analyst put a rush on extracting the data from Claire's phone. He called me fifteen minutes ago to say he'd emailed the results. I forwarded his message to you, too. You should read it. There was a text message exchange between Claire and Hemphill the night she went missing. She asked him to come get her."

"I see. Where are you now?"

"I'm on my way over to the friend's place. I'm hoping Claire is still there. I already found his address because he was one of Claire's social media connections on my list of people to track down."

"I thought you were going to take a night off," Bauer said, a hint of frustration in his voice.

"I never said that. Besides, if I had, we wouldn't know where Hemphill lives."

"Touché." Bauer paused. "You think Ryan Gilder knows where she is, too? After all, he did have the phone in his possession for almost two days before handing it over. He must have read that message."

"Doubtful. It was deleted. Probably by Claire."

"You know what this means, right?" Bauer asked.

"It means I might finally get some answers," Patterson replied.

"It also means it's unlikely Otto Sharp had anything to do with her disappearance, even if it was him who stole back the box of TexFest paperwork."

"Yeah. I know. It looks like Claire disappeared of her own volition."

"She must have left her purse and phone in the car so that she couldn't be tracked by her cell signal or credit cards." There was another moment of silence as Bauer processed the situation. "Which begs the question, was she trying to avoid you because of your questions about Julie, or was she hiding from her boyfriend?"

"When I find her, I'll ask. Maybe she did disappear to clear her head, as Gilder claimed she had done on previous occasions."

"Let's hope. Either way, it's a relief to know she probably isn't a victim of foul play."

"Right."

"You want me to meet you at the location?" Bauer asked.

"No. The GPS on my phone says it's only ten minutes away, and I'm almost there now. I'll assess the situation and let you know if I need backup."

"All right," Bauer said grudgingly. "I'll get dressed anyway and wait for your call, just in case."

"Sure." Patterson swung into the parking lot of the apartment complex listed as Leonard Hemphill's most recent address. She told Bauer to stand by, hung up, and then studied her surroundings.

The apartments, converted from an old warehouse complex comprising four buildings in the city's Design District, sat on a large tract of land bordering Trammell Crow Park, a long strip of Greenbelt following the course of the Trinity River. It was a trendy, chic development that still retained a grungy atmosphere. The words 'Trammell Art Lofts' had been painted in tall white lettering across the brickwork at the top of the largest building— standing six stories high—where the original warehouse name would have been and illuminated by downward-facing lights. A vinyl banner strapped to the building below this proclaimed: Now Leasing. One and Two-Bedroom Studio Living Spaces for Artists, Musicians, and Other Creatives.

This made sense. Leonard Hemphill's online profile identified him as a visual artist. He regularly posted his paintings and drawings.

Patterson sat in the dark parking lot for a moment and centered herself before proceeding. Her car's dashboard clock said it was almost one-thirty in the morning. The storms that had rolled through the area earlier in the evening were now gone, and the night sky was mostly clear, smudged only by a couple of thin streaks of cloud. The moon was almost full and cast a silvery light across the landscape. Lights burned from behind a couple of apartment windows like lonely beacons, but most of the building's occupants were fast asleep in their beds.

Patterson climbed from the car and closed the door as quietly as possible, then made her way across the parking lot to the building's entrance. As she went, a sudden thought occurred to her. What if the apartments had an entry system? She wouldn't be able to get inside. During the day, it would be easy. She would hang around outside until a resident came along and then flash her badge after they swiped their entry card and follow them inside. Alternatively, she could go to the leasing office and ask them to give her access. Now, in the middle of the night, with everyone tucked up in bed and the office closed, those options would not be available to her. But she needn't have worried. The building was not secured, and she was soon in the lobby.

She checked Hemphill's address on her phone as she made her way to the elevator. He lived on the fourth floor. It only took a moment to ride up, and soon she was in a corridor with polished concrete floors and rough brick walls illuminated by industrial-style lighting that kept the ware-house vibe. Large black and white photographs of the indus-trial building in its early days adorned the walls, lit by downward-facing spotlights.

There were eight studio apartments on this floor. Leonard Hemphill's unit was at the end of the corridor on the left. Patterson pressed the bell and waited. There was no sign of movement from within. Hemphill was probably sleeping. With any luck, Claire Wright was also asleep inside the apartment.

Patterson rang the bell again, hearing the faint buzz from beyond the door.

When there was still no response, she gave the door a sharp knock—quiet enough to be heard by the occupants in the apartment but not loud enough to wake those in other units.

Except that instead of her clenched hand meeting firm resistance, her blow caused the apartment door to swing slowly inward.

FIFTY-SIX

WHEN THE DOOR SWUNG INWARD, Patterson reached for her gun. She slipped the Glock service weapon from its shoulder holster and held it in the ready position while peering past the opening into the darkened apartment beyond. She listened, straining to pick up any sound from within the unit, but heard nothing.

She contemplated withdrawing to the safety of the parking lot, where she could call the situation in, speak to Bauer, and wait for backup to arrive. But there wasn't time. Her sixth sense told her something was very wrong.

She stood in the doorway and called out, all concern for disturbing the neighbors now gone. "Armed federal agent. If there's anyone inside the apartment, please identify yourselves."

There was no response.

She tried again, repeating the warning that she was an armed FBI agent.

As before, silence was her only reply.

She steeled herself to enter, but then she heard a soft click from her rear. She glanced over her shoulder to see the apartment door on the other side of the corridor cracked open. A startled female face peered through the gap.

"What's going on here?" she asked, her eyes widening with fear when she saw the gun in Patterson's hand. "Who are you?"

Patterson flashed her credentials. "FBI."

"Oh, my." The woman's face fell. "Is everything okay?"

"That's what I'm here to find out." Patterson turned toward the woman. "Do you know your neighbor, Leonard Hemphill?"

"Yes. Such a nice man. He's always very polite."

"When was the last time you saw him?"

"About a week ago," the woman said. "I've been out of town visiting family. I only got back a couple of hours ago."

"I see. Have you heard any noise from the apartment since you got back? Seen any activity?"

"No. Nothing. But Leonard's a quiet neighbor. Doesn't even play his music loud."

"Has anyone come or gone?"

"I wouldn't know. I've been unpacking."

"Okay. Thank you." Patterson nodded. "Now go back inside and lock your door."

The neighbor watched her for a second more, then pushed the door quietly closed and engaged the deadbolt.

Alone again, Patterson took a deep breath. Her sense of foreboding had risen to a crescendo. Every nerve in her body tingled. With her heart thumping against her ribs, Patterson stepped across the threshold and into the gloom beyond.

The apartment was more extensive than she expected. The lights were off so that she couldn't see into the furthest reaches of the space, but she sensed the openness around her falling away in all directions.

Patterson reached for her phone with one hand while

keeping the gun at the ready with the other. She activated the flashlight and swept it across the room, advancing slowly.

This was not a usual living space. There was an open-plan kitchen to her right, with what looked like a blender sitting out on the countertop next to a glass half full of a dark liquid she couldn't identify. Beyond this was the main living area, which was more an art studio than anything else. An easel stood close by, holding a large canvas filled with blocks of color, the start of a composition not yet fully realized. A bench littered with half-empty paint tubes and brushes of all shapes and sizes stood near the easel. An odor of turpentine and linseed oil hung in the air. A rainbow flag hung on the wall, with the word 'pride' written across it. Patterson's gaze lingered on it. If Claire had come here, it was unlikely to be because she was having an affair, at least with Hemphill. All the evidence pointed to the fact that he didn't have any interest in that regard.

Moving on, she stepped past the easel, deeper into the apartment. Here there was a couch and a TV on a rustic stand. In between the two was a small wooden coffee table that had been tipped over. A smashed coffee mug lay on its side; the contents spilled across the roughhewn wide-plank wood boards that were probably the original warehouse floor. Crumpled sheets and a pillow that still bore the impression of a head covered the couch. Someone had been sleeping here.

But it was what she saw beyond this that made Patterson stop in her tracks. A man's body lay sprawled near the sofa, one leg bent at forty-five degrees. He wore boxer shorts and a light-colored T-shirt, the front of which was stained like some grotesque piece of modern art. Only unlike the canvas standing behind her, this was not paint. It was blood.

Patterson inched closer, playing her phone's flashlight beam across the body. He stared back at her with milky, lifeless eyes. His face was frozen in a rictus grimace. There was no doubt this person was dead.

She looked down at the corpse, knowing instinctively who it was. Leonard Hemphill.

Her mind flew to Claire Wright. Was she in the apartment when this happened? Patterson turned and searched the rest of the living room, then moved through a short corridor that led to an empty bathroom and a bedroom that contained a king-sized bed with crumpled sheets. A closet with louvered doors stood to Patterson's right. An exercise bike had been placed opposite the bed.

She went to the closet and pulled the doors back, raising her gun in case someone was hiding there, but it was empty except for shirts and pants arranged on hangers. Beneath this was a jumble of boxes, a suitcase, and several pairs of shoes.

A breeze tousled her hair, causing her to turn around.

Tall windows—probably original to the building when it was a warehouse—filled the far wall, giving the bedroom's occupant a stunning view of the Dallas skyline beyond. Someone had swiveled one large pane upward on its center hinge.

Patterson crossed over to the window and stuck her head outside, expecting to see a sheer drop to the ground below. She was surprised to find a fire escape balcony instead with a set of metal steps leading down to the next floor. She looked up to see another set of steps climbing toward the roof.

Pulling her head back inside, she turned and swept the flashlight beam across the bed and the nightstand, then out toward the living area. Apart from the corpse next to the couch, Patterson was alone. If Claire Wright had ever been here, she wasn't anymore.

FIFTY-SEVEN

FORTY-FIVE MINUTES LATER, Leonard Hemphill's apartment was abuzz with activity. Patterson stood in the corridor outside the unit and watched as forensics technicians, police detectives, and the coroner went about their work investigating the grisly scene. Despite their protests, the other apartments on this level had been cleared, and the occupants ushered downstairs into a communal area next to the lobby. Now the fourth floor was the sole domain of the Dallas Police Department's homicide squad.

She watched the proceedings for a few minutes more, then made her way to the elevator and rode down to the lobby. Out in the parking lot, she called Bauer.

When he answered, there was concern in his voice. "Is everything okay? Did you find Claire?"

"No. Not so much." Patterson took a long breath. She studied the gaggle of emergency response vehicles that painted the building's façade with their lights in flashes of red and blue. "Hemphill is dead, and Claire is gone."

"What?" Bauer's voice rose in pitch. "You want me to

come down there? I'm already dressed. I can be there in less than thirty."

"No need. You might as well go back to bed and get some sleep. I'm probably going to be here all night. At least one of us should be fresh tomorrow morning if there are any new developments."

"You sure?"

"I'm sure."

"Well, alright," Bauer replied. "But while I'm on the phone, you might as well fill me in. How did Hemphill die?"

"Knife wound to the chest. Coroner says it punctured his heart and probably killed him instantly."

"Crap. Is there any indication of who did it?"

"If you mean was it Claire? I don't know. There were signs of a struggle. Coffee table knocked over. Smashed mug. I'm sure she was there, though. There's only one bedroom in the apartment, but the sofa had been made up into a temporary bed. I assume Hemphill was sleeping on it and Claire was in the bedroom, given the position of the body. Front door was unlocked and ajar when I arrived, but there was no sign of forced entry."

"Which means Hemphill must've answered the door to someone," Bauer speculated.

"There's something else. The bedroom window was open, too. There's a fire escape at the back of the building and it would've been easy to climb out and down. I'm guessing Claire made her escape through the window, which makes it less likely that she was the killer."

"Right. Because there would be no reason for the front door to be unlocked if Claire killed Hemphill and then left by the fire escape."

"Exactly," Patterson replied. "Given the evidence at the scene, it's likely that Hemphill and Claire were in bed or preparing for bed when someone arrived at the apartment.

Hemphill answered the door and let them in. He was subsequently killed after a struggle . . ."

"While Claire Wright, who was probably in the bedroom and heard the commotion, escaped out the window and down the fire escape."

"Which might be the only reason there aren't two bodies in that apartment."

"Or it could be a cleverly staged scene, and Claire really is the murderer."

"What reason would she have?"

Bauer snorted. "You've worked enough murder cases. Sometimes there is no reason that makes any sense to a sane person. Don't forget, Claire was struggling with depression."

"Being depressed doesn't make you a killer," Patterson said.

"What about the boyfriend, Ryan Gilder?" Bauer asked. "You know he's going to be suspect number one in this, given that his girlfriend was in the apartment of another man."

"I'm sure that once they have a time of death, Dallas PD will send someone around to his house and see where he was during the window of opportunity. But I don't think Claire was having an affair with Leonard Hemphill."

"Why do you say that?" Bauer asked.

"He had a pride flag hanging in his living room."

"Oh." Bauer fell silent for a moment, processing this. "He's homosexual."

"He was until someone put a knife in his chest," Patterson responded dryly. She swore. "I was so close to finding her. I was sure this was going to be it. My chance to ask about Julie."

"We'll find her," Bauer said. "I promise."

"I'm not so sure. She's doing a pretty good job of staying one step ahead."

"Doesn't sound like she was trying to avoid you when she

went out that apartment window. Sounds more like she fled for her life."

"I know. It's a fair bet that whoever killed Hemphill was looking for her, probably with the same intention. He just got in the way. If it wasn't Ryan Gilder—and we don't know that it wasn't—then Claire must have gotten herself involved in a really bad situation."

"A situation worth murdering for," Bauer said. "You still think this has something to do with Julie?"

"At this point, I don't know. If Gilder is the killer, then it's probably just a domestic that got out of hand. Claire might have killed Hemphill for whatever reason and then fled. In that case, it's probably not about my sister. If someone else went to that apartment intending to kill her, then who knows? Maybe Otto Sharp is involved in this after all. He could have sent the same thugs who attacked me to take care of Claire."

"You really believe that?"

"I believe that a man is lying dead in his apartment and that Claire is either the intended target or a cold-blooded killer. Beyond that, your guess is as good as mine."

"You absolutely sure you don't want me to come down there?" Bauer asked. "I can take over for a while so you can go get some sleep. You must be exhausted."

"I'm beyond exhausted," Patterson admitted. She could feel the tiredness creeping around the edges of her consciousness. She was also still sore from her confrontation with the intruders who broke into her apartment. Her ribs might not be broken, for which she was thankful, but the bruising was severe. Still, she wasn't willing to relinquish control of the situation. If there was a break in the case, she wanted to be there. "I appreciate the offer, but I'll be fine. I'll head back to the motel and get some rest when forensics wraps up."

"You are one stubborn woman, Patterson Blake." Bauer

sounded frustrated, but there was a touch of admiration mixed in, too. "I'm here if you need me."

"I know," Patterson said before hanging up. She stood for a while in the parking lot, relishing the calm early morning air. Then she made her way back inside the building, past the throng of gawking residents who had assembled in the lobby to see what was happening and returned to the crime scene.

FIFTY-EIGHT

BY SIX AM, after being at Leonard Hemphill's apartment all night, Patterson was beginning to regret turning down Bauer's offer to switch with her. She'd barely gotten any rest since arriving in Dallas the previous Monday. So much had happened, it felt like she'd been here forever instead of a short seven days.

There had been a steady stream of investigators tromping up and down the corridor from the elevator since the first police units had arrived after her call four hours prior. Aside from this, the building's common areas were practically deserted now. Uniformed officers had gone door to door and searched every apartment in the building, and most of the tenants on the fourth floor, who had been asked to leave earlier, were now allowed to return. Only the three apartments surrounding Hemphill's were still off-limits, mainly because the police didn't want curious neighbors gawking at their activity.

Patterson stood near the apartment door and watched as a pair of employees from the coroner's office wheeled a gurney past her. The black body bag on top contained the earthly remains of Leonard Hemphill, whose corpse the homicide detectives had finally allowed to be removed. From here, it would go to the medical examiner, who would perform a more detailed autopsy. Not that it mattered. The preliminary cause of death, multiple stab wounds, one of which penetrated the heart, was unlikely to change. Defensive cuts on the victim's arms provided further evidence of what had occurred in the apartment. Hemphill had not gone down without a fight.

"You look like hell," a voice said over her shoulder.

Patterson drew her gaze from the gurney and turned to find Dallas Police Detective Bob Costa standing there. This was the same man they had spoken to before interviewing Ryan Gilder at DPD headquarters several days before. She tried to force a smile but failed. "It's been a long night."

"That it has." He glanced back into the apartment. "We found a woman's blouse in the dryer, so it looks like Claire Wright was definitely here."

"I figured as much," Patterson said. "Have you spoken to the boyfriend, Ryan Gilder, yet?"

"That's what I came over to tell you." Costa dug his hands into his pockets. "The ME placed Hemphill's time of death between ten PM and midnight."

"Really?" Patterson swallowed hard. That would put the murder around the time she called Hemphill and got his voicemail. If she had left right away to come here, instead of going to bed, she might have been able to save his life. But even as the thought crossed her mind, she dismissed it. Hemphill was probably already dead when his phone rang. After all, the medical examiner had said the fatal wound pierced his heart, killing him within seconds. There was nothing she could have done. Besides, she didn't find out about Claire's text until later, so she would have had no reason to come here. "Where was Gilder between those times?"

"That's the problem. The officer who went to his house didn't get an answer. He's not there. We can't find him."

"Where would he be at this time of the morning?"

The detective shrugged. "Wherever it is, he didn't take Claire Wright's car or his truck. We've issued a BOLO and we're watching his house and the property he's been renovating. If he shows up, we'll bring him in."

"And Claire Wright?" Patterson asked. "She's still out there, too. We need to find her."

"There's already a BOLO out for her, thanks to you. Ryan and Claire are the only two suspects we have right now, so if either of them surfaces, they'll be taken downtown for questioning."

"Good." Patterson nodded. She yawned.

"You're just about dead on your feet, pardon the expression," Costa said, watching her through narrowed eyes. "Why don't you head out? We've got this."

"Are you sure?" Patterson didn't want to be back in her motel room sleeping if there was a break in the case, but she wasn't sure how much longer she could stay awake.

"I'm sure." Costa took her by the arm and led her toward the elevator. "If we find anything, no matter how small, I'll call you right away."

"You promise?"

"Cross my heart." Costa pressed the call button and stood with her until the elevator arrived. He ushered her inside. "Good night Special Agent Blake. Sleep tight."

"Hate to tell you this," Patterson said, "but it's already morning."

"Not in your case," Costa replied as the elevator doors slid closed, cutting him off from her view.

She slumped back against the wall, momentarily allowing

exhaustion to get the better of her. Then, when the elevator door opened, she stepped out and walked through the lobby, ignoring the curious looks of the few tenants that remained there, hoping there might be another opportunity to satisfy their morbid curiosity.

She crossed the parking lot and climbed into her car, then pointed it in the direction of the motel. It was Monday morning and rush-hour traffic was ramping up. She sat behind a tractor-trailer and inched along at an infuriatingly slow pace, unable to see past the large vehicle to the road ahead. It took almost twenty-five minutes to travel the same distance that had taken ten minutes going the other way in the early hours.

She pulled into the motel parking lot and found a space close to her room. But as she climbed out of the car, her phone rang. She answered without looking at the screen, thinking it must be Special Agent Bauer, but instead, a female voice filled her ear.

"Special Agent Blake? This is Cindy Lorenz from Lulu's Hair Academy. I don't know if you remember me?"

"I do," Patterson replied, wondering why the woman would be calling her now. The question got answered seconds later.

"Good, because I didn't know who else to call. Claire is here. She was waiting when I arrived to open the academy this morning."

"Claire Wright is at the hair school?" Patterson asked, climbing back into the car.

"Yes. She's in a helluva state. Almost incoherent. Crying. She says someone tried to kill her."

"Get her inside and don't move," Patterson said, slamming the car door and pushing the key back into the ignition. "I'll be right there."

FIFTY-NINE

PATTERSON SPED out of the parking lot toward Lulu's Hair Academy. Being a Bureau car, her vehicle had no flashers. She avoided the interstate, which was bumper-to-bumper, but even so, she soon ran into traffic, which she weaved around like a crazy person, laying on the horn.

As she drove, Patterson called Bauer.

He answered on the first ring. "Hey. What's up?"

"Claire Wright just showed up at the hair academy," Patterson replied. "She's hysterical. Said someone tried to kill her. I'm on my way there now."

"I'll meet you there," Bauer said. Patterson heard rustling in the background as he moved around, then a clink as he grabbed his car keys. "Heading out the door right now."

"Good. I'll see you there." Patterson ended the call and dropped the phone onto the seat next to her. She concentrated on driving, slipping in between other vehicles whenever there was even the tiniest space. In return, she elicited angry horns and the occasional obscene gesture, but she didn't care. She would not let Claire Wright slip between her fingers again.

When there was a break in the traffic, she pressed on the accelerator, urging the car faster. Up ahead, there was an intersection. As she approached, the light turned yellow. Patterson floored it and shot forward, speeding through as the light turned red. Another angry honk trailed behind her.

I could really use a car with flashers; she thought to herself as a bus pulled out ahead of her, forcing Patterson to slam on the brakes. For five agonizingly slow minutes, she trailed the lumbering vehicle until it pulled over at a bus stop, and she could scoot around it. As she passed by, engine revving, she caught sight of a startled face peering through the bus window down at her. Then she left it behind and was making up time.

Finally, after what felt like a frustratingly long journey, she pulled into the parking for the strip mall where the hair academy was located. The car had barely come to a standstill before she was jumping out, but then, before she could race around to the back and up the stairs to the second-floor catwalk, her phone rang again.

It was Bauer calling back.

"What is it?" she asked, taking large strides toward the building.

"You might want to hold up a minute before you barge in there," Bauer said. "I just heard from the intelligence analysts we had researching the boyfriend, Ryan Gilder. He's not who he seems. Until four years ago, he lived in Seattle and went by the name James Gilder."

"What?" Patterson stopped in her tracks. "His real name isn't Ryan?"

"Middle name. He started using it when he moved to Dallas."

"Why would he change it like that?" Patterson looked up toward the second floor and the row of windows there. Somewhere behind that glass, Claire Wright was waiting for her.

"Because he was trying to escape his past . . . or hide from it. He had a fiancée named Miranda Olson up in Seattle. She was younger than him."

"How much younger?" Patterson asked.

"Twenty-three years old. He's thirty-five now, so he would've been thirty when they were engaged. A difference of seven years."

"That still doesn't explain why he would move to another city and start using his middle name." Patterson sensed there was worse coming. She was right.

"Miranda Olson is dead." Bauer paused a moment to let that sink in. When he spoke again, his tone was grave. "She was killed in a home invasion a year before Gilder moved to Dallas. He was a suspect, but he had an alibi. A friend said they were at a concert in Tacoma on the night his fiancée was murdered."

"Tacoma and Seattle aren't far from each other," Patterson noted. "And people have been known to lie for their friends."

"Right. But the police couldn't find any physical evidence of his involvement, so they had to let it go. The murder is still unsolved. Officially, it's categorized as a home invasion robbery gone wrong because some of her jewelry was missing and the place looked like it had been ransacked. But that's not the worst of it. The murder weapon was a knife. Miranda Olson was stabbed to death."

"Just like Leonard Hemphill." A chill ran up Patterson's spine. "If Gilder was involved in his fiancée's murder back in Seattle, he could easily have staged the scene to look like a robbery."

"That's what I'm thinking." Bauer hesitated. "Do you see Gilder's truck anywhere in the parking lot?"

"No." Patterson glanced around anyway, even though she knew it wouldn't be there. "His white truck and Claire's car were still parked in the driveway when the police went round to question him earlier this morning, but he wasn't there. They have a BOLO out on him."

"Shit. He could be in another vehicle. I'm still fifteen minutes out, but I've called for backup from Dallas PD, and they should be with you sooner. Don't go up to that hair school until they arrive."

"Okay." Despite Bauer's request, Patterson started forward again, heading down the covered walkway that led to the stairs at the rear of the strip mall. It was quiet and empty back there. No students had arrived yet because the school didn't open until eight AM, and there was still an hour to go. Cindy Lorenz must've come in early to prepare for the day and found Claire already there, hiding from the man who tried to kill her, who Patterson now suspected was her boyfriend, Ryan Gilder. Why Claire hadn't gone straight to the police was anyone's guess. Maybe she wasn't thinking straight and went to the first place she knew would be safe. Not that it mattered. Patterson was here now, and before long, the Dallas Police Department would be, too.

She told Bauer to be careful, hung up, and then slipped her gun from its holster. She didn't enjoy waiting around and resisted the urge to charge straight up to the hair school. This impulsiveness had gotten her into trouble before. A couple of weeks ago, while she was in Oklahoma City, a crazed serial killer had taken her hostage, mostly because of her leap first and look later attitude. That situation had worked out for the best in the end, but it almost cost Patterson her life. She didn't want to make the same mistake again. But at the same time, the person she had been looking for was so close.

She was still wrestling with whether to head up the steps to the second floor and find Claire or wait for backup to arrive as she had agreed, when a scream rang out, shrill and terrified.

SIXTY

THE SCREAM CUT OFF ABRUPTLY. The silence that rushed in behind it was eerie and surreal. A prickle ran up Patterson's spine. Something bad had occurred above her on the second floor. She took a deep breath. The decision had been made for her. There was no time to waste. Patterson started up the steps, taking them two at a time until she reached the catwalk above.

Now she stopped, assessing the situation. There was no sign of a disturbance, no indication that anything was amiss, but Patterson was not fooled. People didn't scream in terror for nothing.

She took a step forward and advanced along the catwalk at a slow pace, her Glock at the ready. She checked the door of each unit as she went, wary of her surroundings. Rushing ahead without due caution was a good way to get yourself killed. The instructors at Quantico had taught her that.

When she reached the hair academy, the door stood open a couple of inches. This must be where the scream had come from.

She stopped and listened. Hearing nothing, she pushed

the door open with the toe of her shoe and stepped back, gun raised, and stared into the empty lobby beyond.

She moved forward on high alert, her eyes sweeping the small space, but saw nothing. She approached the only other door, the same one that Cindy Lorenz had emerged through, yelling that she was late the last time Patterson was here. The woman had mistaken Patterson for a hair model, which, she supposed, was a compliment of sorts. This time, the employee of Lulu's Hair Academy did not appear.

The door was closed. Patterson turned the handle and let it swing open, taking a defensive stance. As before, an empty and silent space greeted her.

Patterson stepped over the threshold and found herself in a short corridor. On the right were a pair of toilets, both unisex. Patterson nudged the first door and peered inside. There was a toilet, sink, and a small metal rack that contained cleaning supplies. Other than that, it was empty.

When she opened the second door, she stifled a gasp. An unconscious woman sat slumped in the corner between the sink and the toilet, blood seeping from a nasty gash on her forehead. It was Cindy. Patterson glanced around but saw no one else. She stepped into the room and kneeled by the prone woman, noting that her chest was rising and falling with some relief. Other than the wound to her head, Patterson could see no other obvious trauma. She made a quick assessment and decided that Cindy was in no immediate danger.

She stood and returned to the door, checking the corridor beyond once more before entering. Claire Wright had been here, Patterson knew. But so had the man who called himself Ryan Gilder. Thankfully, he hadn't killed Cindy, but Claire might not be so lucky. The question was, had Gilder taken his girlfriend and left already, or were they both still on the premises?

Patterson had to find out, and quickly.

She turned her attention to a set of double doors on the other side of the corridor. She pushed against one with her shoulder and opened it just enough to step inside. The large L-shaped room beyond occupied the rest of the unit. This must be where the teaching took place. There were rows of hairdressing stations that took up one side of the floor space. Along the far wall, Patterson saw sinks with chairs that tilted backward so that students could wash their model's hair. An area set up like a classroom was to her right, with rows of plastic chairs facing a podium. A projector screen hung down from the ceiling.

At first, Patterson thought this room was empty, and Gilder had fled with his girlfriend. But as she moved further in, she saw something that made her stop in her tracks.

A smeared trail of blood led from between the chairs to a door on the far side of the room.

The hair stood up on Patterson's arms. Blood rushed in her ears. This was too much to be from the wounds inflicted upon Cindy Lorenz, and it ran in the opposite direction. There was only one person who could have left this ghastly trail.

Claire Wright.

Patterson felt a moment of panic. Was she too late? Had Gilder killed his girlfriend already and fled?

There was only one way to find out.

She stepped between the chairs and followed the grim trail to the door, then reached out with a shaking hand and gripped the knob, turning it.

Beyond the door was a small kitchen and break room with four sets of tables and chairs, a couple of microwaves sitting on the counter, and a refrigerator. And on the floor near the first table, lying on her back with her arms at her sides as if she were asleep, was a woman in her early thirties who might have been attractive if it wasn't for the bruising that was already coloring her face, her split lip, and the blood that seeped from her ruined nose. But this wasn't what had caused the sticky red drag trail across the tile floor. That was due to the copious amounts of blood that oozed through her ripped top and now pooled around her limp form.

Patterson sucked in a quick breath. This must be Claire Wright.

She stepped into the room and kneeled. Holding her gun with one hand, she felt for a pulse with the other. It was weak and erratic. Claire Wright was still alive, barely.

Patterson's gaze drifted down the woman's torso until she saw the stab wound. A puckered slit beneath her right breast was visible through her shredded blouse. There might be other wounds, but Patterson didn't have time to find them. She took out her phone, dialed 911, and then identified herself as a federal agent. A moment later, the dispatcher confirmed paramedics were on the way. Patterson only hoped it would be soon enough. She hung up and was about to call Bauer when she heard a noise somewhere behind her in the classroom.

Patterson sprang to her feet and whirled around. In her haste to save Claire, she had become distracted and forgotten about the greater danger. The murderer who might still lurk in the building. An image flashed through her mind of an obese, shirtless man lumbering toward her with a pitchfork. The last time Patterson had become distracted, it had almost cost her life during a raid on the serial killer's rural lair in upstate New York. She would not let that happen again. She was also determined not to let Ryan Gilder escape if he hadn't already.

She returned the phone to her pocket, then went to the door and stepped back out, gripping the gun with both hands and holding it steady despite the butterflies that swarmed inside her stomach. Backup was coming, but she was on her own until it got here.

Another noise, this one fainter.

It came from the direction of the lobby.

Patterson crossed the room, weaving around the chairs and hairdressing stations. She stepped back into the corridor and entered the lobby.

Nothing. It was empty.

She felt a mix of annoyance and relief. Ryan Gilder, it appeared, had indeed escaped. But he wouldn't get far. She would make sure of that. Besides, there were more urgent matters, like the two injured women.

Patterson turned to make her way back inside, lowering her gun. She moved along the corridor and was about to step back into the main room when she caught a flicker of movement from the corner of her eye.

She turned in time to see a dark shape bearing down upon her from the second of the two unisex toilets. She let out a startled cry and lifted the gun, finger falling to the trigger, but it was too late.

A flash of steel, and Patterson felt searing pain explode across her forearm. Enough that she cried out a second time and relaxed her grip long enough for the gun to fall from her hands even as she tried to prevent it.

The next thing she knew, the knife was descending again, and this time it wasn't aimed at her arm.

SIXTY-ONE

THE KNIFE ARCHED DOWNWARD.

In the split second it took for Patterson to realize what was happening, she had lost her gun, eliminating her ability to end the attack quickly. She was also wounded. The pain was intense. She could feel the blood flowing freely down her arm from what was surely a deep laceration. But there was no time to focus on it. She dodged sideways, avoiding what would have been a death blow. Instead, the wicked-looking blade sailed harmlessly past her, mere inches from its mark.

Now she saw her attacker for the first time. A large man wearing a red Halloween devils mask beneath the hoodie that hid his features. But Patterson knew all too well who this maniac was. Ryan Gilder. He must have heard her enter the building while he was attacking Claire. How he had avoided detection as she swept through the building was anyone's guess. Still, somehow he had circled behind her, probably while she was tending to one of the victims, and concealed himself in the previously empty bathroom where he waited to ambush her.

That Gilder hadn't fled came as a surprise. It also meant

that he had no intention of trying to escape—at least, not before Patterson lay dead. Which meant the only way to stay alive was to take him out. And quickly. The best way to do that was to go on the offense. Which is what she did by driving her elbow backward as hard as she could into Gilder's exposed stomach.

He grunted as the air exploded from his lungs and took a step backward, repositioning himself with the knife.

Patterson dodged a second assault, jumping back as Gilder changed his tactics and brought the knife up in a quick stabbing motion toward her torso that would have gutted her. Even so, she didn't avoid further injury as the knife nicked her just below the ribs, in the same spot that was still healing from the previous assault back in the motel room.

She let out an involuntary cry of pain and staggered backward into the lobby. Instinctively, she reached for the backup weapon that should have been strapped to her ankle, but it wasn't there. The Glock 27 subcompact was back in Queens, New York, locked in the wall safe she had installed in her apartment within a week of moving in. This was because she had been on suspension from the Bureau when her search for Julie started and hadn't intended to end up in dangerous situations such as the one she now faced.

It was an avoidable mistake that might now get her killed because Ryan Gilder was charging at her like an enraged bull, with the hunting knife he'd used to stab his girlfriend only minutes before held high.

She looked around, frantic, for some way to defend herself. Anything she could use as a weapon, but the lobby was empty except for a row of hard plastic chairs along one wall.

It was better than nothing.

Patterson rolled sideways and gripped the nearest chair, picking it up and swinging it toward Gilder just as he started to bring the knife down. It deflected the blow and sent the knife tumbling from his hand and clattering across the tile floor, followed by the chair.

Gilder let out an enraged bellow and spat a single word in her direction. "Bitch."

She thought he was going to scramble for the lost knife and was about to do the same, but instead, his clenched fist came up and smashed into her stomach, almost lifting Patterson from her feet.

Her lungs emptied in a mighty whoosh of escaping air. She fell backward, the force of Gilder's attack upsetting her balance, and toppled into the remaining chairs, her head smacking into the wall so hard she saw stars.

Now Gilder went for the lost knife.

He turned and ran toward the weapon, which had come to rest near the opposite wall, hand outstretched to scoop it up.

Patterson saw what he was doing, pushed herself up, and then leaped forward. She lunged across the lobby in a low dive and slipped under Gilder's arm, grabbing the knife before he got there.

She landed hard and rolled onto her back, lifting the blade to defend herself, but Gilder anticipated the move and swatted her hand, sending the knife tumbling away again. Then he fell to his knees, straddling her, and lifted his fist to deliver another crushing blow.

But Patterson had no intention of letting him punch her a second time. She might not have a weapon, but she wasn't entirely defenseless. She lifted her arms, placed a palm on each side of his head, inserted her thumbs through the eyeholes in his devil mask, then pressed into his eye sockets with all her might.

Gilder screamed and backpedaled. He scooted backward, and in doing so, the mask slipped off his head. Patterson ended up holding the empty devil's face with her thumbs still looped into the now empty eyeholes.

She discarded the mask and took the opportunity to regain her feet, clenching her jaws against the onslaught of pain that threatened to derail her efforts. The cut on her arm was bleeding badly, and her bruised torso felt like it had been hit by a truck. She might have sustained a concussion, too, when her head smacked into the wall.

But none of that mattered.

Gilder had climbed to his feet as well and now observed her with a wary stare, his nostrils flaring.

For a moment, the two adversaries faced each other without moving. A momentary respite that Patterson was grateful for. But the reprieve was brief.

The knife now lay by the hair academy's front door, just waiting for one of them to retrieve it and win this battle. Patterson knew she couldn't let it be Gilder, because if he got his hands on the knife again, it would be over. She didn't have the strength to keep fighting, and Gilder had no intention of letting her walk away with her life.

Which was why, when he made a sudden dash for the weapon, she took the only available option. She was nearer than him but stood with her back to the knife. But there was no time to turn and pick it up. He would be on top of her again in an instant. It would be a toss-up which of them came up with the blade. Instead, she stepped sideways into his path and tensed for the impact.

Gilder was taken by surprise but had no time to react. Their bodies collided even as he tried to pivot around the tenacious FBI agent, driving both of them toward the door.

Patterson's back smacked into the plate glass inside the door's frame, and for a second, she was sandwiched there as Gilder's heavy body threatened to crush her. But then there was a loud popping sound, and the glass door shattered into thousands of tiny ball-shaped shards. With the resistance at her back now gone, Patterson was driven out onto the catwalk by Gilder's forward momentum.

Her back met another obstacle. The catwalk's railing.

This time she was expecting it, and gripped Gilder's shirt with both hands, then used her own momentum to pivot sideways and pull her attacker forward.

His waist hit the railing even as he tried to put the brakes on. But there was no time. His top half kept going as Patterson released her grip, and Gilder pitched forward with a shriek and dropped from sight.

A second later, she heard a thud as his body hit the concrete below. Then, as if backup were waiting for her to finish with Gilder before showing up, the distant wail of sirens reached her ears. Patterson grimaced and slid to the ground, her back against the railing, and closed her eyes.

SIXTY-TWO

PATTERSON SAT in the back of an ambulance and let the paramedics tend to her injuries. The laceration on her arm from Ryan Gilder's knife was deep, but they had stopped the flow of blood and bandaged it. Even so, she would need stitches. But when they tried to take her to the hospital, Patterson had refused. That could wait until later.

The strip mall parking lot was chock-a-block with police vehicles, some of them unmarked. A mobile command unit had just rolled in and parked up, too. Uniformed officers had set up a cordon around the building, and the hair academy on the second floor was teeming with detectives. A photographer with a digital SLR camera was photographing the spot where Ryan Gilder had contacted the pavement. All that was left to prove that he was ever there was a pool of now dried blood. They had taken him away clinging to life with a fractured skull, and probably many more broken bones as well.

Claire Wright was in the back of a second ambulance, which departed only moments before. Like her attacker, she was maintaining a tenuous grip on life. Having suffered several stab wounds to the chest and stomach, Patterson wasn't sure the woman would survive.

She closed her eyes and breathed a silent prayer as the paramedic cleaned the wound under her ribs and dressed it with an adhesive bandage. If Claire died, whatever she knew about Julie went with her.

When Patterson opened her eyes again, Special Agent Marcus Bauer was standing peering into the ambulance with the sun at his back.

"You have a knack for getting into trouble," he said with a grin, but she could see the concern in his eyes.

"What can I say? I'm a natural." Patterson winced as a fresh stab of pain shot up her arm.

"That's one way to put it," Bauer said. "If you'd waited for me before going into that building, you might not have come out looking like the last survivor in a slasher movie."

"If I'd waited for you, Claire and Cindy would both be dead." Patterson's gaze shifted from Bauer to the steps leading down from the catwalk where a paramedic was assisting Cindy Lorenz. By some miracle, the woman had only suffered a blow to the head that knocked her unconscious. She didn't know why Gilder hadn't finished Cindy off when he had the chance. Maybe he was too eager to get at Claire and was intending to complete the job later. Or maybe he just didn't care enough about her. Either way, Cindy was lucky to be alive and walking out of the situation on her own two feet. Patterson looked back at Bauer. "Would you excuse me a moment?"

Bauer glanced toward Cindy, then nodded. "Sure. But don't keep her too long. They want to take her in and get her x-rayed. Make sure she didn't fracture her skull."

"I won't." Patterson stood and stepped out of the ambulance despite the protests of the paramedic who was working on her. She stepped around Bauer and reached

Cindy as she was crossing the parking lot. "How are you feeling?"

"Like someone hit me over the head with a baseball bat," Cindy replied, climbing into the back of her own ambulance and perching on a stretcher. "How's Claire? No one will tell me anything up there."

"It's not good." Patterson could see no point in lying. "She's badly injured and has lost a lot of blood."

"Dammit." Cindy hung her head. "It's all my fault."

"No. It's not." Patterson leaned against the ambulance and watched the paramedic fuss over Cindy. "You were trying to help her."

"I'm the one who caused all this." Cindy looked distressed. Tears welled in her eyes. "Before I called you, I texted her boyfriend to tell him where she was. I figured he would be worried about her. That he'd want to know that she was alive."

"That's how he knew to come here," Patterson said as the pieces fell into place.

Cindy nodded. "Claire was hysterical. I could barely understand what she was talking about. She said a man in a mask had attacked her friend. I didn't know it was him."

"There was no way you could. I doubt she even knew."

"Maybe." Cindy took a deep breath. "If she dies, I'll never forgive myself."

"She's in excellent hands," Patterson said, doing her best to reassure the distraught woman. "And she's hanging in there, which is a good sign."

"You really think so?"

"I do," Patterson said, but deep down, she wasn't so sure. It would all depend on what damage Ryan Gilder's knife had done.

"Ma'am, we really need to get her to the hospital now," the paramedic said.

Patterson nodded and stepped back.

The paramedic leaned out and grabbed the double doors at the back of the vehicle, swinging them closed. A moment later the lights flickered on, stripping red and blue, as the ambulance inched forward and weaved its way past the police vehicles out onto the road.

Patterson watched it go, then turned and walked back toward Bauer and her own waiting ambulance. Every footfall caused a fresh jolt of pain. Over the last few weeks in Oklahoma City and Dallas, she had been abducted, beaten, left in a car to die, cut with a knife, and more. She wasn't sure how much more punishment her body could take. All she wanted to do was go back to the motel and sleep for a week.

Bauer watched her approach. "You ready to go to the hospital yet?"

"Sure. Why not," Patterson replied. She really ought to get stitched up. Gilder's knife had sliced her almost to the bone, and now the adrenaline was wearing off, the discomfort was ramping up. She didn't like taking strong medications, but in this case, she hoped there were some prescription-strength painkillers in her future. "But I'm not going in an ambulance. I'm not *that* bad. I'll drive myself."

"Like hell you will," Bauer said, cutting off the paramedic, who was just about to lodge her own protest. "If you won't ride with the paramedics, then I'll drive you."

Patterson shrugged. She had no fight left in her. "Whatever."

SIXTY-THREE

IT TOOK LONGER to get fixed up at the hospital than Patterson would have imagined. They cleaned her wounds and stitched her arm, subjected her to another round of x-rays to make sure she had broken nothing in the brawl with Gilder, then gave her the painkillers she'd been hoping for. She picked them up from the hospital pharmacy and then made her way over to the trauma unit where Claire Wright had been taken, after texting Bauer to see where he was.

It was midnight now, and visiting hours were long over, even if Claire had been in any condition to receive a visitor, which she most certainly was not. Her badge soon took care of any protests by the hospital staff, and she found Bauer right where he said he would be in the empty waiting room, browsing on his phone.

When she entered, he looked up. "They finally let you go, huh?"

"Didn't give them much choice," she said without elaborating on the doctor's request that she stay overnight for observation because of the nasty bump she'd taken to the back of her head. Concussion was, he said, not to be trifled with. She had refused, and after seeing the look in her eyes, he'd backed off. "I thought you might have waited for me."

"I did for the longest time, but I spoke to a nurse who said you were doing just fine, so I came over here to get an update on Claire Wright."

"And?" Patterson was too tired to stand up. She walked over to a seat and dropped into it with a measure of relief. For the second time in a week, she had a bottle of prescription painkillers in her pocket. She still had a few remaining from her last visit to the ER, but these were better. She couldn't wait to go back to her motel room, take one, and crawl into bed.

"She's in surgery. The damage was pretty extensive, but they're doing what they can."

"Do they think she'll pull through?"

"Not sure. The doctor I spoke to said she'd flatlined on the table once, already, and they brought her back. It will be touch and go for the next several hours while they work on her."

"Shit." Patterson buried her head in her hands. "If only I'd gotten there a few minutes sooner."

"You shouldn't blame yourself," Bauer said, sitting next to her. He put a hand on her shoulder. "She wouldn't be alive at all if it wasn't for you."

"Even so . . ." Patterson breathed a silent prayer that Claire would pull through, and even though she felt it was selfish, at least a little of the reason was because of Julie. She looked at Bauer. "How could I have been so wrong?"

"What do you mean?"

"All this time, I thought that Claire Wright had disappeared because of what she knew about my sister. But I was way off base. This appears to be about Ryan Gilder. She must have been hiding from him. But I still don't understand why he wanted to kill her in the first place? It makes no sense."

"Does it need to make sense?" Bauer asked. "He was already a killer. I think it's pretty clear that he stabbed his previous fiancée, Miranda Olson, up in Seattle."

"There's always a reason. You know that." Patterson refused to believe that Ryan Gilder's violence was completely motiveless. "Even if that reason doesn't make sense to a sane person."

Bauer shrugged. "Maybe we'll find out when and if Claire Wright can talk."

"Maybe." There was still something bothering Patterson. Claire might have disappeared to escape her crazy boyfriend rather than avoid Patterson's questions about Julie, but there was still the matter of who broke into her motel room and stole the TexFest documents. The answer would come if only she could sort out the facts. But her sleep-addled brain refused to let her think straight, and she gave up. That was a question for another day.

Bauer was watching her with narrowed eyes. "How about I drive you back to the motel?"

Patterson shook her head, stifling a yawn. "I need to stay here. If Claire regains consciousness . . ."

"I already told you, she's going to be in surgery for a couple more hours, at least. After that, she's going to be in no condition to answer your questions, at least for a while. Sitting around here and waiting is pointless."

"Maybe you're right," Patterson conceded.

"I am." Bauer stood and held out his hand. "Come on. Let's get out of here. I've left instructions for the hospital to inform me the moment they know anything."

"All right. You win." Patterson took his hand and let Bauer help her up. She followed him out of the trauma unit and through a maze of corridors to the parking garage on the other side of the hospital. She climbed into his Dodge Charger with relief, reclined the seat, and leaned her head back against the headrest. As they exited the parking garage, another thought occurred to her. "What about Ryan Gilder?"

Bauer waited a moment to answer, distracted by traffic as he pulled out onto the road. "He's alive but in a coma. Turns out his head wasn't as hard as the pavement. Doctors say his brain is swollen."

"That's a shame," Patterson said ambiguously.

"Because he's in a coma, or because he's still alive?" Bauer asked, shooting her a questioning look.

Patterson didn't answer. Instead, she took a deep breath and closed her eyes. The next thing she knew, they were at the motel.

SIXTY-FOUR

THE NEXT MORNING, Patterson arrived at the field office still sore but feeling more rested than she had in days. She had slept through the afternoon and into the evening the day before, rising only long enough to order takeout, which she had delivered to the room, and then she flopped back in bed and slept through the night, partly because of the prescription painkillers. Bauer was already there when she entered the office, hunched over his laptop. On her desk was a pile of paperwork that she recognized.

"That's the TexFest stuff stolen from my motel room," she said with surprise. "How did it get here?"

"DPD dropped it by last night," Bauer replied. "They found it while they were searching Ryan Gilder's house."

"What?" Patterson was stunned. "That doesn't make sense. Why would Gilder have it?"

"It makes perfect sense." Bauer leaned back in his chair with his hands behind his head and watched as she rifled through the paperwork. "Think about it. Ryan Gilder was a murderer. He moved to Dallas from Seattle to escape questions surrounding the death of his previous fiancée. Then, while he's out looking for Claire, he finds out that an FBI agent is also looking for her."

"Because Cindy Lorenz from Lulu's Hair Academy told him about my visit when he went there to see if Claire had shown up at school." Patterson sat down and placed her laptop bag next to the TexFest documents.

"Exactly. That's the reason he went to the police and reported her missing."

"He was covering his tracks. Trying to look like the concerned boyfriend." Patterson was mad at herself for not seeing this connection earlier. "He probably had no intention of getting the police involved before he found out about me."

"And when he did find out, he grew concerned that he was the target of a federal investigation into his previous activities."

"That still doesn't explain why he took the TexFest documents, or how," Patterson said. "He couldn't have been one of the two men who attacked me at the motel because we were with him at Claire's abandoned car. It would have been impossible for Gilder to reach the motel before me. Besides, how would he even know where I was staying?"

"I can answer that question, too," Bauer replied. "Remember when we interviewed Gilder, and he told us about his job flipping houses?"

"Sure." Patterson wasn't sure where this was going.

"He worked with a crew of men. Four guys he knew very well. The police brought them all in for questioning overnight since Gilder was in no condition to talk. Two of the four are ex-cons, and they spilled the beans. Apparently, Gilder used them when he needed muscle. And I'm not talking about lugging two by fours and sheetrock. They were known to DPD already because of a complaint filed last year by a subcontractor Gilder had used a couple of times. An electrician. Gilder had refused to pay him, saying the work wasn't good enough. When he wouldn't let the matter drop, Gilder sent the guys around to persuade him with their fists. The electrician reported Gilder and his goons for assault but later dropped the complaint, no doubt after a little more persuading."

"It was those guys that broke into my motel room," Patterson said.

Bauer nodded. "He had you followed when we left police headquarters after interviewing him last week. That's how he knew where you were staying."

"I knew someone was outside my room that night."

"Right. Then, while we were with him at Claire's car, he gave his men the go-ahead to search your room because he knew you weren't there. He told them to steal a vehicle and conceal their features in case someone saw them at the motel."

"That makes sense. He needed to know if we were investigating him," Patterson said. "When I showed up back at the room unexpectedly, I disturbed his men, who snatched the bankers box and ran."

"Assaulting you in the process when you got in the way."

"Don't remind me," Patterson said. "That still doesn't explain why Claire disappeared instead of meeting me or why Gilder tried to kill her."

"No, it doesn't." Bauer scratched his chin. "But you'll be able to ask her that yourself once she is in a condition to talk."

"She pulled through the surgery?" Patterson's hopes rose.

Bauer nodded. "She's still critical but stable. They were able to repair the damage done by Ryan Gilder's knife. She should make a full recovery . . . in time."

"That's wonderful news," Patterson said. "What about Gilder?"

"Still in a coma. If he ever comes out of it, he'll stand trial for the murder of his fiancée in Seattle, Leonard Hemphill, and three counts of attempted murder at the hair academy. I'm sure there will be more charges, too."

"In that case, I hope he wakes up. Because I want to see him behind bars for the rest of his life."

"That's not all," Bauer said. "There might be other victims. His high school girlfriend drowned a week before she was due to leave for college. He was never a suspect back then, but it's being re-examined."

"Holy crap," Patterson breathed. The man had left a trail of death wherever he went.

"Really. If he were female, Gilder would be a regular black widow." Bauer studied Patterson from across the desk. "Changing the subject, how are you feeling this morning?"

"About as well as can be expected," Patterson replied. She touched her bandaged right arm. Twelve stitches held the wound inflicted by Gilder closed underneath the dressing. She would have a permanent scar to remember him by. The cut under her ribs was not so bad, but it still needed three stitches. Other than that, she was banged and bruised, with more aches than she could count. As always, her thoughts turned to Julie. There was still one outstanding thread. "I guess Otto Sharp is in the clear, huh?"

"Looks that way," Bauer said. "He wasn't the one who sent those guys to your motel room. DPD's gang task force is still keeping an eye on him after what Angel told us, but I dare say nothing will come of it. At least not in relation to your sister's case."

"You're probably right." There really was no link between Otto and Julie except that she attended the music festival he organized. Now that Patterson knew Otto wasn't involved in stealing back the bankers box, his trip to Las Vegas after the TexFest fiasco was starting to look more like a coincidence. After all, a lot of people went to Vegas, especially if they were in showbiz, and there was no evidence her sister had ever even met the man. She decided to let it go. There were more important things to worry about. Like Claire Wright recovering enough to talk to her. Patterson's throat was dry. She looked around and realized that there were no cups on the desk. She'd gotten used to Bauer bringing her a coffee every morning. "Where's the cup of Joe today?"

Bauer shrugged. "I was running late, so I didn't stop. I didn't know if you were going to come in this morning or not, but if you did, I wanted to be here when you arrived. You've taken such a beating over the last couple of days. I was worried. I almost called last night to see how you were doing, but I figured you'd probably be sleeping."

"That was very sweet of you."

"Meh." Bauer waved off the compliment.

"But really, you could have stopped long enough to get coffee, for heaven's sake."

"Let's fix that right now." Bauer grabbed his jacket from the back of the chair and stood up. "Come on."

"Not so fast. We have to write a report on this mess for SAC Harris." Patterson wasn't sure what was worse—being attacked by a knife-wielding maniac or the reams of useless paperwork that followed.

"The report can wait an hour." Bauer looked over his shoulder. "Besides, you haven't exactly played by the rules so far. Why start now?"

Patterson thought about this for a moment, then smiled as she stood up. "Good point."

SIXTY-FIVE

FIVE DAYS LATER

PATTERSON WAS BACK at the hospital, but this time she wasn't there for herself. She had come to see Claire Wright, who was now awake and recovering from her injuries.

Special Agent Bauer walked next to her as they made their way to the ICU where Claire had been moved from the critical care unit once she was stable.

They were accompanied by a nurse who warned Patterson not to take up too much of the patient's time. Claire was still very weak and on a lot of meds.

When they reached her room, the nurse entered first to make sure Claire was awake and coherent enough to receive visitors. After a minute, the nurse exited and allowed Patterson to go in while Bauer opted to remain in the corridor.

Claire looked as bad as she must have felt. Her bruises made Patterson's own welts look superficial. One eye was swollen shut. Her scalp was bandaged. There were, no doubt, more dressings beneath the covers that were pulled up over her chest. She was connected to a dizzying array of machines. Her bed was raised at forty-five degrees so that she wasn't lying flat.

"You must be Patterson Blake," Claire said in a croaky voice.

Patterson nodded. She moved close to the bed.

"They tell me you're an FBI agent." Claire's good eye, the one that wasn't closed, swiveled in Patterson's direction.

"Yes. That's true." Patterson nodded again. "But I'm also Julie Blake's sister."

"Julie Blake," Claire echoed, then grimaced. She was clearly finding it hard to talk.

Patterson knew she must be quick. There was no telling how much stamina, or lack thereof, the woman lying before her might currently possess. "I just have a few questions. I won't take up any more of your time than necessary."

Claire licked her lips. Her hand found the controller, and she raised the bed a little higher. "That night when you called me . . ."

"Yes?"

"I really did mean to meet you the next day. I didn't intend to run."

"Why did you run?" Patterson asked. She was more interested in what Claire might have to say about Julie, but there were still unanswered questions about Ryan Gilder, too.

"After I hung up, Ryan wanted to know who was on the phone. I told him it was nothing. Just someone asking about an old friend. He flew into a rage. Said I was lying." A cough racked Claire's body. She drew in several faltering breaths.

"Take it easy," said Patterson. "There's plenty of time for this. You don't have to tell me—"

"I want to." There was a defiant look in Claire's good eye. "That bastard tried to kill me. He murdered Leonard."

"He can't hurt you ever again. He's in a coma." Patterson didn't bother to say that it was her that put him there. "If he ever wakes up he'll be going to prison for the rest of his life."

"Good." A tear pushed its way from Claire's eye. "I had no idea he could be so violent. When we first met, he was charming. Loving. He said I was his world. But after I moved in with him, everything changed. He became possessive. Paranoid. Told me I couldn't see my friends anymore. He even wanted me to stop working, and I did, for a while. But I got so bored. Wanted a life outside of our relationship."

"That's when you signed up for the hair academy?"

"I figured he would be okay with it because it was all women there. He always got so jealous. We couldn't go to bars and restaurants anymore because he thought the men were looking at me. By the end he wouldn't even let me go shopping on my own."

"But he wasn't okay with the hair academy."

"No. He became convinced I was seeing someone else, even though he followed me there a couple of times and saw me go in. That's why he got so mad when you called. He thought I was talking to another man. We argued. He'd never hit me before, but that night he did. Slapped me across the face. Said I wasn't going to the hair academy anymore. That I was to quit the next day and stay at home from then on. I was terrified. I grabbed my purse and car keys and told him I was going out to get gas. He tried to stop me, but I ran. Managed to . . ." Claire's voice cracked.

"It's okay," Patterson said. "Take it easy."

Claire nodded. "I didn't know what to do for the longest time. I drove around. Then I found this bar and went in. I sat there thinking and realized I couldn't go back. Couldn't live like that anymore. When the bar was closing, I sent a text to this artist friend I had, asked him to pick me up."

"Leonard Hemphill."

"I'd known him for years. He said I could stay at his place until I figured out what to do."

"Why did you leave your phone and purse in the car?"

"Because I knew he could track my credit cards if I used them, and I was sure he'd put some kind of app on my phone that told him where I was at all times."

"So how did he find you?" Patterson asked.

"Because I was stupid. In my haste to get away, I forgot to delete the text messages before I put the phone back in the car. By the time I realized it was too late. I couldn't go back there in case he was waiting."

Now Patterson understood. Ryan Gilder had found the text messages, which led him to Claire, then deleted them before he handed the phone over to herself and Bauer in an attempt to make himself look innocent. His only mistake was not knowing that the FBI could recover those deleted messages.

Claire sniffed. "I knew he was crazy, but I never imagined in my wildest dreams that he was a killer. When he showed up at Leonard's loft, I was in the bedroom sleeping. I heard shouting, went into the corridor, and saw Leonard grappling with this man wearing a devil mask. There was a knife. The masked man stabbed him. When I saw that, I turned and ran. Opened the window and went down the fire escape. I didn't even realize it was Ryan until he showed up at the hair academy. I still don't know how he found me there."

"Why did you go to the hair academy instead of the police?" Patterson asked. She didn't bother to mention that Cindy Lorenz had notified Ryan Gilder of Claire's whereabouts, not realizing that it was him she was running from.

"I don't know. I couldn't think straight. It was the middle of the night, and I thought Leonard's killer would come after me next because I was a witness, so I went to the only place I knew and hid in the doorway until Cindy showed up."

Patterson was about to press her for more details when Bauer stuck his head inside the door. "FYI—The nurse says you've got two more minutes, and then your time is up. If there's anything else you need to ask, you'd better do it now."

SIXTY-SIX

PATTERSON THANKED Bauer and turned back to Claire. "I appreciate you telling me what happened, but I really need to know about Julie now."

"Sure. I'll tell you what I know, but it's not very much."

"I appreciate that." Patterson gathered her thoughts. "You said that when your brother's band came to town sixteen years ago, they slept on the floor of your parent's garage."

"That's right." A faint smile touched Claire's lips. "Honestly, the band wasn't very good, but they practiced like crazy for days in that garage. Julie had nothing to do, so we hung out together. Karissa was more Julie's age, but she was doing band stuff, not that it mattered. It was hard to get her to talk about anything but music."

"So the pair of you became friends?"

"Yes. At least while she was there. We went to the festival together. I think I told you that already on the phone."

"You did," Patterson said.

"I liked her. She was easy to talk to." Claire's smile grew wider. "She even sent me a couple of postcards after that. After they moved on."

"The band moved on?" Patterson was aware of the time closing in on her. She prayed the nurse wouldn't interrupt them just yet.

"Not all of them. Martin had finished college, so he stayed here in Dallas. He knew the band was crap, that there was no future for them. Karissa stayed for a while because she and Martin were seeing each other. They broke up the next spring. I don't know what happened to her after that."

"And the others?" Patterson asked. "My sister?"

"They left a couple of days after the festival in the van and Julie went with them."

"Where did they go?" This was what Patterson had come to Dallas for.

"Amarillo. They'd all been playing together since their first year of college, and this was kind of their farewell tour. Everyone going their own way."

"Why Amarillo?"

"Because that's where the bass player lived."

Patterson wracked her brain to remember his name. "Mark Davis."

"Mark. He kept in touch with me for the longest. I guess I had a bit of a teenage crush on him."

"What happened to Julie and Trent Steiger?"

"Not sure. All I know is that Julie spent some time in Amarillo. That's where one of the postcards was from. I can't remember if the second one came from there or not."

"Do you still have the postcards?" Patterson asked. She couldn't believe there were more cards from Julie out there.

"I can't imagine. Haven't seen them in years. They probably got lost in the move after my parents got divorced. Sorry."

"That's okay." Patterson was disappointed. "Do you know where any of the band are now?"

"Mark is still in Amarillo. He sends me a Christmas card every year. As for Karissa and Trent, who knows?"

"Mark Davis is in Amarillo?" Patterson's heart was beating fast.

"Yes. If I still had my cell phone, I could give you his details. They're in my contacts. After I get out of here, I'll try to find one of his old Christmas cards. His address might be on that."

"There's no need," Patterson said. "Your phone is in the evidence locker at the FBI Field Office."

"Good." Claire rested her head back and closed her eyes. Her breathing was labored. Patterson sensed she had said all that she was going to. The woman was physically and emotionally exhausted.

Not that it mattered.

A second later the nurse breezed in. "You have to leave now, FBI or not. This woman needs her rest."

"It's fine, I'm going." Patterson said goodbye to Claire and stepped out into the corridor.

Bauer was waiting. "Well? Did you get what you came for?"

Patterson smiled. "Yes. I got what I came for."

SIXTY-SEVEN

PATTERSON RETRIEVED Claire Wright's phone from the evidence locker as soon as they got back to the field office. She took it back to the windowless room with two desks that still reminded her of a janitor's closet and set to work. It didn't take her long to find an entry in the contacts for Mark Davis. To her dismay, there was no phone number, just an address in Amarillo. But it gave her a direction to go in. Julie had left Dallas with two band members and continued on her journey. Whatever fate befell her, it hadn't occurred here. This new information also erased any lingering doubts she had regarding Otto Sharp. He wasn't involved in Julie's disappearance, even if he did travel to Las Vegas after the disastrous TexFest music festival.

"You okay?"

Patterson looked up to see Bauer standing in the doorway. "Yes. I think so."

"You'll be leaving us now, then?"

"I have to follow my sister's trail." Patterson thought she detected a glimmer of disappointment in the rookie agent's voice.

"Right." Bauer nodded slowly and sat down. He put his feet up on the desk and leaned back with his hands behind his head. "I guess this is the appropriate moment to say that you will be missed."

"You don't need to say it," Patterson said jokingly. "I'm well aware that you'll be lost without me."

"Might as well resign now," Bauer shot back.

Patterson was about to respond when there was a light knock on the door. She looked up to see Vanessa Klein, the admin assistant tasked with getting her settled when she first arrived. Given Patterson's attitude that day, it wouldn't be a surprise if the woman had come to see her off the premises personally. But that wasn't the reason for her visit.

"SAC Harris would like to see you in his office, pronto," Vanessa said. She paused, then added, "That was the exact word he used. Pronto."

"Huh." Patterson exchanged a look with Bauer.

"Better not keep him waiting," Bauer said.

Patterson stood up. "He probably just wants to give me a big old hug before I leave."

Bauer grinned. "That must be it."

SIXTY-EIGHT

YOU WANTED TO SEE ME, SIR?" Patterson asked, stepping into the office of Special Agent in Charge Walter Harris.

"Take a seat, Special Agent Blake." Harris motioned toward a chair on the other side of his desk.

Patterson did as she was told.

Harris waited until she got settled before he spoke again. "Congratulations are in order, I believe. You pursued a situation that no one else took seriously, including the Dallas Police Department, saved two lives, and solved a cold case murder in Seattle. On top of that, you managed to get the authorities to take a second look at a decades-old drowning that had been previously ruled an accidental death."

"I really didn't do anything, sir," Patterson said. "I was just trying to—"

"Save the humility, Special Agent Blake. I must confess that when you arrived in Dallas, I thought the kudos you received for the events in Oklahoma City were unjustified. That you were nothing but an unwitting pawn in Marilyn Kahn's power games."

"Sir, I—"

"I haven't finished yet," Harris interrupted.

Patterson fell silent.

"That's better." Harris stood and walked to the window. He looked out for a moment, then turned back to Patterson. "As I was saying, I sincerely believed Kahn was using you. My opinion on that score has not changed. Marilyn and I go way back, and I know her better than she would like. As the expression goes, I have her number. That said, I can't deny that you have a knack for ignoring the rules and somehow coming out on top. You've also solved more murders in the last few months than an entire field office."

"I just got lucky," Patterson said. Not that she felt lucky considering the beatings she had taken while solving the cases in Oklahoma City and Dallas. She wondered how much more punishment her body could take.

"What one person might call luck a person with a different mindset might call prowess." Harris placed his palms flat on the desk and leaned on it. "And right now, I have a situation that requires such prowess."

"Sir?" Patterson had a feeling she wouldn't like what was about to come.

"I've spoken with Marilyn Kahn, and we have agreed that you will stay on here in Dallas for a while longer."

"I can't do that," Patterson said, jumping to her feet in alarm. "I have a new lead on my sister in Amarillo and I need to get there soon as possible."

"I know all about Mark Davis," Harris said. "He's been living in Amarillo for a decade and a half, he won't be going anywhere in the next few weeks, I assure you."

"You can't do this," Patterson said, aghast. "I was given free rein to pursue my sister's case."

"And I'm not taking that away from you. I'm merely asking for you to lend your expertise to a disturbing case here in Dallas for a few weeks first. I need an investigator who can see what other people cannot. Someone who gets results even if they need to bend the rules. In short, I need you."

Patterson didn't know how to respond, so she stood in silence and swallowed her anger. There was no use arguing the matter. Walter Harris was in charge, and he was assigning her to a new case with the approval of Marilyn Kahn whether or not she liked it. And really, what choice was there but to agree? She needed the Bureau's resources for her own quest to find Julie. Resources that might be withheld if she caused trouble. In the end, she took a deep breath and said, "Fine. I'll stay."

Harris smiled. "I thought you would. And if it's any consolation, I'm keeping you paired with Special Agent Bauer."

"What?" This was too much. "He was supposed to be shadowing me, that's all."

"And you work well together, which is why I don't want to break up the team."

For the second time in as many minutes, Patterson swallowed her annoyance. "If you don't mind me asking, sir, what is it you want us to investigate?"

"I was getting to that. Three weeks ago, a teenage girl was snatched while riding her bike home from school. No one has seen her since. The kid had a troubled home life, and DPD was working on the assumption that she was taken by her estranged father. They issued an amber alert, but it did no good. The father was located, and he didn't have her." Harris let this sink in before continuing. "Yesterday afternoon, a second girl was taken while also riding home. There were no witnesses to either abduction. Their bikes were found on the side of the road. DPD has asked for our help in finding these girls and catching this person before they strike again. Given the circumstances, I harbor little hope of finding either girl alive."

Patterson digested this for a moment. "You think there's a fledgling serial killer out there."

"Yes," Harris replied. "At best, we have a serial abductor. At worst . . ."

Patterson nodded. Harris didn't need to finish the statement. She pushed her hands into her pockets. Julie would have to wait, at least a little while longer.

Read the next book in The Patterson Blake FBI Mystery Thriller series.
All The Dead Girls.

ABOUT THE AUTHORS

A. M. Strong is the pen name of supernatural action and adventure fiction author Anthony M. Strong. Sonya Sargent grew up in Vermont and is an avid reader when she isn't working on books of her own. They divide their time between Florida's sunny Space Coast and a tranquil island in Maine.

Find out more about the author at
AMStrongAuthor.com

Made in the USA
Middletown, DE
29 January 2024

48726193R00191